WILD

THE PACK OF ST. JAMES

NOELLE MACK

BRAVA

KENSINGTON PUBLISHING CORP.
http://www.kensingtonbooks.com

BRAVA BOOKS are published by

Kensington Publishing Corp.
850 Third Avenue
New York, NY 10022

All Kensington titles, imprints, and distributed lines are available at special quantity discounts for bulk purchases for sales promotion, premiums, fund-raising, educational, or institutional use.

Special book excerpts or customized printings can also be created to fit specific needs. For details, write or phone the office of the Kensington Special Sales Manager: Attn.: Special Sales Department. Kensington Publishing Corp., 850 Third Avenue, New York, NY 10022. Phone: 1-800-221-2647.

Brava and the B logo Reg. U.S. Pat. & TM Off.

ISBN-13: 978-0-7582-2275-6
ISBN-10: 0-7582-2275-0

First Printing: March 2008
10 9 8 7 6 5 4 3 2 1

Printed in the United States of America

for my favorite wolf

Also by Noelle Mack

ONE WICKED NIGHT

NIGHTS IN BLACK SATIN

JUICY

RED VELVET

THREE

Anthologies with novellas by Noelle Mack

PERFECT KISSES

SEXY BEAST

SEXY BEAST II

THE HAREM

Published by Kensington Publishing Corporation

1
_____

London, 1815. October . . .

"A woman is most beautiful when she is waiting to be kissed," Kyril said. He looked down at her, a sensual fire in his gaze, and his thumb traced the line of her chin. He tipped her face up to his. "And you are the most beautiful woman in London."

Vivienne Sheridan did not mind if he thought so. Her lips parted as she began to reply to his gallant compliment—but he spoke first.

"May I kiss you, Vivienne?"

He wasted no time. Neither would she. "Yes," she murmured. A kiss was only a kiss.

Kyril smiled. "Well, then. Come a little closer."

She obeyed without saying a word. His arm encircled her waist. Her eyes closed as his hand moved down to the side of her neck. He stroked the sensitive skin with his fingertips, easing away every trace of her nervousness. To be touched so tenderly felt wonderful. Blissfully aroused by what he was doing, Vivienne sighed, wishing she was not . . .

In her drawing room. Fully dressed.

His strong hands made her feel naked. How she wanted his kiss.

But his lips only brushed hers before his mouth moved to her ear and he spoke again, very softly. "May I stay the night?"

She had not expected that. Or at least not so soon. Her answer came quickly. "N-no."

"Why not?" His low, very masculine voice was as persuasive as his caress.

Vivienne straightened up, a motion that made her bosom rise within the snug-fitting bodice of her gown. She quickly tugged at the décolleté neckline, aware that the delicate lace edge might not be enough to conceal—she stopped when she saw him glance down at it and then up again at her face.

He was too tall not to have seen her nipples.

They tightened. She quelled a wanton urge to wind her arms around his neck and press her breasts against the fine linen of his shirt. But Vivienne was unwilling to leave his embrace and equally unwilling to give in too easily.

"Why not? Ah—I would rather sleep alone."

Her new bed was her sanctuary, a bower in which she retreated from the world, piled with soft pillows and hung with rose-embroidered curtains. No man had ever shared it.

"Really?"

He drew her body back to his. He inclined his head and nibbled her neck precisely where he had stroked her. Vivienne tried not to moan. The pleasurable stimulation was almost too much to bear, and the light trace of stubble on his chin only added to her excitement.

"Yes. Really."

"Hmm." He ceased his gentle biting and relaxed his hold somewhat. But she did not move away from him.

He pressed his lips to her forehead, his gaze heavy-lidded and dreamy when he finally looked at her face again. He touched the small emerald in her earlobe, toying with it. That too was stimulating. It was clear enough what was on his mind.

"Pretty earrings," he said at last. "The same green as your incomparable eyes."

"Not quite."

"You do not like compliments."

"I do not trust them. But I like them well enough."

"I meant it when I said you were the most beautiful woman in London."

"No doubt you did."

He gave her a level look that held a hint of amusement. Then he touched the other earring. "Can I persuade you to take these off?"

As a prelude to . . . she would do well not to think about taking anything off if she was going to refuse him. "No."

"Then I will take them off for you." Before she could stop him, he removed both jewels and dropped them down her bodice. "There. They will be safe enough."

Her eyes widened with surprise. A master thief could not have done the trick more deftly.

"Oh!" Her indignant protest faded away when he bent down again to take her earlobe in his mouth and suck it gently. "You—mmm. Never mind."

He released it. "Should I stop?"

Determined beast. She did like what he was doing. "Not yet," Vivienne answered. "But you must go soon. You do understand that I *like* to be alone."

"If you say so." He turned his attention to the other earlobe and sucked it harder than the first.

His lips and tongue were warm and wet and tight on that tiny part of her body. What he was doing felt so good. So very good.

"Everyone knows that I do," she managed to say.

He let go and laughed against her ear, a throaty sound, almost like a growl. "Yes, I have heard a few rumors to that effect. I am glad to have no rival."

"That is not what I said—"

"I know." He radiated self-confidence as well as heat. His hands moved to her shoulders, stroking her bare skin until languorous warmth spread through her. "But I suspected as much."

Vivienne arched her back, wanting and not wanting a more intimate embrace. She placed her hands upon his chest to push him away, then felt the strong beat of his heart and let them rest there.

Kyril kissed her neck once more and lifted his head. She could not help but meet his unfathomable gaze. His eyes seemed to take in everything but they reflected nothing. Not the candles or the fire in the drawing room. No detail of her face.

He gazed down at her and Vivienne felt a dizzying sensation of vertigo.

What was—*that*? For a fraction of a second she saw something strange in the darkness of his eyes. A glimpse of a wild and forsaken land . . . an otherworld buried in blue-white snow . . .

She blinked and the illusion vanished. She told herself she'd had too much champagne. She was tired. Imagining things. She would not explain.

He seemed to understand, though, that something had upset her. He brushed away a tendril of the dark hair that clung to her cheek and then his hand slid over her shoulder to the bare skin of her upper back. He stroked her there, taking his time.

She rested her head against his chest, limp with pleasure. His shirt had a pleasant fragrance, as if it had been washed in herbal water. There was a much more masculine smell mingled with it—the warm smell of his skin underneath the shirt. Kyril clasped her nape, calming her. Her neck curved in graceful submission. She could not move, did not want to move. For a moment, the feeling of falling ebbed away and Vivienne felt deliciously safe.

No woman is safe with Kyril Taruskin . . .

The thought vanished in an instant.

"Come away with me," he murmured. "The drive to my house is not long."

She could not think of a very good reason to say no. She came up with a merely serviceable one. "My servants will see."

"They are abed."

"But—"

"We can continue this conversation on the way."

"Kyril, if you—"

"We do not have to talk, of course. But a carriage with closed curtains is a wonderfully private place. As private as a confessional. Intimate secrets, softly voiced—there is nothing more exciting."

The warm hand on her nape stayed where it was. Vivienne tilted her head back to smile at him. "Perhaps. But I have no significant sins to confess."

"Give me time. You will."

Vivienne laughed a little but made no reply.

"Just tell me what you want, my darling. Let me satisfy you."

"Kyril, I cannot think when you hold me like this." She did not really want to think. Such was the power of his touch. His strong hand upon her nape was deeply soothing and stimulating at the same time. "No—do not move your hand—not yet."

He gazed down at her, his eyes dark with passion. "Grant me one night, Vivienne."

"Ahh—"

"My coachman will bring you back in the hour before dawn. No one will know."

She hesitated. "It is already past midnight."

"Is it?"

"The church bells rang. Did you not hear them?"

He shook his head and moved his hand from her nape, tucking a fallen lock back into her upswept hair. The passion in his eyes was shadowed with tenderness.

The candles had burned low. Without his hand upon her skin, Vivienne felt a sudden chill down her spine. The fire had dwindled down to a broken mass of gray and scarlet embers, dancing with shivering little flames. She avoided his intent gaze, not wanting to see his mouth so close to hers.

He still had not kissed her—not really. She had said yes to that. But nothing more.

Vivienne steeled herself to resist whatever came next. The tenderness in his eyes had vanished. His moods were mercurial. Now Kyril was smiling down at her in a wicked way. Ready to pounce.

He *was* wicked. She was well aware of his reputation. And he was wild in equal measure, for all that he dressed so elegantly. Kyril Taruskin's dark clothes were set off by a pure white linen shirt, its tall collar filled with a black silk cravat. Above that, a strong jaw and sensual mouth. An aristocratic nose. And those odd eyes. Intent upon her.

With a start, she felt Kyril's hands trace her collarbone and then move lower, over the swell of her breasts.

She gasped but she did not say no.

He cupped the lush flesh and gently squeezed, again and again. The sensation was deeply erotic. Suddenly all she wanted was to lie down with him, let him suckle her until she cried for joy, running her fingers into his dark hair while he buried his face in her breasts . . . She swayed against him, feeling something small and hard prick her skin—the earrings.

Breathing hard, Kyril released her breasts and circled his palms over the erect nipples nestled in the lace of her bodice, looking into her eyes now with intense desire. Teasing her. Exciting her. He would have her dress up to her waist next to fondle her bare bottom if she let him—how far was he going to go?

As far as you let him.

No. However handsome, however gifted in the art of pleasing women, Kyril Taruskin was not going to have her tonight.

"That is enough," she said softly. "I will not go with you and you cannot stay here."

He nodded, a curt motion at odds with the sensual slowness of his caresses, and ceased what he was doing.

"As you wish, Vivienne. When a lady commands, a gentleman obeys."

It was rather the other way around, she thought nervously. His tone was neutral, his words polite, but there was an unmistakable steeliness behind both. His reluctance to concede was obvious—he was no longer stimulating her nipples but his hands had moved down again to clasp her waist.

Vivienne drew in her breath and his grip tightened ever so slightly. It was easy to imagine how good those hands would feel on her if she were naked before him, her dress upon the floor in a silken heap, her dark hair tumbled over her shoulders, her corset unlaced and tossed aside . . .

But he might insist on you wearing the corset and nothing else. To start.

Her breasts ached, not from his sensual fondling of them but from wanting more of it. Her flesh betrayed her. Still and all, his expert caresses had not left her dress in disarray. Her breasts were nicely uplifted and pressed together by the exceptionally fine corset that he was not going to see. Her damned nipples were as hard as the emerald earrings he had playfully dropped into her décolletage. The faceted stones pricked her but she was not going to fish them out. He would only look at her, eyes hot with desire, while she retrieved them—and then she would have no chance at all. No, her dress would stay on and her hair would stay up. Vivienne pressed her lips together and held back a sigh.

There was no real reason to refuse him. But it would be interesting to make Kyril wait for what he wanted. His lust for her would know no bounds—and his erotic ingenuity would come to the fore to win her. The moment of ultimate surrender would be intensely pleasurable for them both.

Vivienne favored him with a look that she hoped was stern. The gossip that she had tried to ignore in the last months was not wrong. Kyril Taruskin had a legendary talent for seduction and making love. His conquests were many. Now she understood why.

Of course, no one had ever mentioned him *loving* anyone. Yet it did not matter, not to Vivienne. Certainly it would be foolish of her to think that she was or would be different, somehow, from the others. Still . . . she wanted him.

He cleared his throat with a slight cough. "Where were we?"

She cast a meaningful glance at the door.

"Now I remember. You want me to go."

"Yes."

He gave her a wry look. "But you are not sure."

"I am quite sure of what I want, Kyril."

"Are you?" He grinned at her. Deep-carved dimples appeared, framing his sensual mouth.

Annoyed by his amusement, she tipped her head to one side. "You need not grin like that."

"Like what?"

"Like a damned wolf."

Kyril laughed. "Perhaps I am one. I do follow my instincts and I can sense your mixed emotions."

"How?"

"By what I see." He gestured at her glass on the low table near the fireplace. "Champagne left unfinished. The ashes of a fire that has burned too low."

She almost smiled. "As good a way as any to describe the end of an evening."

"Is it?"

His gaze locked with hers. Damn him—the mixture of intelligent amusement and sexual desire in his expression made her feel hot all over again.

"Vivienne . . ." His voice was deep and yearning.

She shook her head and Kyril let go of her at last. Vivienne was almost disappointed.

Until he pounced. His full lips captured hers for a kiss that made her tremble. Encircled once more by his arms, lifted slightly, she barely felt the floor beneath her thin-soled evening shoes. Her stockinged toes curled and wiggled under the embroidered flowers on her silk shoes as freely as if she were barefoot.

Kyril's lips were soft, his technique sensual in the extreme. Opening her lips, his tongue tasted her mouth as if he found her utterly delicious. His kiss was tender but not in the least tentative. His self-assurance and his skill compelled her to respond fully, pressing her body to his at last, arching with the pleasure of allowing so powerful a man to claim her, however briefly . . .

But the kiss went on and on.

Vivienne was the one who ended it. When he stopped to draw breath, she placed her hands on his chest once more and pushed him away with firm resolve. He stood his ground. She was the one who moved.

Kyril studied her. A few candles sputtered and went out, their hollow stubs filled with molten wax. A thin thread of smoke rose from one extinguished wick and hung in the air. He neither moved nor spoke.

He seemed taller and more masterful, growing in apparent size as the light diminished. Another illusion. Vivienne reached up a hand to rub her eyes and he caught her by the wrist. Her fingers curled into a loose fist, as if to defend herself, but his long thumb gently forced her fingers open.

That done, he pressed a tender kiss into her palm. Then he released her and she let her arm fall to her side, feeling suddenly bereft. How had he ensnared her with such ease?

"Kyril . . . when will I see you again?" She bit her lip. That had sounded far too eager. Almost girlish.

Kyril only shrugged. "Soon." He looked at her and murmured a few words in Russian under his breath.

"What are you saying?"

"That you are utterly alluring. And dangerous."

The first part of his reply was flattering, but the last puzzled her. It was he who was dangerous. To her peace of mind. And to her heart, if she was not careful.

Still, she was feeling reckless. It had been too long since she had let a man get close to her and Kyril was no ordinary man.

"Will you not—" She hesitated, looking at him warily.

"Stay?" He shook his head, looking down at her parted lips. "No. Forgive me, Vivienne. As it happens, it is for the best that you asked me to go. I have just remembered that I was supposed to meet someone."

Highly unlikely. But she supposed it served her right for putting him off.

"After midnight?"

"As a matter of fact, yes. I cannot be late."

He could not possibly be telling the truth. No, they were playing the same game with each other. Advance and Retreat.

"Then it is a good thing you remembered it."

He only nodded.

She would not ask one word more. Vivienne silently reproved herself for her pique. She hoped he did not see the tinge of angry scarlet in her cheeks.

They got through the adieus politely enough. He turned to go without touching her again.

The sound of his boot heels on the stairs died away and the front door closed behind him. Vivienne went to the window. She pulled the heavy drape aside and looked out in time to see him stride to his black coach. Its windows were shielded on the inside of the glass with rich material she could just see under the streetlamps. Their light revealed the falling rain, turning it into sparks of gold that pattered down upon the black-lacquered top of the coach.

The sight was beautiful but it filled her with melancholy. Rain often did. There were times when she could not stand the sound of it against the windowpanes.

How long had it been falling? The night had been clear when her other guests departed one by one. Of course, that was hours ago. In Kyril's arms, kissed so well, she had not heard the storm blow in.

The horses shook their heavy heads, jingling the bits in their velvet mouths as their master approached. They were stamping their hooves on the wet cobblestones, eager to be off. As he passed a dark doorway, Vivienne saw something move. She narrowed her eyes when a man stepped forth from it.

His long, matted beard and ugly coat gave him the look of a beggar or a lunatic. The sleeves were so long his hands were covered and the hat he wore was strangely shaped.

Vivienne studied him. He might be only a poor foreigner. London was full of them.

Kyril did not seem to see the man. She put a hand upon the window, ready to open it and warn him . . . no, it was no longer necessary. The rain drove the bearded man back into the doorway. Vivienne retreated behind the drapery.

The coachman turned around and tipped his hat to Kyril, spilling the rain accumulated in its rolled-up brim upon his own greatcoat. She imagined the fellow's curse—she could not hear it. The heavy rain obliterated the sounds outside.

Kyril spoke to him before he got into the carriage, swinging up one long leg and entering without a backward glance at her house. Damn the man. Where could he be going after midnight? She regretted her decision to make him wait. She ought to have let him have his way with her, permitted herself the physical pleasure he was so determined to give her, however fleeting it might be. Men's hearts were fickle.

As was her own, she reflected. Not that she had always been cynical. But London was a sophisticated city that did not hold love in high regard. After some years of dwelling here, she no longer hoped to find it again. She had loved once and loved well—but not wisely.

Her gaze fell upon a closed case on the nearby shelf, a flat thing that looked like a little book but was made of engraved metal. It held a miniature that she often looked at. She had taken it out from her desk just that morning. She had painted the image herself, with mousehair brushes on an ivory oval, of a small face, like an angel, with closed eyes. It was a face she had seen only once, as if in a dream, when she had been nearly out of her mind with grief. But she had captured its delicacy of features and expression. The miniature had become a sort of amulet that she always kept nigh, but not where anyone would see it.

Vivienne crossed in front of the window and swiftly picked it up. She opened a drawer in her desk and put the little case away, then happened to touch the letter that had come for her today.

Her hand drew back as if she touched something filthy. But the folded paper was immaculately white, folded to hide the lines penned upon it. It had come from someone demanding a meeting. Someone she knew well—and never wanted to see again. But she would have to.

If only. . . . Suddenly she wanted Kyril to hold her, right now, until the sun came up. For whatever reason he pleased. He might do as he wished with her. She craved his warmth, his sensuality, his amorous determination—animal qualities that had nothing to do with romantic nonsense. Not loving but definitely life-giving. He might ease the coldness in her heart. That would be enough.

The wheels of the black coach moved slowly forward, then back, as the horses strained against their harnesses. Radiating misery from his dripping hat to his drenched back, the coachman settled himself stolidly upon his high seat and flicked the whip at the horses. The carriage lurched a little over the cobblestones of Cheyne Row and rolled on. She watched it rattle away around a corner.

He would be home soon. She had never been to his house but she knew that Kyril lived only a few miles away, near Grosvenor Square. She pulled the drape closed, imagining the place for a few seconds.

His clothes were not at all showy; his house was likely to be just as sober. It would have, oh, tall columns framing the entrance. It would be built of pale stone blocks fitted together with the utmost precision. A paneled black door with no glass inserts and no hint of what was beyond it. She added just one touch of whimsy to her mental picture: a polished doorknocker in the shape of an animal's head, holding the heavy ring that did the actual knocking in its brass jaws. He was not British, so it did not have to be the obligatory lion. No, a wolf would do nicely.

He had money. What of it? So did she. But she was not sure where his came from. Months ago, a mutual friend had explained the Taruskin family's long association with the British Society of Merchant-Adventurers. She had not listened closely, preferring to look at Kyril.

Now, with nothing else to do but think, she tried to remember what bits she had heard. The immense wealth of the Russian aristocracy . . . the vast country's unexploited riches, there for the taking . . . the necessity for the Society's foreign agents to learn excellent English . . .

Glancing constantly at Kyril as her friend spoke, captivated by everything from his handsomeness to his height, she had paid little attention to any of it.

Her former lover, a duke who lived apart from his cantankerous duchess, had introduced her to Kyril—without explanations—shortly after his arrival in London. Horace had seen to it that Vivienne was often thrust into the company of the dashing newcomer at the assemblees and balls they attended, social occasions at which the duchess never appeared.

Had Horace hoped Kyril would sweep her off her feet when he was bored with her?

It had not happened. Kyril had been the soul of propriety until tonight. Horace had been forced to take up with someone else and incur the expenses of two mistresses for a while. The duke had complained that Vivienne was as serene as a statue when his eye wandered elsewhere.

He had not been entirely wrong about Kyril, however. Her attraction to him had been obvious to an old roué like Horace. Vivienne had been curious about Kyril, invited him to several soirées of her own, hoping to draw him out or at least overhear if he talked of anything more personal than the theater and music and books. But he never had. Kyril was discreet to a fault.

He had reason to be, she supposed. Tonight had been her first encounter with the man behind the gentlemanly façade. So far, he lived up to his legend. The breathless whispers about his prowess as a lover—she had overheard those—were undoubtedly right. The subtlety and skillfulness of his lovemaking made her want more. Far more.

Vivienne opened the window at last, heedless of the rain. She needed a breath of air. Without his vital presence, the drawing room seemed dull and stifling. She was restless, as she so often was at night, hating to be confined.

During the hours of daylight, she might walk out when she

pleased, unaccompanied, but night was a very different matter. The duke had seldom come to her then, saying that once the sun went down, she became a different woman.

Her own woman. Not properly attentive to his dull anecdotes or his sexual demands. Those at least had the advantage of being quickly satisfied at any hour of the day.

She looked again for the beggar in the long coat but saw no sign of him. He was hidden in the shadows or no longer there at all. Drawing a deep breath, Vivienne closed her eyes, refreshed by the cool air. Despite the storm, she could just hear the Thames, flowing through the darkness of the London night toward the distant sea.

After a few minutes, Vivienne closed the window quietly. She might as well retreat to her study and read through the lonely hours that remained of the night. Kyril's kisses had stirred her too much to sleep.

Sexual desire, if satisfied, was as good a cure for loneliness as any. Love was not. A dalliance with the mysterious Russian would do no harm. How odd that he thought of her as dangerous. Surely he was teasing.

Once downstairs, she entered the study and locked the door behind her. A servant had lit an oil lamp some hours ago and forgotten to blow it out. The golden glow brightened the pleasantly cluttered room. Vivienne pushed aside a small crate with her foot. She still had not unpacked everything she had brought from her apartments in Audley Street.

But the house already looked like hers. Most of the rooms were furnished to her taste, if haphazardly. She sank with a sigh upon the chaise. There were books stacked upon a small table by its side, not very neatly.

She looked at the titles imprinted in worn gold letters upon their spines and picked out one Kyril had given her months ago. Folktales, translated from the Russian.

Vivienne kicked off her embroidered shoes. Then she swung

her legs up and made herself comfortable, opening the book without looking inside it. She set it down upon the front of her dress, and got a pillow behind her neck.

Lying down, relaxing, she could not help but think of Kyril and wish again that he were lying by her, holding her in his strong arms, warming her body with his own. His expert kisses—his masterful strength—his passionate whispers and his repeated invitations to come away with him—ah, she had been far too quick to say no.

He intended to become her lover, though love would have nothing to do with what she wanted from him. However, she intended to say yes the very next time she saw him.

Vivienne let her eyes drift closed, seeing his dark blue ones as clearly as if he were above her. Her hand rested on the book of fairytales.

Imagining him pressing down upon her, his long thigh between hers as he worked her dress up to her waist, arousing her with ardent caresses ... then ... naked ... their bodies entwined ... her sensual fantasy became a dream of pure pleasure.

Vivienne did not remember falling asleep.

She wakened just before dawn. The lamp was still lit, but the clear oil in the reservoir was nearly gone. She glanced at the clock on the mantel to confirm the hour: five o'clock. Then she looked down at her disheveled dress, remembering what she had done. She must have pulled it down to keep herself warm.

She hugged a pillow to herself, pretending it was Kyril.

Something was poking her in the side—the book of folktales. In his own way, he was with her. The thought pleased her and she took it up again. Vivienne yawned and stretched with the book in her hand. Once awake, she rarely went back to sleep. She opened the small volume, not awake enough to read, either, but willing to glance at the illustrations. She rifled through it and stopped at a thin sheet of crinkled, transparent paper protecting a hand-colored page underneath.

This she lifted carefully, revealing a picture of a Russian church, its onion-shaped domes decorated with dazzling touches of real gold. Peasant women in bright skirts and shawls stood by its massive doors.

Then, before her disbelieving eyes, the doors in the picture swung open and the women passed between them, their skirts swaying. She even heard their voices, tiny, sweet, and distant—and was that thread of smoke issuing from the sanctuary . . . incense? She swore she could smell it.

No. It could not be.

For the second time in one night, she had seen things that were not there. She was awake but still somehow dreaming. The solution to that was to go to her bed. Something about the comfortable chaise made her indulge in wayward fantasies, and Kyril had made them worse.

Unless there was some hidden magic in the book of Russian folktales . . . she dismissed the thought as impossible and slid the thin ribbon bound into the spine over the page to mark her place.

Vivienne raised her head, looking toward the window. Black, utterly black, the sky showed not a trace of morning light. The darkness outside seemed to press against the panes. She was glad for the circle of light that the lamp provided.

Her bedroom would be just as dark and her bed would be cold. If the chambermaid had brought up a warming pan of coals, the effect would be long gone. Slipping between chilly sheets by herself did not appeal to her. She decided to stay where she was. Vivienne opened the book at random to another page and began to read.

In the far, far north lived the Roemi, men like no other, warriors of legendary strength, born under the blue sun that never

*sets. They were magi, endowed with supernatural powers . . .
and masters of the great ice wolves that are no more. The Roemi
rode the freezing winds that howled down over the vast steppes
of Russia . . .*

The tale captivated her. So did the illustration of a Roemi
warrior. She marveled at his fierce beauty. For all that he was
standing in snow, he wore a loincloth and not much else. There
were tattoos upon his bare chest that outlined his muscle.

The picture was beautifully detailed. She could see the stip-
pled patterns on the soft boots laced with hide that covered his
calves. His mighty thighs were bare, bulging with more muscle
that looked real enough to touch. The warrior was about to
throw a spear, his brawny upper body half-twisted, his throwing arm drawn back. His hair was long and dark, with thin
braids at the temple.

Vivienne admired him, noting with an inward smile how
much he resembled Kyril, who was also tall and dark and beautiful in a very masculine way. His movements had the same
quality of utmost readiness as this imaginary warrior, eternally
poised to strike down an unseen enemy.

She read more of the fanciful tale, then turned back to the
picture, touching the Roemi man with a fingertip. He felt . . .
warm. How very odd. She touched the middle of his chest
and—dear God—felt a faint but unmistakable heartbeat. Vivienne flung the book away from her.

It fell facedown on the floor and lay there. She put a hand
over her own heart, willing it to stop racing, and breathed
deeply.

She sat upon the chaise and extended her foot toward the
book, pushing it away from her with a stockinged toe. Nothing
happened. She heard no sound, however faint. But she was not
going to pick it up again.

Not until morning. The sun would most likely shine
strongly tomorrow after such a heavy rain, with matter-of-fact

cheerfulness that would erase her weariness and her strange thoughts. Her restless hours of sleep had been worse than none at all. Exhaustion was causing her to imagine things.

Vivienne stood, stepping carefully around the book, and went to the mirror on the study wall. Her hair was half up and half down, badly tangled where her head had pressed against the pillow. She lifted the lid of a small box that contained a hairbrush and ivory hairpins, and set to work.

When her dark chestnut hair was once again arranged and pinned up to her satisfaction, Vivienne smoothed her rumpled dress. If a servant should come in, hard at work before dawn to clean the grates and lay new fires, she would not look too disheveled.

Of course, she was not supposed to care what servants thought, but the role of mistress of a household was still new to her. The Cheyne Row house was hers, certainly. Horace had deeded it to Vivienne at the conclusion of their love affair.

She had furnished it to her own taste with the large sum of money he had given her as well. Owning things that were new and entirely hers was a very great pleasure. That was why no man had yet slept in her rose-curtained bed—knowing that Kyril was likely to be the first made her smile at her reflection.

It had been worth enduring the duke's awkward caresses now and again. He had become her lover because she was beautiful and remarked upon by everyone—a female worth having simply because everyone wanted her. Easily distracted, he had moved on eventually to someone else, an event that had troubled her not at all.

His regretful letter of farewell had explained everything. She remembered it but hadn't bothered to keep it.

I shall remain, my dear Vivienne, ever your champion and obedient servant, and wish you happiness in each and every day of your life without me. Do understand that it is I who am unworthy, and not you. But I have met . . .

A brassy-haired actress who had all of London at her rather large feet. Vivienne had seen her, but only from a distance.

She did not miss the duke as a lover, if that word could be used to describe him. But she was very grateful to him. She straightened up tall as she looked at herself in the mirror. Being bought off was not the worst thing that could happen to an intelligent and independent woman. The philandering duke had provided handsomely for her.

Vivienne went to the shelves and began to set her other books to rights, tucking in the ones that went on and off the shelves, novels and the like. Their worn covers showed her affection for them. She blew the dust off more worthy volumes, leatherbound and ponderous, that she had yet to crack. She felt calmer now. What she had seen was only an illusion.

Seen, heard, smelled, said a little voice in her mind.

She ignored it. Her fatigue—and frustration had left all her senses overly stimulated. In any case, the volumes of folktales was a thoughtful gift and could not be left on the floor. She pushed over the leaning books on one shelf, and slanted one to hold a space open. Then she went to where the book still lay facedown, picking it up.

How silly she was to imagine herself bewitched by it. Forcing her actions to seem casual even though there was no one there to judge her, she slid a finger between its pages, hearing a familiar crinkle of transparent paper. Another illustration. She flinched when she opened the book to look at it.

It showed a Roemi warrior, fallen in battle, his broken body lying alone upon the killing field. His wounded face was still beautiful, even in death.

She dared not touch the page. The hand-colored blood seemed so fresh as to be real. As respectfully as one might shroud the dead, she covered the valiant hero with the transparent paper again, half-expecting to see the scarlet pigment seep through.

It did not. The blood—the paint, she told herself fiercely—was quite dry.

Very slowly she looked through the pages and found the first Roemi warrior she'd seen.

He had thrown his spear.

Vivienne gave a soft cry. If this was a trick, it was a very good one. Kyril must have expected that she would say something about it to him, but she simply accepted his gift at the time, feeling awkward for weeks afterward because she had not yet read it. Not even skimmed it so that she could pretend she had.

Was Kyril only a conjuror and a charlatan, and not a rich Russian gentleman, after all?

His air of mysteriousness had been noted and commented upon nearly as often as his sexual magnetism. That too could be practiced just like magic, she thought. He had been charming women ever since he arrived in London, according to all reports. Perhaps his paramours each got a little book like this.

No. The old volume was unique, and probably quite valuable. There could not be others like it, not with richly colored illustrations like that.

She turned the pages again, looking only at the pictures. The words behaved themselves, staying on the paper in neat rows of black type. Then she came to the concluding illustration.

Scolding herself for being so gullible, she lifted its protective page and gasped. Her eyes widened. The picture showed a wild and desolate land, buried in towering drifts of snow and ice.

She snapped the book shut. It was the otherworld she had glimpsed in Kyril's eyes.

2

After Kyril's departure from Cheyne Row...

He asked not to go north to his house near Grosvenor Square as his coachman expected but to the east, following the road along the river. Tom Micklethwaite hunkered down as if his massive shoulders could protect the rest of him against the rain, and urged the four black horses on with a slap of the reins. No whip. His master did not like animals to be mistreated.

Miles away, an hour or more later, he stopped where Kyril had told him to, pulling up the reins and looking about nervously. They had come out from under the storm. Here, the wind was blowing from the opposite direction, pushing the clouds and rain back.

Tom heard his master open the door and step down quietly. The coachman reached for the stout cudgel that he kept under the seat. In sight of the Thames, the ramshackle houses leaned upon each other and there was no telling who lurked in the alleys between them. If heads had to be broken, he would break them and ask no questions.

Kyril looked up and saw Tom slap the cudgel against his rough palm. Once. Twice.

"I hope we will not need that, Mr. Micklethwaite. But the boat is coming. I will soon be on my way and you can go home."

The coachman peered into the darkness, seeing nothing out on the water. They had stopped by a flight of stairs leading down to the river, slippery with moss and filth. Someone had left a lamp there, but its light was feeble.

Kyril gave a soft halloo when a bright point of answering light appeared in the distance, reflected in shattered fragments by the black, rushing water. Little by little, the light came closer and he heard the soft dip and splash of oars.

"Here he is."

"An invisible man," the coachman grumbled, "in an invisible boat. I wish you luck, sir."

Kyril made no comment. Tom Micklethwaite was blunt by nature. But the Pack had needed a coachman who knew his way through the intricate web of alleys and crooked streets along the river, especially at night. The Thames waterfront was a maze that often trapped the unwary, with stairs and docks and landing places that took a lifetime to learn. Born in Stepney, Tom had proved to be their man and he was trustworthy.

"Coming about," the man in the boat said in a low voice. He gave a final hard pull on the oars to propel himself to the narrow dock at the foot of the stairs, then kept one in the water to turn the boat around with.

Kyril handed the lantern on the stairs to Tom and, sure-footed despite the slime on the stairs, went down to the boat. The other man drew both oar handles through the oarlocks and trapped them under a planked seat, keeping the wide, wet blades up in the air. They dripped into the river, gleaming in the isolated light of the lantern attached to the bow. He threw a line in a loop around a half-rotted piling, securing the boat to it.

"Neatly done," the coachman said softly. "If that bad wood holds."

"It will hold long enough." Kyril clambered down into the rowboat. "I will be gone for some time," he said over his shoulder to Tom, trying to stay on his feet. "Return the carriage to the mews and—" He swore under his breath when an unseen swell rocked the boat.

Lukian Taruskin leaned to the opposite side to steady it.

"See to the horses, Tom, and yourself—it was a long while to wait in bad weather and then the gallop—damnation!" The boat tipped to the other side.

"Sit down, cousin." Lukian spoke in Russian. "The tide is turning and we must be off. Tom has not failed you yet."

Kyril finally sat down.

Tom tipped his hat to his master once he was safely down and slapped the reins over the horses' backs, turning them and the carriage in the opposite direction from which they had come.

The darkness swallowed the sound of their pounding hooves just as Kyril reached up to extinguish the little flame in the lantern. "Thank you for fetching me. We will not need this now."

"No," said Lukian, "perhaps we did not need it at all. But I wanted to be sure you would see me and I was prepared to wait. I saw the storm blow in over your part of London some hours ago."

"The rain was very heavy."

"I am glad we are not in the thick of it."

"So am I."

Lukian set to in earnest, pulling rapidly on the oars to get them well away from the treacherous bank.

After a little while he spoke again. "How did you get through the streets? London is ankle-deep in muck when it rains hard. I was surprised to see you at the dock." His efforts took the boat straight through the strong current of the placid-looking Thames. Like Kyril, he was a powerful man.

"Micklethwaite made good time."

Lukian's breathing was deep and regular. He seemed to be enjoying the vigorous exercise.

"And where were you before this, Kyril?" he asked with amusement. "You smell of flowers."

"Do I?"

Lukian snorted. "Let me guess. You were not picking violets in a churchyard. Who is she?"

"That is for me to know and you to find out."

His cousin rowed on, thinking it over. "Hmm. Of the ladies of your acquaintance, there is only one who likes that particular perfume. I met her once. You dragged me to a soirée at her house when I was the worse for drink."

"Are you speaking of—"

"Yes, her," Lukian said impatiently. "The woman you hold in such high esteem. I don't think she liked me. You know exactly who I am talking about."

Kyril did, but something in his cousin's tone struck him as odd. Lukian's bad temper was nothing new, but his snappishness was. He was a lone wolf by nature, prone to dark moods which he usually managed to keep to himself. It was impossible to see his expression clearly now that the lantern had been put out.

"I doubt she remembers you," Kyril said at last.

Lukian shrugged, which interrupted the rhythm of his rowing. The oars bounced on the water and splashed. "Good. What was her name again?"

"Vivienne Sheridan."

"Yes, of course. She must have rubbed herself against you very thoroughly, Kyril."

"Do not be so rude. She did not rub, as you put it. We embraced."

"Aha. How romantic. Do you love her?"

There was a thin, razor-sharp edge to that unexpected question. Why on earth did his cousin even care? Kyril cleared his throat. "She is very beautiful."

"So she is."

"And highly intelligent."

Lukian snorted. "A paragon of womanly perfection, I suppose. Worthy of a pedestal."

"Yes, Lukian. But not at all like a statue. She is extremely sensual," Kyril added. "So much so that I very nearly forgot my meeting with you."

Lukian's eyes gleamed in the darkness. "Then I will count myself lucky. I suppose she refused you?"

"She did not."

"Then why are you here?"

"It seemed best not to send one of my brothers in my place."

Lukian laughed. "You are lying, Kyril. Though Semyon and Marko are good men. But they lack your experience at skulking around."

"That is because they are still cubs."

"Tall ones."

"But cubs."

"Have it your way, cousin." Lukian returned his attention to his rowing, lost in thoughts that Kyril could not read.

Kyril let the matter drop, thinking of Vivienne instead. How ardently she had pressed against him, how much she had seemed to want him—why had she said no?

It had worked out for the best, of course. If Lukian had come to the north bank of the Thames, following the beacon that a confederate had set out before Kyril's arrival, and not found him there, he would have been angry indeed. Given Lukian's current mood, they would have come to blows over it.

Kyril sighed. Family was family, but his relatives were sometimes too fond of fighting. But there was nothing he could do about that. For reasons of security, the members of the Pack of St. James had to stick together and he had not found it easy to make friends among the English in any case.

If truth be known, his feelings for Vivienne were a combustible mixture of raging lust and the first, worshipful stirrings of tender love—a love that was likely to consume him if he was not careful.

She most likely wanted him for only one reason. And yet she seemed loving as well as sensual. But she was reserved. She had been wounded in some way years ago—he sensed as much. He would have to find out her secrets. It might not be easy. She did not reveal herself in artless chatter as so many females did.

No, she waited and listened and bided her time—

"Tell me more of Vivienne," his cousin said. "Do you mean to make her your mate?"

"Lukian . . ." Kyril's voice held a warning. "She is human and mortal."

"And so she will remain. Unless you take her as yours forever in the rites of our kind."

"I know that," Kyril said a little irritably. "In any case, it is high time for me to—"

His cousin interrupted him. "To what? Find one woman and give up your wild ways?"

"Yes."

Lukian gave a disrespectful snort. "You have been made welcome in a hundred beds, some say. And I hear that women will not wash the sheets after you leave. They vow to treasure them forever."

"Ridiculous. And mostly untrue."

"Oh?" Lukian inquired. "What part of it *is* true? The one hundred women or the sheets that bear your manly mark?"

"Who have you been talking to?"

"I did not make up these wild rumors," Lukian said solemnly. "And I cannot trace them for you."

Kyril was silent. Had Vivienne heard such tales? She was too intelligent to believe them. She would dismiss them as boozy jests. Or so he hoped.

The oars splashed in the water as Lukian laughed rudely. "No one is as good at being bad as you are, cousin."

"A year ago I would have taken that as a compliment. But now . . ." Kyril did not finish the sentence.

"Since you met Vivienne," Lukian prompted. "Go on. You still have not told me much about her."

"We are friends."

"Hah."

"Perhaps not for much longer," Kyril conceded.

"Of course not. We are wolves at heart."

"We are men, Lukian. To all outward appearances. And we follow the conventions of men."

"More's the pity."

Kyril felt the hair at the back of his neck rise. An ancient response . . . but the threat he sensed was somehow new. His cousin, blood kin, seemed deeply troubled. Lukian's mind should have been easy enough for Kyril to read. But something seemed to have clouded it and Kyril could not pick up very much at all.

He did not understand Lukian's irritable mood or his interest in Vivienne. Perhaps it would be best for Kyril to assert his claim upon her now so there would be no misunderstanding later.

"I am considering Vivienne for the rites," he said at last. "Of course she must understand fully who we are and the nature of our mission in England, and that will take time. The men of the Pack mate for life but we are—"

"As wild as we want to be otherwise," Lukian growled. "And rough. The women of London adore us."

Kyril knew what he was talking about, but he had no wish to satisfy Lukian's unwelcome curiosity about his own sensual adventuring. Kyril was quite sure that his feelings for Vivienne went far deeper. But they had been inspired by physical passion.

"I would never treat Vivienne with roughness, not even in play. She is different."

Lukian rowed on. "All females are the same, cousin."

Kyril made no reply to that, occupying himself by looking from side to side. Theirs was not the only boat on the river but it was too dark, even for him, to make out many details of the others. Some craft had lanterns at the stern, some at the prow. A few had no light at all.

It was possible that they were being followed. The agents of the Tsar were everywhere, now that the Congress of Vienna was over and the Russian eagle was spreading its imperial wings.

It seemed hardly fair that one powerful man could decide the fate of millions, Kyril thought. His own clan included. But they numbered only in the hundreds, even after generations of intermarriage.

They might vanish in a few more.

He pushed aside his forebodings and looked at Lukian, whose unerring sense of direction was keeping them on course. *Nose to the wind.* The old Pack motto. Whatever was clouding his cousin's conscious mind did not seem to affect his instincts.

Perhaps the enfolding darkness heightened those. Kyril gave heed to his own and allowed himself to enjoy the journey. Moving swiftly over water in the night was a sensation something like flying. There was a tang of brine in the air. He inhaled deeply. The sea was not all that far away—if they continued around the Isle of Dogs, following the great loop of the

Thames, they would soon join the ships heading for the open ocean.

But they would not. They were only to observe and take notes upon the unloading of a Russian ship, the *Catherine*, at the Baltic Dock on the south side of the Thames. She had been listed as missing in the shipping news, but had been sighted two weeks ago and boarded by the officers of another, faster ship, who reached London first and relayed the news of her slow, perilous progress through drifting ice.

It was early in the year for that. The ship had sailed from Archangel on schedule, well before the port was locked in by winter, loading at the wharves of the Dvina before entering the White Sea and going on through the Baltic.

But northern seas were notoriously unpredictable and too many of the captains who sailed those dangerous waters were drunken brutes. The owner of the *Catherine*'s cargo, a wealthy man named Phineas Briggs, did not trust the ship's master, whom he had not hired. Nor did he trust his Russian factors or his English middlemen. Kyril and Lukian had been recommended to him by a friend, and the deal had been sealed with a handshake and a few well-chosen words.

Phineas Briggs did not believe the story about the ice and held that the *Catherine*'s captain had detoured to a remote island to pick up something that was not on the cargo manifest. In a word, he suspected smuggling.

Someone would be clapped in irons, Kyril knew, or several someones, and a great fuss kicked up in the Admiralty. Then everybody would go right back to smuggling again.

He could not help that. He respected Mr. Briggs's shrewdness but it was not as if he or Lukian needed the man's money. Nonetheless, the case provided an excellent cover and a reason to be on the docks, should English officials inquire as to the reason for their presence.

And the Taruskins had intelligence of something else that

was likely to be in the *Catherine*'s hold. Agents of the Tsar, traveling incognito. They apparently knew who many of the other members of the Pack were, if not precisely *what* they were.

Kyril sighed. He and Lukian would soon be on the south bank and at the warehouses on the dock, where they could observe the passengers leaving the ship in the morning—that would take place before the unloading.

They would have to memorize faces. The secret communiqué from their Archangel headquarters had given general descriptions, but warned that the information was not complete.

The *Catherine*'s captain might very well have picked up new agents who were not mentioned in the communiqué at all. The thought was troubling. Absently, he listened to the oars in the water. Dip, pull, up, dip. Over and over again. The sound was hypnotic.

"You are thoughtful, Kyril."

"I suppose I am. Has the *Catherine* docked, by the way? I forgot to ask you."

Lukian shook his head. "Not yet. But our man got the harbormaster roaring drunk and extracted a little useful information. He said she is downriver, riding low in the water. Her progress is steady, though."

"Her cargo must be heavy. Did you obtain a copy of the ship's manifest and the bills of lading?"

"Yes. Stepan Wisotsky boarded her at Gravesend in the guise of a customs inspector and made them wait while he inspected and memorized both. He was only able to make a cursory inspection of the cargo but he penned fair copies of the paperwork when he disembarked. A messenger brought them to me."

"Very good. Stepan has prodigious powers of recall."

"Yes. He was a bookish cub, as I remember. He would never come out to play in the Archangel winters."

Kyril laughed in a low voice. "I remember that. Stepan was no fool."

"How pure the snow was there and how white. Blindingly white." Lukian sighed. "London snow is grimy even when it falls. Full of soot and ashes."

"Yes, yes, the city runs on coal," Kyril mused. "Does the *Catherine* have any in her hold? It is a risky cargo and sometimes explodes."

Lukian shook his head. "Mostly timber, according to Stepan."

"That is what Mr. Briggs is shipping. Nothing out of order there."

"Stepan thought he saw a container marked as khodzhite."

Kyril raised an eyebrow. "Indeed. I am sure our client knows nothing about it. Khodzhite is valuable and very rare. And far more dangerous than coal."

"The shipment is safe enough. The container was made of lead."

"Did Stepan estimate how much of it there is?"

"A thousand pounds, he said."

"Hmm. No wonder the ship is slow."

Lukian interrupted him. "The Russian captains overload their ships, no matter how valuable the cargo or perilous the voyage. They would sacrifice their own mothers for a kopeck."

Kyril nodded. "Indeed." He remembered the captain on his voyage out to England two years ago. The tightfisted bastard had served his passengers spoiled meat and the sailors had to subsist on hardtack. Lukian, on a different ship leaving months later, had been far worse off, with a very devil at the helm.

"They treat their men brutally. Even an officer can be flogged."

Kyril knew that Lukian bore the marks of the cat upon his powerful back, deep scars that would never fade. Posing as a naval attaché on his way to England, his cousin had protested an ill-advised shortcut through drifting floes—the Taruskins had made the voyage in generation after generation, and a few of them could read the changing sea as well as their native ice.

Lukian had told Kyril much later that the captain seemed to suspect his otherness from the beginning—or had been told to break him.

The agents of the Tsar had already been looking for the Pack and gathering intelligence as to their travels, and their confidential assignments for the British Society of Merchant-Adventurers. None of whose members had been on Lukian's vessel to intervene for him.

For daring to question the captain's judgment, Lukian had been shackled for three days, unable to move. The captain made his punishment an object lesson to the others. He had been stripped to the waist in freezing weather, tied facing the foremast and flogged until his skin burst and the blood poured from his torn flesh, an agony he had endured in silence.

He had been taunted for that, loudly mocked by the captain and the petty officer who had flogged him, but still he said nothing. Then salt water was thrown by the bucketful upon his open wounds to wash away the gore and shredded flesh—and make his agony worse. But Lukian could not be broken by mere men, however cruel they were. He revealed nothing, not one secret of the Pack, or who and what he really was.

He was taken down half-alive, brought belowdecks and left alone to die. He hadn't. Before the sun came up the captain was found in his cabin with his throat savagely ripped open, his dead body draped with the corpse of the man who'd whipped Lukian. Both were naked.

And mutilated.

Their balls had been ripped from their groins, then stuffed, sac and all, into each other's mouths—no, their fate was worse, the sailors whispered. Their mouths had been stuffed before they were killed. To keep them from screaming. Before they drowned in the blood gurgling down their throats from the stumps of their severed tongues.

Persuaded, the first mate turned the ship and went the long way, around the ice, arriving in London a few weeks late.

The dead men had been buried at sea, wrapped in red-splotched shrouds of canvas and tipped into the waves. No holy verse was read and no tears flowed. And no one was the wiser in England. The dreaded execution dock of Wapping, built out in the mud of the Thames, did not creak under the last steps of the killer and no one was left in a noose for the tide to wash over him three times. Lukian left the ship and simply disappeared into London, finding his way to the Pack's lair near the Palace of St. James's, where he had healed.

Kyril had a great deal of respect for his cousin's temper. And his toughness.

"They are fools as well as brutes," Kyril said at last. "But captains earn nothing if they are forced to wait out the winter in Archangel and this fellow made it through."

"We are supposed to think so. I for one agree with Phineas Briggs." Lukian pulled harder on the oars, battling the swift current in the middle of the river. "But the northern seas will soon be choked with ice. It is lucky that the *Catherine* did not sink."

They turned their heads, hearing distant shouts in the dark. Sailors called to each other and a bosun's whistle piped. Kyril's ears pricked. He thought he heard the name of the vessel they sought, though he could not see the ship. "That may be her."

His own excellent hearing was not quite enough. But sounds traveled over open water in an uncanny way. In a little while his guess was confirmed.

"Well?" Lukian asked.

Kyril listened intently. "Yes, it is the *Catherine*. Her crew took advantage of the incoming tide."

"Perhaps they kedged her."

"A tedious business. Letting go an anchor and dragging to it makes for slow going. And I do not hear the rattle of chains."

Lukian exhaled. "Then they are relying upon a pilot or a tug."

"They would have to. Sailing upriver on so dark a night is treacherous."

Lukian left off rowing and listened too. "The watermen guided them. The sons of the Thames are a race apart, like us. Sometimes I think they share our powers of perception, Kyril."

"Perhaps." Kyril smiled slightly. "But they are not as we are."

Bobbing in the water, they looked in the direction from which the distant shouts had come, at last seeing the shape of a square-sterned cargo vessel riding low in the water. Looming in the darkness, it seemed unreal, a ghost ship under black sails, groaning.

Lukian set to the oars again, bringing them at last to the other side of the river and the Baltic Dock. They were well ahead of the *Catherine* and the smaller boats that attended her, their lights pinpricks in the dark. Lukian looked over his shoulder only once as he rowed, pointing the bow toward the open side of a ramshackle boathouse.

Here, though they were still in London, the sky seemed wider and higher, a great, dark bowl over the flat and marshy land of the docks. To the east, they saw the beginning of dawn.

Lukian nodded toward the horizon. "First light."

"Well done. We are here. No one saw us."

His cousin rowed almost silently now, angling the oars so that they cut into the ripples with even more precision. Kyril looked over Lukian's shoulder at the boathouse, its open side a gaping, dark mouth that would soon devour them.

They shot in and the rowboat bumped against a thick mat of fibrous stuff at the other end. Kyril gripped the seat to keep from falling backward and Lukian laughed under his breath.

"You are safe. Dry land awaits," he said.

Kyril made an obscene but cheerful gesture at his cousin.

"The same to you." Lukian drew down the oars and watched Kyril tie up. He pulled a leather bag from under his seat and tossed it onto the boathouse floor. "Time to change clothes."

"I had not thought of it," Kyril said, using a cleat to pull himself up and out of the rowboat.

His cousin did the same. "That is because Miss Sheridan has got under your skin."

Kyril pulled out a coarse shirt and trousers from the bag and scowled. "And if I wish to save my skin, I suppose I will have to wear these. The shirt stinks of sweat."

Lukian made a sound of disapproval at Kyril's finickiness. "And a good thing, too. You are much too handsome to go about among dockworkers and sailors smelling of women's perfume and dressed in fine clothes. The manly ones will beat you to a quivering pulp if they catch you alone and the others will make indecent offers. It would serve you right."

Kyril swung a fist, mostly in jest, and Lukian dodged it.

Lukian was already dressed in rough clothes, but his face was clean, Kyril noticed. Had his cousin forgotten that important detail?

He had not. The bag was lumpy. There were other things in it. Lukian rummaged and brought out two squat jars stopped with thick corks. "Rouge and powder." He pulled out the corks and stuck his fingers into the first and then the second, smearing his face with grease and ashes. Then he cleaned his filthy fingers by dragging them through his hair. "How do I look?"

"Alarmingly ugly."

"You are next."

"Give me a moment. I am tying these shoes. What dead body were they taken from? Anyone we know?"

"I don't think so," Lukian said gravely.

The crudely made shoes were damp inside and the less said about the way they smelled, the better. Disgusting. But Kyril was grateful to Lukian for thinking of everything.

His cousin was not far wrong about Vivienne Sheridan getting under Kyril's skin. He had stayed too late at her house tonight, hoped for more than she was ready to give—fie. Kyril prided himself upon his skill at knowing when a female was ready. Still, in her naive way, she was good about keeping her secrets. He had been told by someone else of her affair with the duke, of course, and that he'd provided for her.

He knew nothing about her family. She was well-bred and well-educated. Given her beauty, it was a puzzle to him why Vivienne had not married well. She had been very young when the duke made her his mistress, Kyril knew that much.

Howard? Horace? What was his first name? The old fellow had paid for the soirées at her Audley Street apartments and, in the end, deeded her the house on Cheyne Row and provided for her comfortable retirement from the business of love.

A business that was conducted like any other in London— prudent terms set in advance, a reasonable outlay of money, a dash of goodwill, and a final nod from the solicitor who looked over the necessary documents to end it.

Sealed with hot wax and a cold kiss.

The experience seemed to have left her curiously untouched. Almost innocent. Or as innocent as a nobleman's plaything could be.

It would be amusing to find out what else Vivienne might be keeping from him. Kyril had time to find out. He might go so far as to return to her tomorrow night.

In another minute they were walking through the boathouse door. The Baltic Dock was less than a quarter-mile away from it and the *Catherine* was entering the connecting canal. They hastened to the empty warehouse in which they would hide to watch the unloading.

Kyril took out a heavy iron key that opened a rear door, and both men stole inside. There was nothing to trip over or bump into—the walls echoed their every footstep as they climbed to an upper floor.

They sat down to wait, familiar with the tedious process that was about to unfold.

Lukian patted his pockets and found his tobacco and his pipe, lighting it and smoking while Kyril looked out a dusty window.

The light of dawn streamed in by the time the ship had entered the calm, flat water of the dock's immense pool. Men swarmed over her, uncoiling massive ropes as thick as their own arms, throwing them as easily as cats played with yarn. Cranes swung huge hooks and slings over the *Catherine's* deck and hatches began to open. The work of unloading was beginning. It would take most of the day and they had been told to stay there until the bitter end.

Kyril's belly grumbled but he ignored it. He had come away so quickly from Vivienne's house, disturbed that he had forgotten all about meeting Lukian at the river until she had finally told him to go. He had not thought of what he would eat the next day and it had not occurred to him to ask Tom to stop the coach and buy something.

But they would feed well at their lair tonight near the Palace of St. James's. A traditional Howl had been planned to welcome a new member of the Pack, a man he did not know.

Lukian heard his cousin's belly rumble. He reached into the leather bag and took out two small parcels wrapped in paper.

"Here you are. Bread and meat." He tossed one of the parcels at Kyril.

Kyril caught it. "You think of everything."

Lukian snorted. "I have no mate and no distractions."

"I am not impressed. Celibacy is nothing to brag about."

"I did not say I was celibate, did I?" The other man laughed, then stopped quickly. Both men heard an animal whine. There was a dog in the warehouse.

"Probably a stray," Kyril whispered. "But we should be careful."

Lukian stood up, unwrapping the other parcel as he walked to the landing of the stairs. There at the bottom was a very large, short-haired dog. Its ribs showed and its belly was hollow, lifted up almost to its protruding spine. Its penis trembled. The dog stared at Lukian, who stared back. The dog's lips drew back in a snarl that ridged its muzzle.

"Hello, my friend," Lukian said calmly.

The dog only growled.

Kyril saw his cousin press his lips together. Lukian was about to respond in kind. One touch of the tongue at the top of his mouth and long, tearing teeth would descend over his human ones. Most of the Taruskins had the trait. But they seldom used it.

Lukian smiled, fangs bared. The dog's tail curled between its back legs and it lowered its head. But it kept its wary eyes on Lukian.

"I see that we understand each other," he said. He separated the meat from the bread and threw it down to the dog. "Eat that. You are starving. Go in peace."

The dog snapped at the meat, devouring it in an instant. It looked up hopefully.

"Kyril . . ."

"Yes, yes. I am coming." Kyril joined Lukian at the top of the stairs and threw down his portion of meat. Minus one bite. He was no saint.

*　*　*

In another hour the first passengers paused at the head of the gangplank, a little unsteady on their legs at the end of their long voyage. Kyril and Lukian ran downstairs to another window where they would have a better view. There were scores of people jostling each other on the deck.

The English left the ship first. Lukian checked and counted them silently against the manifest. Traders in fur, lumber, jewels, coal, and minerals. Red-faced, boisterous, and glad to be home.

Then came the Russians, at least the richer ones.

Merchants led the procession—there was no mistaking their pompous air or their plump bellies. Their wives waddled after them.

Several other men of various nationalities followed. One wore pince-nez and carried a valise. Kyril cast an inquiring look at his cousin.

Lukian hazarded a guess. "The ship's doctor. He carries the most valuable cargo of all."

"Which is?"

"Morphine." His cousin's tone was curt. "Cheap to buy but worth more than gold when a man needs it."

Then a bearded boyar wearing ankle-length robes and a fur hat strode down the gangplank, swinging his arms inside his long sleeves. His wife followed him.

Kyril straightened. "Who is he?"

His cousin looked at the scribbled copy of the ship's manifest in his hand. "Not anyone who is looking for us. There are only two Old Believers listed. As you know, they have some understanding of our kind—"

"Lukian, what is his name?" Kyril wanted to know before the fellow and his wife were engulfed by the others like them on the dock, waving handkerchiefs and smiling through their tears.

"He must be . . . Vladimir Kromy of Moscow. And that is his wife Lizaveta."

"Ah! I have heard of him. Deeply religious and a thorn in the side of our dissolute nobility. But what are they doing here?"

Lukian only shrugged. "Meeting that horde of relatives, I suppose."

"Their faith is strict," Kyril said. "They will find London a perfect Sodom and Gomorrah."

"They are not wrong about that," Lukian said shortly.

The next passengers to disembark were a mixed lot. Kyril guessed at the nationality of each, then looked at the manifest to see if he was right. A massive Dutchman. Rawboned Germans, tall and strong. Ukrainians and Swedes, blond as angels. Several strapping African men, laughing together, their kit bags over their shoulders. Their bearing was proud, not like the hangdog look of ordinary swabbies. Kyril glanced again at the manifest in Lukian's hand. There they were. Three harpooners, two ship's carpenters, and one cook.

On and on. More came, clutched the ropes of the gangplank, made their way down. No one stood out. If there were agents of the Tsar on board, they ought to have appeared by now. Perhaps Kyril had not recognized them.

Then a horde of peasants, the men in caps and the women in shawls, stormed up from steerage, disheveled and exhausted, children clinging to their mothers' skirts as they were swished along in them to the bewildering strangeness of a new land.

"Hmm. Is that all?"

Lukian looked down at the manifest. "Wait. There are more to come. I have been counting."

The officers and crewmen of the *Catherine* were still onboard, running about yelling orders to the dockworkers they would supervise. They ignored the five tall fellows dressed like

English laborers who came to the top of the gangplank and paused.

"There they are," Kyril said. He had never been surer of anything.

"Yes. The officers are pretending not to see them. I expect they were told to make them look like Englishmen. They did not succeed."

"They look like what they are—Cossacks. Bloody-minded Cossacks."

Kyril nodded as he memorized their faces. Their upper lips were pale, he noticed. The long mustaches, the mark of their tribe, had been shaved off. "It would not be more obvious if it was stamped upon their foreheads."

Their height, their swagger, their ferocious cockiness—they would be easy to avoid. Or to hunt down, if it came to that. They would not be killed by any member of the Pack unless they killed first.

The five men still waited, as if someone was about to join them. A man who was even taller than they came up behind them, his coat collar turned up and his hat brim turned down. He spoke to one of the others, who nodded respectfully.

"Wait—I think my count is off by one," Lukian said. He stared at the manifest as if he could mentally add up all the people who had flowed down the gangplank once more.

The very tall man looked up. His gaze swept the pool of the dock and the quay teeming with laborers. He looked at the immense warehouses, built in ranks, strongholds that bore a distinct resemblance to prisons.

There was something about him that suggested he had once worked in one. His watchfulness, for one. For a few seconds, he seemed to be looking at the very window behind which Lukian and Kyril stood.

Even from here Kyril could see the livid scar that ran from

his temple to the corner of his mouth—and that his eyes were the color of ice. Bleak and freezing cold. He kept still, aware that he and his cousin could not be seen, given the direction of the light. The man's gaze returned to the Cossacks.

Kyril realized that they were only his bodyguards. The imperial secret service had not needed to send a team of agents. The man with the icy eyes was capable of slaughtering the entire Pack by himself, given time and the right weapons.

"No, Lukian. Your count is correct. I suspect that man, the last one, was exempted from appearing on the manifest. By special order. An order that had to be obeyed."

"What the devil are you talking about?"

Kyril pointed and made sure that Lukian's gaze followed. "That devil. His identity is a closely guarded secret."

"Then how do you know it?"

"I had an affair with the wife of the head of the Tsar's secret service. In St. Petersburg. A talkative woman. She described him well."

"Were you trying to get us all killed?"

Kyril clasped his hands behind his back and shook his head. "At the time, and that was two years ago, it was the only way to find out anything about the man. And she was very pretty."

"Who is he, Kyril?"

Kyril stared fixedly out the window. "That is Volkodav. It must be. Have you not heard of him?"

"No."

"Otherwise known as the Wolf Killer?"

Lukian nodded, his expression suddenly grim. "That name is one I know."

Several hours later . . .

He had left Lukian stationed where he was to observe the

complete unloading of the ship. Phineas Briggs was a powerful man and it would not do to accept his fee and not find out more about the smuggled goods aboard the *Catherine*.

The matter of the khodzhite was intriguing. As far as Kyril knew, the rare mineral had never been allowed out of Russia. Military scientists and strategists regarded it as a secret weapon, although its lethal properties made it so dangerous to work with that several had died and been duly rewarded with posthumous medals. And now a thousand pounds of it were about to land on a London dock.

The lead box would protect human beings from its harmful rays until it was unsealed. Nothing would protect the members of the Pack from Volkodav, however. His unexpected arrival might prove disastrous. When one of the clan died—Kyril corrected himself—if one of the clan died, it was as if they were all diminished in strength and spirit. They could not afford to lose a single man.

Kyril had crossed the river unobserved in the crowd on the ferry and followed the men he was watching to Threadneedle Street and the Antwerp Tavern. He sipped a pewter mug of ale, eavesdropping on the conversation of the *Catherine*'s captain. It was a one-sided conversation for the most part. The man sat at a round table about five feet away, blathering about his glory days. His junior officers wore glazed expressions as they listened patiently.

Eager to be out among the whores, no doubt, who greeted every incoming ship with sincere enthusiasm.

Kyril looked up when the captain paused for breath. Most of the younger men rose, made some excuse and departed.

Their places at the table were quickly taken by the Cossacks. The tavern was crammed with Russians—the captains and crews of the ships who sailed the Baltic routes came here.

Volkodav was not with them at the moment, although Kyril had seen him enter the tavern flanked by all five.

As Kyril had thought, the captain went out of his way to be generous and courteous. He greeted them in their dialect. "Welcome, my friends! Sit with me."

They scraped back chairs and sat down, half sprawling.

"Our legs are too long for this country."

"The women have bad teeth."

"English ale tastes like the piss of horses. Is there no vodka?"

"There is gin," the captain said. He spoke to a passing barmaid in English. "The damned English love their gin."

She giggled when he pinched her round arm. "So do the dirty Dutchmen," she said pertly.

"They are dirty," the captain agreed. "Dirty hands and dirty arses—"

The massive man Kyril had noticed on the gangplank stood up and threw the captain a menacing look. "I am a Dutchman and all of you can kiss my dirty arse."

He spoke in Dutch and the Cossacks took no notice. The captain wisely chose to ignore him. The Dutchman looked a little disappointed but sat down again.

"So, Captain Chichirikov, you old rogue," one of the Cossacks said, talking in Russian. "Tell us how to catch a wolf. That is why we are here."

"There are no wolves in London."

Volkodav returned as his bodyguard answered, "We have heard differently."

"Then you heard wrong." The captain signaled the barmaid and asked for brandy.

"Shut up, both of you," Volkodav said. "We may not be the only Russians here."

The girl brought five big glasses of brandy and the Cossacks toasted each other and drank them down in one gulp. The captain ordered another round.

Chichirikov looked around. "No, we are. I know everyone

here, except that fellow"—he nodded at Kyril without catching his eye—"and he is a Cockney. Filthy people. Brawlers and thieves. They barely understand the King's English, let alone Russian. We can talk in safety."

"Good," the first Cossack continued. "We are also looking for a man."

The captain gave the one who had spoken a narrow look. "Describe him."

"He is tall—"

"Many men are. But Cossacks are the tallest of all," the captain said genially.

It was shameless flattery but it worked. The Cossacks ordered the next round and toasted the captain's health.

Volkodav scowled his disapproval of the drinking. "Will you excuse me? I have to piss. I ought to do it on you five."

Kyril wondered how they would take that. But the Cossacks only laughed—carefully. The man with the icy eyes looked at them with contempt and walked to the back of the tavern where the pisspots were hidden behind a screen.

"As I was saying," the man who had spoken coughed, "he is tall and good-looking. A Russian. Dark hair and blue eyes."

"So? He could be anybody," the captain pointed out, wiping his beery lips.

"He passes for a gentleman in London. His name is Taruskin. Kyril Taruskin."

Kyril looked down into his pewter mug, glad that his face was dirtier than the workingman's clothes he had on. His dark hair was hidden under a dockworker's knit cap, the last of the things in the leather bag.

Not even he could take on five drunken Cossacks and expect to survive. Not with Volkodav to deal with at the last. The Wolf Killer was more dangerous than all the rest put together.

Kyril had to wait.

If nothing else, his sense of honor prevented him from attacking them now. None of their number had made a move against him or a member of the Pack. He reminded himself that he had been sworn to defend the English crown as well as his own kind. Picking fights in taverns fell far short of that lofty vow.

"He belongs to a club," Volkodav said. "A very old one, which was founded in Russia. A branch of it was established in London more than a hundred years ago."

The captain seemed unimpressed. "What of it? Every man needs a place where he can gamble and fornicate in peace."

"Yes. But this club exists for other reasons."

Chichirikov guzzled the last of his ale and set his mug down on the table with a thump. "What is it called?"

"The Pack, I believe. Just the Pack."

"Ah. Like a pack of dogs, eh? I suppose they are worthless dogs at that."

Volkodav gave him a thin smile. "Mongrels."

"I see. Well, I am sure this pack can be found. Most gentleman's clubs are in Regent Street or near it. Or in—" He named several more streets, all in Mayfair.

"Our agents have been to all of those. There are more of us than the five who accompany me. They have already fanned out through London."

Good God. Kyril had not picked them out from the crowd, which was now a faceless blur in his mind. Kyril remembered the ale he was supposed to be drinking and put the mug up to his face to hide his shock.

"Have they reported back?" the captain asked.

"Not yet," Volkodav said calmly. "Finding the Pack has always been a problem."

"But surely—"

"The men who belong to it are equally at home in the wilderness or cities. They have a maddening ability to vanish in either one."

"I see. What are their names? The other ones."

Again Volkodav gave the other man an unpleasant smile. "At the moment?"

"Yes."

"Besides Kyril Taruskin, there is his cousin Lukian—a man to be reckoned with."

Yes. He would cut your throat without a moment's hesitation, Kyril thought.

"And Kyril has brothers, Semyon and Marko."

The captain nodded. "Do you have pictures of any? Drawings or miniatures, perhaps? This fellow's description"—he nodded at the Cossack—"was vague."

"It is what I was told," the Cossack said earnestly. "We have to kill him, you know, or risk the firing squad."

The Cossack's loyalty was admirable but stupid. He did not have to return to Russia to be shot. Kyril or his brothers could do the honors here in England.

"Taruskin is no better than an animal," Volkodav said quietly. "He must die first. A degrading, painful death that his brothers will witness. Then it will be their turn. This is the wish of the Tsar."

One of the other Cossacks spat on the floor. He might not be quite so loyal as the others. Kyril studied his face for as long as he dared. If he could turn one of the five against his comrades in time—

"And you are prepared to do this?" the captain was saying.

The Cossack who had spoken opened the front of his coat no more than an inch. Kyril glimpsed a flash of steel.

"At once. As soon as we find him."

"London is a much bigger city than Moscow, my friend."

The captain's comment sparked a ruckus. The men shouted over each other as to which city was greater, claiming Moscow, the beating heart of their beloved motherland, as the fairest metropolis on earth. Anyone who disagreed should expect to be disemboweled, drawn, and quartered.

Sentimental and vicious, Kyril thought. Not an unusual combination.

He hated listening to their bluster. He could not pick them off in so public a place and he wanted to leave. But he had to stay with Volkodav as long as possible.

"Enough!" The captain held up his hand. "I will help you track down this animal—no, this man. Where does he take his pleasure? That is the easiest way to find a fellow."

"He is often with a lady. Blast—I forget her name."

"Brandy," another said.

"That is not a name."

"Of course not. I want more, you fool!" He snapped his fingers at the barmaid.

Another of the Cossacks withdrew a folded paper from his pocket. Kyril strained to see. He mispronounced the name he read aloud but Kyril understood him only too well.

He had said Vivienne Sheridan. Kyril was thunderstruck. How had they known of her? The imperial secret service had a long reach.

But the address the man read next was her old one, in Audley Street. Kyril was thankful for that.

Flooded with fear, he did not know whether to go to her and tell her to flee to the countryside or—it might be best to avoid her entirely. What if he was followed to the house in Cheyne Row?

She could be easily used to bait him. And as far as he knew, she was not in love with him. What if she turned against him— no, the thought was impossible. The secrets he sensed she was keeping were those of a gentle soul betrayed. She was a woman of the world but he truly believed in her essential purity of heart.

Lukian would have told him that he was a sentimental fool for thinking so.

So be it.

Somehow Kyril would protect her, at the cost of his own life if necessary.

You will have to. The thought flashed into his mind when he saw Volkodav come toward the table again.

"Where were you?" one of the men asked.

"I told you, you drunken idiot. I had to piss. But it is time we left. It is hot in here."

The air in the tavern was humid and the windows were covered with mist. Streaks of water created clear spots here and there—Kyril spied a young whore peering in, looking at the new faces. Through the blurry window, she looked a little like Vivienne. Dark hair and dark eyes. Delicate features. His heart ached for her.

By and by, she sauntered in and the illusion of the resemblance vanished. Young as she was, she had been too long at her trade and her careworn face showed the strain of it. But she perched upon the knee of one of the Cossacks as if she were a new girl on the street, afraid of no man.

They roared with laughter, and the man she'd chosen put his arm around her waist. He fondled her bum, squeezing hard through her bedraggled skirts with his free hand. The girl looked nervous but she was game, smiling and joking though she understood not one word of their talk.

"Nice piece of chicken."

"Take her to bed."

"No, save your money. Fuck her on a table. It's cheaper and you can keep your breeches on. And your boots."

"None of that here," the captain said. "There is a brothel close by. The madam is an old friend. She will not overcharge."

"Then we will go there. But first we drink again."

The barmaid brought another round and escaped a groping

hand. The whore was not so lucky. The Cossack's fondling had grown rougher and her threadbare gown showed it. The bodice was ripped and so was the waist.

"I should pull this off you and fuck you in front of everybody."

She smiled desperately, not understanding.

"Then I will give my friends a turn, eh? One of us in every hole you have!"

The men roared with cruel laughter.

"But Grigor—she has only three!" one yelled.

He squeezed her waist so hard she gasped for breath.

"Then we will make her more," he growled. "One in the bum!" He jabbed her there with two bent knuckles. "And one in the head!"

The blow split the skin just above her eye and his knuckles came away bloody.

The girl shrieked with pain, but he opened his hand and boxed her ear with all his strength. Dazed, she still showed spirit and struggled against him. The Cossack tightened his grip and slapped her across the mouth. Her lip split and more blood trickled down her chin.

Something snapped in Kyril. He rose and hit the man on the side of the head as hard as he could with the pewter mug. The Cossack fell backwards in his chair, not releasing the girl even though he was unconscious.

She sunk her teeth into his arm and he let go at last. She scrambled to her feet and ran out the door, wiping the blood from her lip on her sleeve and holding a hand over her injured ear.

A blow like that might leave her deaf. It was a wonder she had escaped with her life—

Volkodav stepped in front of Kyril and took the mug from his hand. Kyril stood his ground.

Icy eyes looked into his. Flat. Expressionless. There were

flecks of steel-gray in the other man's pale irises and his pupils were unusually small. Kyril saw no flicker of recognition.

"You are gallant," Volkodav said in English. "But you are also a fool." He looked down at the unconscious Cossack on the floor. "And so is he." His next words were just as calm. "Go. I have no wish to fight you for his sake."

Kyril dared not answer. Volkodav had not recognized his face but Kyril could take no more chances.

He had to warn Vivienne . . . Kyril realized that the other man was looking intently at him. He should not have even thought her name.

He nodded, ready to walk out the door. He would not run.

Volkodav raised the mug in his hand so swiftly that there was no chance to react. He smashed it into Kyril's face with extraordinary force.

Kyril felt his cheekbone crack and swayed on his feet. Blood filled his mouth. He spat it into Volkodav's face and punched him so hard he could feel the other man's guts give way under his taut skin.

Volkodav's eyes rolled to the whites. He swayed on his feet and bile spurted from his open mouth.

The others stared with shocked surprise as Kyril delivered two more punches and the Wolf Killer joined the Cossack on the floor.

3

Running for his life could get him killed. Kyril slowed down when one too many faces turned toward him in the waning light of day. Long shadows crept forth between the ramshackle tenements, some of which leaned on each other at their tops. The river folk were a suspicious lot and he was a stranger here, after all. On a somewhat more respectable street, he found a hackney cab.

The driver gave him an indifferent glance. "Naow. Move along."

Kyril looked down at his filthy clothes—in his haste to get away, he had forgotten what he looked like. The drying blood had soaked his coat and Volkodav's spewed bile had an acid reek.

He dug out a gold guinea, which the driver squinted at as Kyril began to give his address, then thought better of it, and made up one several blocks away. He had no wish to be remembered.

The driver smirked. "Oho. Near Grosvenor Square. Gone slumming, m'lord? Crawling home to the countess?"

Kyril ignored the man's insolence. He had to get back.

The driver relented. "In you go then," he barked. "And sit up. No leaning back. Yer coat will besmirch the seats."

Kyril was tempted to knock him off his seat and steal the cab. But a wild, careening ride through these streets, pursued by a howling driver, would soon draw a mob, yelling, "Stop! Thief!" just for the fun of it.

He tossed the man another guinea, which he quickly pocketed.

"Much obliged, m'lord."

He got in and contrived to look out the open side, holding a small mirror in his palm so that the street behind them was reflected in it. He had taken it from Lukian's bag of tricks. Supernatural powers only went so far.

No one was following them. He folded his fingers around the mirror and leaned back. The seats were filthier than he was. The hard, jolting ride helped him think.

He would walk home and enter through the back door, making sure that he was still unobserved. Then he would go to Vivienne's house and tell her—

Nothing. She was safe where she was. If he stayed away. He did not know how many men were on their trail, but the combined brains of the Pack and their unique skills should enable them to find all the agents and dispatch them in time.

How to tell her to stay safely within doors until then was a problem. Vivienne struck him as independent to the point of willfulness, though her manners were elegant. Still, the look in her eyes held a hint of wildness.

A very good thing in a female, especially when combined with intelligence.

But he could not, for any reason, tell her of the Pack's existence at this point, or explain his own nature. Certainly not now, when their very survival was at stake.

Volkodav would see to their destruction with pleasure.

He was an enforcer and a killer. A very efficient one. And patient. With the might of the Russian state behind him.

And the silent support of the Tsar. Alexander I's intolerance of difference—in religion, in politics, in anything that might threaten his absolute rule—had forced the Pack to go underground in Russia. Until now, their bastion in England had seemed safe. No longer. The unremarkable town house in Great Jermyn Street, not far from the Palace of St. James's, might be under surveillance.

Then again—perhaps not. The Pack had been recognized, sub rosa, by the King of England himself.

The mad George III. Only his long-suffering attendants listened to him now. Long live the king, thought Kyril bitterly.

An hour later, the hack rattled over smoother cobblestones, a sound he recognized. He was close to home. The driver pulled his nag to a stop, and Kyril got out at the wrong address he had given.

The man was as nervous in this neighborhood as Kyril had been in his. He drove away in haste.

The streets were empty. The houses seemed blank, locked, no doubt, although light shone from many windows, piercing through the shutters.

Using every strategy he knew to ensure that no one was following him, he came to his own house eventually and entered as he had planned. His servants were below—he could hear their voices from the kitchen in the basement. Kyril walked quietly across his front hall, intending to slip upstairs and bathe somehow. The workingman's clothes could be bundled and discreetly thrown away tomorrow.

There was a letter waiting for him on a silver tray. He glanced at it and immediately recognized Vivienne's handwriting.

He almost hated to touch it with his dirty hands but he was consumed by curiosity. He slid a finger under the flap and broke the wax seal.

She had not signed it. She had written only one sentence.

I must see you tonight—come to me.

Kyril left his house as stealthily as he had entered it.

He doubled back several times and went part of the way through Hyde Park. Now and then he glimpsed a figure in the shadows as furtive as himself.

There was nothing for it. He did not know if Vivienne had already been spotted by Volkodav's agents. She might have been already threatened with harm or hurt. His dirty clothes now concealed a loaded pistol and a dagger.

The two miles—no, the way he chose was longer and he felt every extra step—were eaten up quickly by his long strides. Sometimes he ran when he was quite sure that no one was about to see.

At last he came to Cheyne Row. The windows of the houses were shuttered, but very few were lit.

Her bedroom window was, though. He supposed it was her bedroom—the other room had to be her drawing room and that one, her study. Above both was a glowing rectangle of double shutters, over a flower box from which cascaded some night-blooming plant.

Kyril looked around once more and saw no one. He went to her house and knocked softly, hoping that her manservant would not answer the door. He willed her to understand, sending his thoughts to her through brick and plaster, that he had come to her as she had asked. He knocked again.

The footsteps that came to the door were firm.

Hers, he hoped. As feminine as she was, Vivienne was not one to mince her words or her steps—

The door opened. Damnation. It was her manservant, Henry Freke.

Henry slammed the door in his face.

He waited.

Then Henry opened the door again, waving a cast-iron poker at him. "Be off!" he thundered.

"But—"

The door slammed again. He heard the bolt slide into place and a bar come down on the other side for good measure.

Kyril went down the stairs, looking for pebbles to throw. He collected a handful and bounced them off the wooden slats of the shutters.

"Vivienne!" he called, hoping she would hear.

In a minute, the window inside was open and the shutters that protected it were folded back. He saw her heart-shaped face looking down. Her eyes widened when she saw him. Kyril pulled off the knit cap and waved it at her.

Her lips parted. She recognized him, battered face and all.

He went up her front stairs again, hearing her inside explaining the matter to Henry, who muttered some reply. Evidently she had sent her manservant away—he was nowhere in sight when Vivienne opened the door herself.

She pulled him in, looking with fearful puzzlement at him, searching his face.

"Kyril—what has happened?" She reached up a hand to touch his bruised, swollen cheek and thought better of it.

"I had business to transact in the East End." He kept his voice calm, still determined not to tell her details that could be beaten out of her. But if Volkodav forced his hand, Kyril would tie her up and spirit her out of London to some safe hiding place if he had to. Immediately.

"Oh?"

Clever woman. She said nothing more. He knew he had been given an opportunity to blurt out everything. Had she bombarded him with questions, he could have done the manly thing and ignored her completely.

But he did have to say something. "The other man did not like my terms."

"I see. Business, was it? I thought there were only a few reasons for gentlemen to visit that part of London. To gamble or to see the prizefights or—" She did not finish the sentence.

Her proud expression made one thing clear. She did not want to ask if he had been whoring.

"I will admit to gambling." True enough. He had been playing a risky game. One he intended to win eventually.

She gave him a cool look. Not the kind of woman who would wring her hands or weep, young as she was. Kyril was not surprised somehow.

"Well, I suppose it could be said that playing at cards is a sort of business. It must have been a low establishment. You are dressed accordingly."

"Forgive me, Vivienne."

She only nodded.

Best not to argue. Or explain. "Thank you."

"Come up to my bedroom. Your cheek needs to be seen to. I was about to bathe—there is hot water and soap."

This was an interesting turn of events. He had not expected to excite her sympathy. No, he had come to see if she was all right. That done, he ought to leave.

He didn't. "I cannot impose—"

"You are not imposing. Kyril, did you get my letter or have you been out all day? Henry sent the boy to deliver it by the early afternoon. It concerns—" She broke off.

"Yes, it arrived. That is why I came. But I was not at home when it did. I only just opened it. What has happened? You said that you must see me."

"It was written in haste. For no very important reason."

He studied her, trying to read her thoughts. She was troubled about something, but he had the feeling that she was afraid.

"Vivienne, you must tell me—has anything unusual happened? Has someone come to see you, someone you don't know?"

She gave him a wry smile. "I am not sure I know *you* very well at all, Kyril. But no one has come to see me."

"Good."

"Why do you ask?"

He shook his head, still not ready to explain.

"You are my only visitor today. And I am glad of it."

"Ah." He was nonplussed. There had been no other woman in his life who would have let him in her house looking like he did. "I would have come sooner but—" He hesitated only for a moment. "Well, here I am."

"I will tell you why I wrote to you upstairs, if you don't mind."

"Not at all."

He had never been inside her bedroom. The thought of her, naked, about to step into her bath, distracted him from the throbbing pain in his cheek. Not that he would see her that way. He would not stay long in Cheyne Row.

She led the way and for the first time Kyril noticed what she wore—a long silk robe sashed tightly at the waist. Nothing underneath. The slithery stuff moved over her round behind in a provocative way as she mounted the stairs. He would have to be a dead man not to appreciate that.

He was suddenly glad that he was alive.

They came to the landing of the upper floor and she swept ahead of him, not looking back as she pushed open the door to her bedroom.

The décor was feminine in every detail. A canopy bed was hung with rose-embroidered curtains that were otherwise sheer. The bottom sheet was rumpled. The coverlet and blankets had been kicked down to the foot of the bed.

He tried not to look at that particular piece of furniture. It was only too easy to imagine her in it, and himself on top of her and—

"Come here."

She pulled up a light chair by the side of the sloped tub that rested on the carpet. There were towels folded next to it on a small table. Wisps of steam rose from the water in the tub.

"The maid only just finished filling it. Please sit down."

Kyril obeyed. An hour ago he had looked death in the face and now here he was in her private paradise.

The fear that drove him to her side seemed to vanish with the wisps of steam rising from the bath. The scene was dreamlike. Perhaps it was nothing more than that—Volkodav had hit him hard. His brain might be swelling inside his skull and affecting his reason.

If he was indeed imagining all he saw, if this was a dying man's dream, then death was kind.

He wished he could take off his coarse clothes and throw them into the fire that warmed the hearth . . .

And step into the hot bath, watched by her . . .

Then rise from it, dripping wet, and let her towel off his naked body . . .

So that he could seduce her slowly, like a gentleman . . .

Which he wasn't. He was ready to pounce. His wolf blood thrummed in his veins.

He sat down anyway. Vivienne picked up a washcloth and trailed it in the hot bathwater, wringing it out and keeping it in one hand. She pulled over a chair for herself and sat in front of him.

Despite the pain, he wanted to kneel in front of her and open her thighs and—he focused on her concerned face. She touched the warm, wet cloth to his cheek.

Kyril flinched. "The bone might be broken. I heard it crack."

"Do you want me to stop?" She looked at him anxiously.

"No."

With tender motions, she cleaned away all the blood, and scrubbed a bit harder at the ashes and grease he had smeared on his face. "Hmm. You went out in disguise, I see. Slumming?"

The hack driver's contemptuous word. "And what do you know of that?"

Vivienne reached for a basin and filled it with water to continue cleaning him. "The duke used to visit dens of vice, as he called them. He liked actresses and low women."

"I see."

She gave him a thoughtful look. "Perhaps I should not have told you."

"What he did is no reflection on you."

Vivienne only shrugged.

He thought again of how little he knew about her. "Did you assume that I was with another woman?" he asked suddenly.

"No." She soaked the washcloth again and got the rest of his face clean. "I do not think the cheekbone is broken. But you will look ugly for a few weeks. Any woman who looks at you will turn away."

That seemed to please her. So she was jealous, but too proud to say so. Kyril understood that particular mix of emotions.

She set the cloth aside and looked into his eyes. He saw compassion in them—and feminine pique—and some other emotion he could not name.

"That does not bother me. So long as you do not."

What else was there to say? *If you will not tell me the reason for your letter, then I really must be going. There is a man—no, five men—who need killing.*

No. He would stay with her for a little while longer. If Volkodav or any of the others had tracked him here, he would find out soon enough.

A look of sympathy softened her beautiful green eyes. He would definitely kill to protect her.

She laughed lightly. "Shame on me. I am sorry, Kyril. I should not have said you were ugly. Your face must hurt terribly. You look—"

She broke off again.

"What is it?" he asked. "There is something on your mind and it is not the way I look. Will you not tell me the reason for your letter?"

Vivienne considered her words before answering him. "Do you remember the book of folktales you gave me?"

"Yes. That was some time ago."

She rose and walked about the room. "You look like one of the Roemi warriors in the illustrations. Although the one I saw was stripped nearly bare."

If only he could do the same and step into the steaming bath to wash away the violence he had seen. The deliberate cruelty of the man who'd hit the poor little whore had stained his soul.

He needed to be purified somehow to take her as he passionately wished to do.

"Ah yes," he said politely. "The Roemi. Some say they were a Scythian tribe. The Taruskins might have descended from them. No one really knows."

She seemed intrigued. "I thought the Roemi were fictional."

"The stories about them are," he said carefully.

"There was a picture of one about to throw a spear. He looked very much like you."

"Poor fellow." Kyril touched his face and winced.

"Well, he was unmarked." She sat down facing him again. "But there was another who had been hurt. A wounded warrior dying heroically on the battlefield. His face had been beaten, more badly than yours. But even so. . . ."

Kyril scarcely knew what to say and so he said nothing.

"I suppose it is an odd time to bring it up but your resemblance to the Roemi is extraordinary." She threw up her hands. "I will confess, Kyril—"

"One of us ought to."

She raised an eyebrow. "And what do you mean by that?"

"Nothing. But do go on." He slipped off his coat. "I am getting warm. Do you mind?"

"Not at all."

She reached for the coarse garment he removed and folded it over her arm, standing there. She looked charmingly domestic, like a young wife putting away her husband's clothes.

"I fell asleep after you left . . . was it only last night, Kyril?"

So much had happened. But she was right. It had been just twenty-four hours ago that he had said good-bye to her and driven away in the rain. "Yes."

"I was on the chaise in my study—I had picked up the book of folktales to read myself to sleep. And then . . ."

She hesitated, looking intently at his face. Kyril raised a hand to touch his cheek. Was he bleeding again? He glanced at his fingertips. No. They were dry. If not clean.

"The pictures seemed to come alive."

"That is odd."

"First it was the picture of the peasant women going into the church—I thought I could hear their voices, like little dolls talking. And then I found the first warrior and the story of the Roemi and the wolves. He was about to throw a spear—oh, Kyril, this is silly."

"No. Please go on."

"He looked so real that I touched the paper." She hesitated, giving him a worried look.

"And?"

"It felt warm. I happened to touch his chest. He had a heartbeat. I know I felt it."

"How very curious."

"I looked again and he had thrown the spear."

"No."

"Yes!" Her next words tumbled out in a rush. "I flung the

book to the floor. But I could not resist picking it up again and that is when I saw the second warrior."

"Vivienne, I—I scarcely know what to say. I bought the book on an impulse and only glanced at the pictures."

"In England?"

"No, in Russia. But I do not remember much about it."

She studied him for a long moment before she spoke again. "The very last picture was of a landscape. A desolate place but beautiful. Covered in snow. There were mountains. Black, jagged mountains."

Kyril gave a start. She had described the land of his birth, a place he had not seen since he was a very young cub.

His mother had made the long journey through the frozen wastelands of northernmost Russia to Archangel, carrying him on her back to join their relatives there, some of whom had prospered beyond their wildest dreams. He had grown up in that port city on the Dvina. Living as he now did in London, never far from the Thames, often put him in mind of that river. But the Dvina was featureless by comparison, and its banks were mostly empty of people.

Like so many of the exiles of the Pack, he had not considered even Archangel home. It was just a way station on an endless journey. Their true home was forever out of reach—but was it so surprising that there would be a picture of it in a book about the Roemi?

No. He was only surprised that the illustrations had captivated her so. He felt a wave of irrational happiness that had everything to do with the future and not the present. She possessed an instinctive understanding, evidently, of who and what he was.

The rites of the Pack, their ancient history, their customs—none of it would seem strange to her when the time came to explain it all.

"Kyril, where did you get that book?"

"Truthfully, Vivienne, I cannot remember. Let me think."
He paused. "I found it in my library one day and thought to
give it to you. We had been discussing fairytales and poetry, and
it occurred to me that you would like it—"

"I do. Very much."

He tried to recollect exactly where he had purchased it. Not
in Archangel, surely. There were only two or three bookshops
there—no, the old book had not come into his keeping there.

"Ah, now I remember. I bought it in Moscow."

He looked again at Vivienne and said no more.

She seemed disappointed and puzzled, perhaps because he
was frowning. She did not even notice that her beautiful robe
had fallen open over her bare thighs.

Dear Wolf, she was temptation itself. The sight of her pearly
skin, the thoughtful look on her face, her tousled hair . . .

In another instant Kyril forgot everything but her. The fight
in the tavern, the painful injury to his face, the threat of further
harm—his desire for her pushed it all away. It was a good thing
that his workingman's trousers were both loose and thick. He
had a raging erection.

"I had hoped otherwise," she said at last.

"Why?"

"Well, the book is in English. Translated from the Russian."

"Of course." He had not even remembered that, but then he
had given her the book some months ago without ever really
reading it.

"Please think, Kyril."

"Why is it so important?"

"I—I thought perhaps that I had gone mad for a moment
when I saw the illustrations come alive."

"You were tired, that was all. Such things happen. The eyes
play tricks."

"I also thought—this is very silly—that the book might be
magic."

Unlikely. It was only a book. The Taruskins and their clan were the descendants of magi, but their powerful spells were far older than printed words. Their magic came alive in songs, in howls, in the distillation of fear and blood into poems celebrating their gods and their battles, their loves and their lust.

The book was made of paper and ink and nothing more. However, he felt inclined to indulge her.

"A charming idea. You would certainly feel sure it was true if you saw the bookshop. A quaint place and very old. It was in the oldest quarter of Moscow, as I remember."

"Do you suppose you could go back there and ask the owner if—"

"No, Vivienne," he said gently. "That part of Moscow was all built of wood. I am sure it burned down when the city was put to the torch."

"I see," she murmured. "A pity."

"Napoleon thought so. There was nothing left for the Grande Armée to steal."

It occurred to Kyril that he might have been conscripted to fight them all the same. It was just as well he had left the country before the French invasion. In his wolfish way he had considered himself a patriot but no longer. Volkodav had not known who Kyril was but his icy gaze made it clear what the Wolf Killer thought of men who were not like himself.

He stood up and went to look at himself in the mirror over her chest of drawers. To his amazement, the swelling had gone down.

Pah. He might look better but he was suddenly seeing tiny stars from standing up too quickly. He would not tell her that. But more than ever he knew that his injury had affected his reason. And his sense of time. Here, with her, it seemed to stand still.

"You have a healing touch, Vivienne."

"Nonsense."

"You do," he insisted. "I believe the bone is not broken after all."

She rose and moved behind him, looking over his shoulder at his reflection. "Hmm. You do look better." She wrinkled her nose. "But you smell bad."

That would be because you make me sweat when you stand so close, Vivienne. She could not read his mind, fortunately. "Do I?" was all he said.

"The heroes in the book did not," she said pertly.

He gritted his teeth. "They were only pictures. I am real."

If she stepped forward just one more inch, her nipples would brush his back. If his clothes—and her robe—were to vanish, her nipples would touch bare skin.

If only they could step into a picture in the book themselves and leave the world as they knew it behind.

His groin tightened unbearably. His cock pulsed. Kyril rested his hands atop the chest of drawers and moved forward himself, away from her. Without her knowing it, he pressed his achingly erect flesh against an ornate brass handle until it hurt . . . and subsided.

But he could not stop looking at her. Her reflection in the mirror was not real, but she was. Heartbreakingly so. Knowing that she was behind him, close enough to capture in his arms if he turned around and followed his instincts—

He was ready to shatter the looking-glass with one blow. The intimacy of their position was overwhelming. A mood this sensual had no beginning and no end—he wanted it to go on forever.

He fought for self-control. He reminded himself of the threat that might have already cast a shadow over her quiet street. And he racked his aching brain for a pretext that would allow him to stay just a little longer.

He turned around. "May I see the book, Vivienne? I really do not remember it all that well."

"Of course. It is in my study."

She drew her robe more tightly about her and went to the door. Kyril sighed with relief. He would have a chance to compose himself.

Not likely. Not in a boudoir like this. The waiting bath, the fragrance of her fine soap—it was a new cake, he noticed.

How he would love to soften it in the hot bath and rub her all over with it . . . then rinse her lovingly . . . and watch the water roll down her velvet skin . . .

Vivienne came back in and held the book out to him.

"Here it is."

Kyril took it with a nod. The volume was even smaller than he remembered, not useful for concealing the erection that had stiffened his cock to its full length. He would have needed an encyclopedia for that.

Thank God she looked at the book in his hands, then at his face, and not down.

He opened it, leafing through without reading it. He noticed the illustrations she had described and came to one that she had not.

She lifted the crinkly sheet that protected it.

Just that gesture—the fragile paper held in her fingertips and lifted up while her beautiful eyes widened with appreciation—made him want to ravish her. Kyril groaned inwardly.

The picture was of a Roemi warrior but he was not throwing a spear or dying on the battlefield. This warrior had been vanquished by love. He was carrying his lady upon his saddle, riding in front of him through a meadow surrounded by thin trees showing the new leaves of spring. They both wore white, flowing clothes. The delicate flowers that encircled her long hair were the same as the ones that dotted the grass.

"He picked them for her," Vivienne murmured, "and made her a crown. How handsome he is."

The stallion that bore them both—the powerful horse clearly was a stallion—wore chains of the same flowers around its neck. Kyril looked at Vivienne as she looked at the picture. Without thinking, she touched a fingertip to the warrior's muscular thigh.

Her lips parted. "He is warm! It is just as I thought—"

Kyril could stand it no longer. "You are imagining it, Vivienne. It is only a picture. A very pretty one."

"But—"

Kyril closed the book and put it on the dresser. He reached out to embrace her. "You are warm. And you are real. Come to me."

She had hesitated and they argued about the book for the better part of an hour. She'd taken it back and he took it away from her again, swearing to discuss it later. Only then would she go into his arms.

Of course, she had not been very far away from them in the first place. But she could not help thinking of how she had ended their first real kiss, fool that she was.

But he had come back. The book had brought them together.

His hands moved down, cupping her behind through the light of her robe, squeezing lightly but sensually, claiming the lush flesh in a masterful way, pulling her to him. He was fully aroused—and had been, perhaps, for some time. Vivienne could feel his magnificent erection, barely restrained by his trousers, against her body.

She might as well be undressed, her skin was so sensitive. The tight sash around her waist felt like she was being gripped by his strong fingers, as if he had already taken her upon all fours—oh God. The thought was highly erotic. She reluctantly broke off the kiss and rested her head against the front of his coarse shirt, not caring that it was dirty, rubbing herself against him, sighing her pleasure at what he was doing.

"Don't stop, Kyril," she whispered. He treated her to another deep, firm, double squeeze, lifting her by the buttocks. "Ohhh..."

Rather more roughly, he kissed her again as he held her in this way, tonguing her deeply. Vivienne felt her lips swell pleasurably under the pressure of his impassioned mouth, but she cried out faintly when he nipped her lower lip, tasting a trace of blood.

He stopped at once. "Forgive me—oh my darling—for a moment I forgot myself. I did not mean to hurt you."

"I know, Kyril."

With a deep, regretful sigh, he let her slide down his body. She would not let him alone—and in another moment she'd found the pistol and the dagger.

"So. What business were you on to need such things?"

Kyril set both aside. "A dangerous business and nothing you need to know more about."

"Hm. I have been put in my place."

"Your place is in my arms."

He pulled her back for another kiss. She went up on tiptoes, pressing herself against him more ardently than before. Kyril's breath came raggedly and he murmured wanton words, Russian words, into her hair. Vivienne blushed, even though she did not understand what he was saying.

Then, craving more, she writhed, begging silently with her body for more of what he had given her. He reached down and clasped her buttocks again. Full and round as her behind was, his large hands encompassed it, giving her even greater pleasure as he listened to her whispers and caressed her there in a rhythm that both soothed and excited her.

Another rough kiss shaded to tenderness when he felt her

tremble. There was no need for him to hold her so tightly now—she had molded her body to his. His arms were tightly wound around her waist and she moved her hips freely, back and forth, side to side, riding his muscular, wool-clad thigh. The friction excited her.

Her hands stretched up and she raked her fingers into his black hair, drawing his face down to hers for a deeply erotic kiss that let her share with him each and every sensation her body was experiencing . . . until the pulsing waves began.

"Ohhh," she moaned helplessly. Again and again. A gentleman to the last, he assisted her to climax, murmuring loving encouragement as she rubbed and rode him, nearly naked and utterly wanton, to a crescendo of bliss.

She swayed against him, quite unable to stand without his support. With one hand, he pushed back the wet locks of hair that straggled down her neck, tenderly whispering more words she did not understand.

Vivienne let him soothe her, aware that she had lost the battle of wills she had contemplated, not caring in the least. He picked her up in his arms and spun her around once, then a second time, laughing with her until he collapsed in the chair she had set by the bath for him, still holding her securely.

She opened her eyes and looked at him with wonder. "What have I done?"

He laughed again. "I think you know. Shall we do it again?"

"Oh, Kyril . . ."

He picked at the knot of her sash and soon had it undone.

"Into the bath with you."

"But what about you?"

"I shall bathe at home."

"That is not what I mean."

He slid the robe off her shoulders and let it fall to the floor. He held her more tightly, one arm still under her bent knees and one around her back, and rose, almost folding her double.

"What are you doing, Kyril?"

He kissed her cheek. "I am about to dip your beautiful arse into the bath. The water has cooled. Imagine how good it will feel upon your cunny."

He bent and dipped her bottom in just as he had said.

"Oh!" She kicked her feet. "It does feel good."

He lifted her and dipped her again.

"Do you want it all the way?"

She twined her arms around his neck. "Yes," she whispered.

He set her down on the bottom of the bath with a bump. Water splashed over the side. Vivienne laughed and extended her legs over the rim. "Again, that was not what I meant."

"Enjoy yourself. I want to watch." He tossed her a sponge. "Soak that. And let the water trickle over your breasts."

"It is not as warm as it was."

Kyril nodded. "Then your nipples will stand out all the more."

As she played with the sponge, he shucked his clothes, revealing a very male body of such beauty that she drew in her breath.

His erection jutted out. She could not help but look. He took it into his big hand, stroking and squeezing until the pulsing veins on it stood out still more.

Then, more gently, he rolled down his foreskin, watching her eyes as she looked at the heavy, plum-colored head. A drop of clear fluid appeared in the small hole at its tip.

She touched a fingertip to it and took her first taste of him.

"Ah, Vivienne," he growled.

"Mmm." She looked up at him flirtatiously.

His groin was taut and so was his flat belly. The musculature of his lightly furred chest stood out. His tight, tiny male nipples did too.

He let go of his cock and bent all the way over, cupping her breasts until her nipples stood out and drawing one into his mouth, sucking it until it tingled. Using the edge of his teeth, he nipped it gently, right where the areola encircled the small column of pink flesh. She cried out with soft pleasure. He sucked her nipple again, then moved to the other.

She held his head, tugging at his earlobes. Kyril's stubble had come in and the slight rasp of it against her damp skin felt wonderful. He moved to her neck, growling and nipping and biting with infinite gentleness upon her ear.

His lovemaking was both animal and human, unlike anything that she had ever experienced.

It felt incredibly good. It had been much too long.

He stopped what he was doing and sat on his haunches by the tub. Like his chest, his thighs were lightly furred. The fine, dark hair did not cover his skin so much as outline his muscles. His cock rose up from a curly thatch of hair that was just as dark, so thick she barely glimpsed his balls.

He adjusted his position slightly to give those parts more room, and then she saw them. Large and round. Bigger than plums.

Vivienne reached out and cupped them. They were heavy in her hand, as if they were full of delicious come.

"Stroke yourself," she whispered. "I want to watch."

"Very well."

She fondled his big, hot balls while his encircling fingers slid up and down his shaft, looking intently at his action.

"I swear," he said, "there is nothing more erotic than your eyes. Watching . . . just watching."

She looked up at him and he bent down to capture her mouth in an ardent kiss.

Like their first, it went on and on. But this time, he broke it off. "Ah. The excitement is too much."

She pushed herself up and out of the bath when he rose. He was not lying. His cock was enormous. The head looked larger than before, tightly bound underneath by the foreskin he had rolled down to free it. How good that soft, engorged flesh would feel driven deep inside her by his strong shaft.

She wanted him. Now.

He took a towel and dried her gently but vigorously from head to toe. He kissed the damp tendrils of dark hair that clung to her neck, wiping away the water that had trickled down from them.

And then he turned his attention to the delicate curls between her legs. Kneeling in front of her, he parted her labia and applied his tongue to the small, hooded rod nestled there. His tongue moved lower and for the first time she enjoyed penetration from him.

Kyril's powerful body was quite flexible, and he lowered his head so that he could thrust his long tongue up inside.

Shaking with pleasure, Vivienne moved her legs wide apart in an open stance. He tongued her deeply again and again, murmuring his pleasure in doing so.

But he avoided her clitoris. Clever man, she thought. She would have come very quickly had his eager tongue lapped at that.

Kyril sat back and looked at the part of her body where his face had just been buried. He seemed about to . . . lick his chops.

But no. He gave a growl from deep inside his broad chest and lay down on his back on the carpet, his own legs sprawled.

"Kneel over my face, my love," he said. "I can fondle your behind while you do that and put my tongue in you even more deeply. Would you like that?"

"Y-yes."

"Then come down. Don't be shy about it. I love a womanly arse. I love the taste of you. You can push down . . ."

She straddled his face and did just that.

His tongue went in and out as he caressed and squeezed her behind, spreading it to get his tongue up in her more deeply.

She reached out to hold onto his cock. It was like having two men. One in her cunny and one in her hand.

But he still would not lick her clitoris.

Frustrated, she squirmed on his face. She saw his belly tighten with suppressed laughter and held his cock more tightly, administering a little punishment.

He rolled her off and rolled up, leaning on his elbows. "Now?"

"Yes, Kyril!"

He picked her up and whirled her around, making her dizzy, making her laugh. His mouth was soft and a little slippery from his attentions to her cunny. He rubbed it clean on her shoulder.

Then he walked the few steps to the bed and put her down respectfully. Almost worshipfully. As if she were royal. A very queen. He seemed to want to be at her command.

"On all fours."

There was nothing very royal about that position. But even a queen had to obey someone.

She rolled over and let him look his fill at her bare behind and thighs, which he stroked. He kneeled once more behind her and this time her clitoris did get a few lashes, just from the tip of his tongue as he ran it over her intimate flesh, preparing her.

He stood behind her. Instinctively, Vivienne got her behind up as high as she could. She felt him position the plummy head just inside her labia. His big hand spread across her lower back to steady her.

In another second, he rammed the entire rod all the way inside, filling her. He grabbed her hips and held her tightly, pulling all the way out and going all the way with every single stroke.

No half measures. No wriggling about. Just deep, thorough, repeated penetration. The feeling of it made her gasp with pleasure.

He sighed deeply and dropped down over her back, supporting most of his weight by the strength of the muscles in his belly. His torso slid up and down as he took her somewhat less deeply, but she found it even more erotic. She could feel his tight nipples, and he in turn tugged on hers, making her breasts sway and bounce.

He nuzzled her neck and bit at it gently, moaning in her ear. "You are beautiful . . . so beautiful . . . my God, Vivienne . . ." His hand reached back between her legs.

"Oh!"

His fingertips found her clitoris, which he rubbed, using her slickness to excite her more.

Dominated and comforted by his strong body over hers, pushing back with each thrust of his long, thick cock, her breasts stimulated and her clitoris teased with expert skill was Vivienne's ultimate undoing. An orgasm began deep within her, an unfolding sensation of pleasure so intense that she screamed.

Both of Kyril's hands moved down, holding the inside of her thighs. His entire body was braced perfectly as he gave her the maximum effort a man could give, thrusting his cock deep and hard into her welcoming cunny, growling in bliss as he ejaculated in hot spurts that she could feel. So good . . . ahh . . . *ahh* . . . it felt so good . . .

He eased off her and collapsed on the bed.

"Stay with me," she whispered.

"Do I look like I am going anywhere?" he whispered back.

Vivienne laughed under her breath and curled herself into the crook of his arm. He tightened it around her and dashed the sweat from his brow away with one hand.

Her toes scrabbled at the end of the bed and she managed to catch a blanket with them, dragging it up until she could get it in her hand. She spread it over them.

"Vivienne . . ." he murmured. "I love you."

She was taken utterly aback. Where had that tender sentiment come from?

"Do you, Kyril?"

He made no reply. His breathing was deep and even. There was a smile of inexpressible joy upon his sleepy mouth.

Dear God. *I love you* was the last thing she expected to hear. Or wanted to hear.

Some hours later, he was still sound asleep and she was wide awake, trying to figure out what had just happened, step by step.

Firstly, he had sought refuge at her house after a drunken brawl in some nameless place.

She had no idea why she had even let him in, looking the way he did, over Henry's protests.

His manners were always so damned perfect, even with his bruised cheek and the blood dripping onto his rough clothes— not his, certainly, although they had fit him well enough. He'd asked to come in as if it were the most natural thing in the world to do in his condition.

Of course he'd had the pretext of her letter.

It had been hastily dashed off and she had not wanted to say in writing what she had seen in the book. She did not know how his house was run, and thought it possible that someone else might read it—his secretary, perhaps.

The long wait for a reply had first irritated her, then alarmed her. As far as the book, his responses had been somewhat evasive, she thought. There was something about it that he was not telling her, she was sure of it.

And why had he asked if anything unusual had happened or if someone had come to see her?

The day had passed like any other. Cheyne Row was not known for excitement.

Vivienne curled around his long body. Damnation. It was only a book and that was that, she told herself. She could not say why the folktales and the pictures had such a hold on her imagination. But, as he had dryly pointed out, he was indeed real.

Very real.

He stretched slightly in his sleep, allowing his powerful thighs to fall open.

His cock nestled in the thatch of dark curls between his legs and the heavy balls that she had fondled while in her bath hung down.

She cupped them. His breathing remained deep and steady.

What dreams he would have, she thought slyly.

Rising from the bed, she soaked a washcloth and gently rubbed away the last trace of stickiness.

She held his soft cock in her fingers and ran the cloth around it, then over his balls, holding them up by the sac and rubbing underneath.

He parted his legs even more. Vivienne smiled to herself. Was he dreaming of being licked as he had licked her? She could make that fantasy come true.

She set the cloth aside and applied her tongue to his balls, warmly licking him there. Then she took his soft cock in her mouth.

He arched a little but made no protest. Whatever mischief he had been up to before he had arrived at her house truly had exhausted him.

She sucked more intently, making him stiffen in her mouth.

Then she felt a hand upon her hair, stroking gently.

So he was no longer asleep. Very well.

But how sweet it was to have a man in this way, as if she were in control and not him.

Her tender cock-kiss was making him breathe ever so slightly faster. But he said nothing. They both kept up the pretense that he was asleep.

As if he were a man she did not know, a man she had happened upon in a wood, sleeping.

In the flickering candlelight, his eyes closed, Kyril looked like a statue of a young god from eons ago. Watched first, then touched by her as he lay dreaming. Naked, without shame, his brawny thighs and what was between them were shown with animal abandon.

Love, bah. She preferred lust. Open desire was an uncomplicated pleasure.

She stopped for a moment, holding herself up on one arm and keeping his cock in her hand as she looked between his widely spread legs.

He held still, his eyes closed, and said nothing. But the cock in her hand stirred and grew longer.

Clearly it excited him to be looked at so intently by a woman. His muscular buttocks were tensed, not sinking into the bed. His large balls had tightened and drawn up.

She could well imagine the ride he would give her when she straddled him. He would push up strongly against her cunny from below, reaching to hold her behind with ease. Even lying down, a tall man was better suited for women's pleasure.

Vivienne let go and she heard him sigh.

She considered other ways to please him sexually—and then it occurred to her that it might be best done by pleasing herself.

In truth, she was still somewhat annoyed with him for making her wait all day for a reply. And for not explaining where he had been. And even for saying that he loved her. He should have prepared her for that.

Kyril sprawled, relaxed. Why was it that men got to do as they pleased so often, and women never?

Hmph.

She rose once more and went to the chest of drawers, pulling open the top one and withdrawing a handful of silk scarves, light as gossamer.

She came back to the bed and let one drift over his nude body, giving him an ethereal caress.

Again he arched . . . but he made no sound. Vivienne knew instinctively that he understood her as well as she understood him at this moment. He would make amends for his ungentlemanly behavior by permitting her a different sort of lovemaking.

He had, in effect, rolled over and displayed his belly.

Vivienne grinned. It was a fine, hard-muscled belly, as tense as his spread thighs. She saw the tendons in them twitch as he awaited her next action.

He was watching on the sly. She caught a gleam of light under his thick, dark eyelashes. His sensual lips parted as he drew in and released his breath.

Vivienne took one scarf and wrapped it around his ankle. He murmured his assent. This she tied to the post of her canopy bed. Then she tied the other. Then she tied his hands to the posts at either side of his head.

He could snap all the scarves in an instant. Such feminine bonds would never hold him. Shackles of cast iron might not even be enough. No, it was his willingness to indulge her wanton whim that kept him where he was.

That intrigued her. As did the way he looked when bound. Vivienne did not have to touch herself to know how wet she was.

Kyril was hers. Tall, powerful, and wicked, he was spreadeagled on her bed, his private parts on display for her eyes only.

She touched his nipples, stroking them in tiny circles with her fingertips. Then she treated him to a very light pinching on each. His chest rose as he sighed with pleasure, reveling in her feminine punishment of his flesh.

"How nice to know that you can be a—" He drew in his breath. "No, perhaps I should not say it."

"The word is bitch."

"A very beautiful one."

Vivienne smiled and let her fingernails trail over his chest down to his belly. She used just her fingers to stroke his groin in low half-circles.

Kyril tensed.

Her teasing made his cock stand up straight.

She took the last scarf, and wrapped it once around the base of his cock.

"No knots," she whispered.

"As you wish."

"I want to be able to tighten or loosen it quickly."

"Do what you will, Vivienne. I am yours."

Indeed he was.

Holding each end of the scarf, she moved over him and took his erect cock into her mouth. Pulling and releasing the silken bond as she sucked brought him to a still higher pitch of sensual excitement. His hips began to move involuntarily. She thought it best to stop. Vivienne sat up, one hand on either side of his body so that the delicate scarf made a strap holding him down.

He opened his eyes all the way. The look in his eyes made her gasp. She had awakened something in him that was wild indeed. Sitting up in one motion, his arms bulging, Kyril ripped the scarves from the upper bedposts. She heard more ripping as he pulled his legs free.

Then it was her turn.

So swiftly she did not know precisely how he had done it, she found herself tied with the now-ragged strips of silk. He had saved one—the one she had tied around his cock.

He let it drift over her nakedness. The sensation was so light and so erotic, she wanted to scream with it. But they were not alone in the house.

"And now, my love, I will give you the pleasure you have given me," he said softly. "No. I will give you more."

He tossed the scarf aside and put a large, warm hand over

her navel. He stroked her belly in sensual circles, then moved up to her bare breasts, using both hands to stroke and squeeze. Stroke and squeeze. He added his mouth to it, holding each breast in turn so that her nipple jutted out and giving each a thorough sucking.

Dear God. The pleasure she felt went deep—very deep.

He pulled his head up and wiped his wet mouth on her shoulder. His grip was firm and assertive, claiming her breasts. Possessing her flesh. Then he spoke into her ear, not letting go. "This is what I would have done had you let me stay that first night, Vivienne."

"Ahhh . . ." She moaned and writhed, pushing her breasts into his hands. "I am sorry that I—that I sent you away."

"But I am glad you did."

He began to caress her breasts again without sucking her nipples, watching her face as he did, hypnotized by her uncontrollable response.

"Why?" she whispered.

"Because it made me want you all the more. I will not be satisfied with this one night."

He released her breasts and Vivienne sighed with disappointment.

"Be patient. There is more pleasure in store for you."

"What is it?"

"You are very greedy."

"Yes."

He untied her wrists and ankles. Vivienne got a good look at his cock, straining toward her with every move he made.

Kyril rolled and lifted her so that she was on hands and knees.

"I must say the sight of you on all fours is extremely exciting. Your arse is so round. And your cunny looks so inviting . . ." He stroked her back with long motions, sparking a deep fire within her.

Then he moved around and knelt upon the floor, so tall that

he could easily apply his tongue to the outside—and then the inside—of that feminine flesh.

His tongue probed and then entered. Vivienne dropped her head upon her folded arms. His lovemaking was incredibly skillful.

His warm hands caressed the sensitive skin of her behind, then spread the cheeks slightly to get his tongue deeper in her cunny.

She groaned, wanting to be satisfied but willing to wait until the sun came up for the ultimate moment. The pleasure he was giving her was intense.

Kyril stopped. "Move up," he said. There was a raw urgency in his tone that thrilled her.

Before she had completed the action, he was on the bed. Unerringly, he put his knob to her labia. She felt his hand on her back holding her still. She breathed very deeply, wanting the moment to last. The anticipation of the strong thrust to come was something to savor.

He too was enjoying it.

Kyril rested his hands on her arse. In another second, he spread her cheeks roughly and rammed all the way inside her cunny. He grabbed her thighs, encircling them with his large hands and raising her bodily from the bed to give her everything he had.

In and out. In and out. His thick cock was all that she knew. His balls were too tight to swing but their heaviness and size were easy to feel, adding momentum to his every thrust. She responded with shameless abandon, supporting herself easily on her outspread hands as he continued to lift her by her thighs and take her from behind, hard.

Hot spurts pulsed through his rod—she felt every one. Once more he cried out his pleasure and her name. Once more he cried out that he loved her.

Vivienne moaned, a ragged sound of surrender that had no words.

4

_____

Two days later . . .

Vivienne sat in an overstuffed chair in a house she hated. Her father's second wife sat opposite her, not moving.

Abigail did not bother to smile. Her round face was unlined, except for her furrowed lips, which looked as if a drawstring had been run through them and pulled tight. She seemed to have decided to let Donal Sheridan do the talking.

It galled Vivienne that the woman simply listened. But her father was indifferent to her feelings. Nothing had changed.

"I assume you read my letter," he said.

"I did." Vivienne had wanted to burn it. But that seemed unwise.

"Then you know what I want."

"Yes."

He crossed one leg over the other, resting his slippered foot upon his knee. "You haven't sent it."

"No, I haven't. And I won't."

"My girl, you owe me something."

"I don't agree."

Donal's eyebrows rose. Of late he had not trimmed them and she supposed that Abigail excused herself from this task. He had gone gray and wispy, and there was not much hair left on his head. His eyebrows, however, had grown thicker, with long tufts that looked almost like horns.

"No, my darling daughter? Are you telling me no?" He favored her with a sarcastic smile. His teeth were yellow and stained, and a few were missing. He looked unhealthy and she noted that his belly was slack and bulging.

He smelled of liquor. His great weakness. He did not have many, but she sincerely hoped that one would kill him.

"I am."

"Ungrateful of you. But then—"

"I am not your darling," she said tightly.

He scratched the white stubble on his chin and looked at her thoughtfully. "That is no way to talk to your old father."

"You no longer control me, Donal. Be careful what you say."

He looked at her narrowly. "Donal, is it? So it has come to that. A sad day, Abigail. A very sad day when a daughter calls her father by his first name."

His second wife pursed her drawstring lips. "Yes."

Vivienne wanted to smack her.

"You are very like your mother, Vivienne. Obstinate."

A quality that had helped her survive. He'd thought nothing of locking her at night in a closet as a child while he rained blows upon her helpless mother in the next room. Just as helpless, Vivienne had heard her cries and pleas for mercy through the wall between them.

"But I will forgive you."

Did Donal Sheridan think she had forgiven him? She never would. Gently bred, the daughter of an earl, Caroline Bentham

Sheridan never fought her ill-use at Donal's hands, and died young, her spirit almost broken by her brute of a husband.

"That is not necessary."

He cleared his throat. "Then I won't."

The two of them stared at each other. Donal's eyes eased away and he glanced at his silent wife.

"Shall we get down to business?"

"I suppose we must."

"Now that you have driven the duke from your bed—"

She barely suppressed her anger. "That was his choice. And it is no business of yours who is in my bed."

"But I am your father," he said pompously. "It is my duty to think of such things."

"Mr. Sheridan is quite right." Abigail spoke up at last. "Your reputation and all that—you should listen to him."

"Leave." Vivienne stood up and spoke sharply to the woman. "Before I make you."

"Well!"

Her father waved a hand. "Please. Ladies should not quarrel."

"She is no lady," Abigail huffed.

Donal only laughed. "What did you just say? You great whore, that is funny, coming from you."

Vivienne did not smile. Her father's second wife was the proprietress of a shop that sold sheep-gut condoms and quack cures for syphilis.

Abigail's eyes filled with tears. "Donal! How can you?"

He shrugged in a lordly way. "Don't give yourself airs, Abbie."

"You live off my money and yet you talk to me like that—"

"I will talk to you however I please. And you will listen. Unless you want a beating. Perhaps the last one did not take."

Abigail pressed a hand to her heart, gasping.

Vivienne said nothing. She stood her ground until her father's wife gave in and left the room, quivering with sobs.

"You two deserve each other."

"Do you think so, Vivienne?" Donal took his foot off his knee and went to his desk, where he sat down and took a ledger from a drawer. He opened it and leafed through the dog-eared pages. "She knows her place. That is good enough for me."

"I am sure that is true."

He hummed idly as he ran his finger down a column of numbers. "You have been conscientious about the payments. Until recently."

"Horace paid you."

Donal chuckled. "Always on time, too."

Vivienne said nothing. Her father, who had regarded her as a burden to get rid of as soon as possible after she'd turned eighteen, had been surprised by the duke's generosity. And taken full advantage of Horace's desire to avoid scandal.

"Dear old duke. He did not want it known that his paramour was a—"

"Shut up." She wanted to shriek the words.

"Oho. I have touched a nerve."

She took a step toward him. He didn't look up, only flipped through the pages, humming again.

"Someone has to pay for your sin, Vivienne."

"I never sinned, not in the way you think."

"Well, it was difficult to prove, either way," Donal said affably. "Sometimes just saying a thing is enough to make it so."

"No more!" she burst out. "Not another cent!"

"Are you sure?" he inquired in a mild tone.

Vivienne began to cry. She hated herself for it.

"Do not snivel." Her father came to a blank page at last. "As I was saying, now that the duke is—"

"He would have his man thrash you if he knew that you—"

Donal held up a hand for silence. "But you never wanted him to know. Has that changed?"

Vivienne held her tongue. Let him say the worst. She would not give in again.

"There was a time," he said thoughtfully, "when you wanted no trouble. You had snagged a rich man to look after you and perhaps you hoped he would marry you."

"The duke was married."

"Oh yes. You did not want the duchess to learn of your existence—he did not tell her. But I am sure her ladyship did. However, she did not know everything. No one does, except me."

"And you are a liar."

He coughed, still looking down at the ledger. "And you are the daughter of a liar. And were kept by another liar. So who will be believed in the end?"

Vivienne gave a bitter sigh. "It no longer matters."

"Yes, it does."

"Explain yourself, you dirty bastard." She hated to show the least sign of anger, hated him to think that he held the slightest power over her. But he did. Still.

"Well, well." He looked up at her at last. "We have gone from 'Donal' to 'dirty bastard.' I have come down in the world."

"Indeed you have." She looked around at the shabby furnishings. The room was crowded with bric-a-brac and smelled of stale tobacco. Abigail's sofas leaked horsehair and the rugs bore the marks of her father's pacing.

He was not doing well and he wanted money from her. She had been his sole source of income for some time. Even though the goods her father's second wife sold were much in demand, there was not much profit in them, and Abigail might turn him out upon the street someday.

"Let me get to the point."

"Good."

"Abigail saw you and Mr. Taruskin in Hyde Park."

Vivienne tensed. They had been out for a stroll after their wonderfully wanton night together. "What of it?"

"Congratulations on your new man. I made a few inquiries. He is a foreigner and a rich one. Possibly richer than the duke. He is a bit mysterious, but it is not as if you can be too picky."

She said nothing.

"And I understand he is kind. Helps his countrymen, gives to charity. A soft touch and a true gent."

Living with Abigail above her shop had coarsened him, Vivienne thought. And even from here, she could smell bad port on his breath.

"You would not want him to know about the child you once bore," Donal mused. "No more than you wanted the duke to know."

She gritted her teeth. "Get on with it."

"Of course, babies are born on the wrong side of the blanket all the time. You were a little fool. I still don't know why you thought any man would marry you."

"Nor do I."

Donal gave her a thin smile. "Perhaps I hit you too often. You were so eager to get away. But then there was your mother. You would not leave her when that young pup abandoned you."

Vivienne felt an abyss open beneath her. Her father had disowned her when he'd finally realized she was with child. Her mother, incurably ill by then, had helped her hide it, sewing loose gowns. Slender as Vivienne was then, her pregnancy hardly showed—and then the baby had come too soon and died.

Her father had pronounced it a blessing in disguise and mocked her grief. That act of heartlessness was among his lesser sins, however.

Donal had come to London to find her months later, living in the apartments Horace paid for on Audley Street. And he had threatened to tell the duke a different version of the story.

"Have you forgotten that I am here?" Donal Sheridan said peevishly.

"No," she said at last, coming back to the present moment. "I would not leave Mama and I would not let her die in pain either. I asked Horace to pay you so that you would go away and leave us both in peace."

"No more than you should have done."

Vivienne wished she was strong enough to hurt him as he had hurt her. And her mother. She drew in a deep breath and forged on. "He loved me then, in his way. And he paid what you asked without complaint."

Horace had given Vivienne plenty of money of her own as well, but her father had not known about that. Still, it had enabled her to bring her mother to London and pay for a nurse for her in the final months of her life. Caroline Bentham Sheridan had died peacefully in her daughter's arms. She had begged for something that broke Vivienne's young heart: that Donal's face not be the last one she saw. She had wanted her daughter.

Caroline would have no other descendants.

The doctor had told that to Vivienne months before.

When she'd found out that her lover had gone and was never coming back, Vivienne had succumbed to profound despair—and given birth too early, helped by her mother. Sweating and screaming, she'd sensed how afraid Mama was for her. She had tried to be brave and failed miserably.

Her newborn baby had barely seemed to breathe and did not even cry, never even opened her eyes. Her daughter's face had looked to Vivienne like that of an angel. Pure. Untouched by the evil in this world and slipping quietly into the next. She had lived but an hour. Vivienne had named her Arielle and held her while her own mother wept.

It was her daughter's face that she'd memorialized in the ivory miniature. Her own angel, if only for a little while. In the one hour of her life, Arielle had been loved. Vivienne had not known that she could love anyone like that.

"Vivenne, pay attention."

She came back to reality when she heard her father's voice. She looked at him with loathing.

"What?"

He tapped the ledger with his pen. "Your new man must also be made to pay. You would not want him to know that you smothered your own infant, would you?"

After Vivienne had stormed out, Donal went straightaway to the secret cabinet that held his wine and whisky. He poured himself a glass of whisky and drank it down in one go. His ungrateful daughter had defied him. Called him insane and worse. Threatened a lawsuit.

The duke must have made a handsome settlement upon her, he mused. What if she did sue him for libel? It was too bad that Horace was much less likely to be interested in suppressing juicy stories about his former love. Donal had liked that variation on the theme of The Fallen Woman. It was funny that his favorite tavern had the same name. Its swinging signboard featured a badly painted picture of a whore with enormous tits holding up a mug of ale.

Her new lover was somewhat of an unknown and it was not clear how he might react. If Kyril Taruskin was a hothead, or obsessed with trivial things like the truth, then Donal might end up shot.

The glass in his hand shook. His nerves needed steadying. He poured himself another and drank that too. But Taruskin was not the only mark Donal had in mind. Another fellow was interested in finding out more about Vivienne and had even sought him out. He too was Russian. A rival for her affections, perhaps. Donal did not know and did not care, so long as he got money. Inventing scurrilous tales about his daughter had been a profitable business so far. And a gentlemanly one.

He had been discreet. He had no idea why she had cried so.

5

Near the Palace of St. James's, a few days later . . .

Kyril had joined his brothers and his cousins and the arriving members of the Pack at the lair, a town house that was unremarkable but somewhat different from the others on Great Jermyn Street. Its walls were unusually thick and its windows were small.

All the better to howl in, long and loud. At the moment, preparations were underway for a Howl with a capital H, an ancient tradition of their clan. The rite had been enacted in secret since the first Taruskins and others of their kind had come to England more than a century ago. Every newcomer to the Pack of St. James was welcomed with one.

He had told Vivienne before they parted that he had to attend a family gathering. He saw no reason to be more specific than that.

In time, his clan would observe a rite still more ancient: the communal and public punishment meted out to those found guilty of violence or harm to one of their number. However, he had neither culprit nor evidence.

Volkodav and the Cossacks had not appeared anywhere near the lair, or Vivienne's house. Kyril kept men stationed there, changing the guard every six hours.

She knew nothing of it, coming and going as she pleased, as usual. His lady love only liked to be controlled in bed, and certainly not always even there. The thought of their wondrous night together still made his cock swell and twitch in homage. She was extraordinarily beautiful in every way. And truly, only a bitch when it amused her. Which amused him no end.

He had not found time to write to her and thought it best, given Volkodav's presence in London, to stay away for a little while. It satisfied him that she was as safe as he could keep her for now.

And she had seemed uneasy about his avowal of his love for her, responding only with a question, as if she doubted him.

He had not been as sleepy as all that when he'd said he loved her. Groggy from a fierce blow to the head, yes. Glowing with their shared passion, certainly. But he'd meant what he'd said.

She could take all the time she wanted to think about it. He was preoccupied with the matter of Volkodav in any case.

And primed for a fight. His passion for her—and their uninhibited, blazing-hot sexual encounter—could and did burn away the fear of death. Guarded by nature, Vivienne was very different in the bedroom. Ah, it had been so good . . .

Kyril forced his thoughts to return to the Wolf Killer, who waited so patiently to strike. As far as he knew—and his instincts were excellent—he had not been followed either, nor had his brothers or Lukian.

Still, he was wary, convinced that it was a matter of time. He knew too well the effectiveness of a surprise attack. Many agents, more than he knew, were all over London. Lukian, who had enlisted others of the clan to monitor the docks, was convinced of it also.

The tension of waiting was mounting. For that reason alone he was very much looking forward to the Howl. So were the others. To a man, they were sticklers for tradition, observing theirs with the devotion of all émigrés.

Semyon, his younger brother, came up and patted Kyril on the cheek, rather too near the remains of the bruise. Kyril glowered at him. "Was that necessary?"

"Oh—I am sorry. Does it still hurt?"

"Now it does. It was healing nicely. Until you walloped me."

Semyon only laughed. "Forgive me, my brother."

Kyril cuffed him. "That is my forgiveness."

"I deserved that." Semyon grinned. "Has that bastard Volkodav or his henchmen shown his face?"

"I have not seen him anywhere in London, nor have my informants. Have you?"

"No one has seen him. So we will enjoy ourselves tonight and not think of him. With so many of us gathered, he will not take unnecessary risks." Semyon turned when another man entered. "Ah—here is Marko."

The third brother came in, looking around the hall before he spotted them and walked over. The Taruskin men resembled each other in their height and strong build, but the younger two did not have Kyril's dark blue eyes. Marko's hair was ash blond and his eyes were brown, while Semyon's was a true black, the black of the Roemi warriors in the old stories, and his eyes were hazel.

Still, anyone looking at the three of them could see that they were brothers, Kyril thought. Semyon and Marko had filled out impressively. Both had been scrawny in childhood, always fighting with each other. Semyon still had a scar on his ankle from a particularly fierce bite that Marko had once given him.

The servants of the Pack bustled about setting the table with zakuski, the appetizers, and bottles of vodka, a spirit that was difficult to obtain in England.

"I hope there will not be as many toasts as the last banquet," Kyril said. "There was not a man standing by its end."

"I was up to the last," Marko pointed out.

"You had to hold onto a chair. And it went down with you."

"Still, I was the only one on his feet," Marko insisted. "I won, fair and square."

"It is no great honor," Kyril said dryly.

He saw Ivan, the butler, pour himself a small shot of vodka to test the flavor, and nodded to him. The man was a distant relative of the three Taruskins, and he and his assistants made their own in the cellar from humble potato peelings. The result was very strong, of crystalline purity, and reserved for feasts and banquets. The greengrocer who supplied the house with pecks of potatoes had once expressed curiosity as to the large quantity on order, but Ivan came up with a plausible explanation and saw to it that his bills were promptly paid. The Pack disliked attracting attention as a rule.

But here in their house and their hall, they might do as they pleased, especially when the non-Russian servants retreated to the kitchen or went home, and their countrymen and women took their place. One of these came in, a girl with long braids and a pointed kokoshnik headdress that framed her high cheekbones and almond eyes. She tapped Ivan on the shoulder and twirled her embroidered skirts for his approval when he turned around.

"Is that Ivan's mate?" Kyril asked.

"Mate to be," Semyon replied. "She will be serving tonight."

"She is a pretty girl. What is her name?"

"Natalya."

The butler clasped her around the waist and kissed her on both cheeks and finished with a kiss on her nose.

"She is very pretty," Marko said. "And I hear she has a very cold nose."

They all laughed. "Healthy, eh?" Semyon asked. "I am happy for Ivan. We will be celebrating his wedding feast soon enough."

"Where is our new member?"

Semyon thrust his hands into the pockets of his light tailcoat and shrugged. "Not here yet. He arrived only yesterday."

"His ship came in at the Baltic Dock, I assume."

"Yes."

Rudolf Panasenko came up to them. Elegantly dressed for the Howl, he had been assigned to the dock for a fortnight before Lukian and Kyril had spent the day there, disguised like them in filthy clothes, his face blackened with charcoal and his hair under a knitted cap.

He had obtained evidence for Phineas Briggs on a related matter of cargo thefts, not smuggling. His investigation was ongoing, and focused on the ordinary sailors and petty officers. However, Briggs was convinced that the orders for the thefts were coming from the Admiralty itself.

Kyril had just come from a meeting with the man. He had been brought in on Panasenko's case as well, to gather intelligence on the government minister who controlled the purchase of materiel for the Royal Navy from the Russian traders. Lumber, iron, hemp for ropemaking—ordinary things, but vital to England's far-flung empire.

Kyril had mentioned the shipment of khodzhite to Briggs, who had not known that it was included—a polite term for smuggled—in the cargo he owned. He was as curious as Kyril as to why it was there, and what it would be used for.

Kyril had not been able to find out one thing about it, and the lead box was nowhere to be found in the warehouses of the Baltic Dock. Their surveillance had been to no avail. It had been unloaded and promptly vanished. Rudolf and the men under him had looked everywhere for it. But at the moment, Phineas Briggs was more concerned with the materiel that had also gone missing.

It was possible that the minister was responsible. The man was close to bankruptcy, owing to the jewelry required to satisfy several demanding mistresses. Kyril and Lukian had found nothing else concrete in the way of evidence against him, nor had Rudolf.

But Kyril found the pursuit enjoyable—it tested his wits and kept him on his mettle.

If not for the recent arrival of Volkodav and his henchmen, Kyril would be inclined to go undercover more often, working on the docks with Rudolf and not sitting in meetings. Strenuous physical labor built muscle and kept it hard. However discreetly, women did notice the body underneath a man's clothes and Kyril was proud of his own. He thought of Vivienne's hands upon his chest . . . and elsewhere.

Kyril smiled inwardly. The rough work sometimes required for his secret assignments had toughened him but not to the point of coarseness. Gentlemen were always appreciated by gentle ladies, and Vivienne was proof of that. Only a few days ago she had let him warm her bed at last—ah, how the memory excited him. Her wanton ways were a delight. The ladylike reluctance she had displayed when he had first got her alone was gone.

He was proud, nonetheless, of behaving with self-restraint—difficult as it had been—upon the night when she had refused him. By the Wolf, he had wanted so to take her then and there. On the chaise in her drawing room, in his coach, in his bed, hers, wherever, whenever, if she had said yes. Her uncertainty had made her doubtful. He had been wise to wait a little longer and let her take the lead. A female should never be forced. No good ever came of it.

His other side had appeared. The growls. The lovebites. But

she had not asked him to stop or to explain himself—she had enjoyed it. In fact, the very first time he had kissed her, she had even presented the back of her neck and allowed him to calm her with a firm grip upon her vulnerable nape. What an extraordinary woman she was. Instinctively sexual. Intelligent. Pounceworthy.

Her eventual surrender was sweet indeed. He had the book to thank for it—no, the book was not magic, but if she thought so, then what was the difference? He had expected her to take longer to give in.

New love was a powerful thing, a force of nature in fact. Kyril's feelings for Vivienne would sustain and strengthen him. Volkodav would never know what hit him when the battle was joined. Even so . . . Kyril heaved a sigh and returned his attention to his two brothers. He corrected himself. His one brother. Semyon. Marko had wandered off.

"Might I ask what you are thinking about?"

"Oh, nothing."

"Nothing, Kyril? I am catching a whiff of . . . something female."

Not possible. Kyril had bathed and scrubbed himself thoroughly at the banya three times since his early morning departure from Vivienne's a few days ago. There was no trace of her scent upon him.

Semyon's nostrils twitched. "Perhaps I am wrong."

"You are, my brother."

Semyon shook his head. "No, not entirely. But I would have to say that the scent is actually yours—I would define it as a male reaction to a female."

It was a popular guessing game among the Pack, but Kyril was not inclined to play it at the moment. Especially not with Semyon, who was exceptionally good at identifying scents.

"London is full of women. One reacts. What of it?"

His brother grinned rudely. "You are experiencing an intense reaction, though. Who is she?"

Damn. There was no stopping Semyon, who had a shameless interest in all matters relating to the fairer sex.

"Vivienne Sheridan," Kyril muttered. There was no reason to not say her name, considering how much time he'd spent at her town house. His brother would figure it out sooner or later.

"Ah! She is the former mistress of a great duke, I believe." Semyon raised a hand as if to give Kyril a congratulatory pat on the cheek, then thought better of it and clasped his hands behind his back. "I have heard that she is very beautiful. Not suitable for a mate, though."

"It is not any of your business, Semyon. I would prefer not to talk about it."

Semyon regarded him thoughtfully. "I see. Very well."

"Perhaps Natalya needs your help," Kyril suggested. He pointed. The girl was balancing a tray that held a huge, layered pie of fish.

"With the kulibiaka? I don't think so. There is Ivan."

Ivan took the tray from Natalya and set it on the table. Semyon gave a small cough. "Speaking in general terms, do you think a mortal woman could be a worthy mate for a man of our kind?"

Kyril let out a groan. "You do not give up."

"No. Neither do you."

"Well, then. I will reply in general terms. It depends upon the woman."

Semyon rubbed his chin. "That one is not likely to obey you, from all I have heard."

"I do not need to be obeyed by a female. Only by my younger brothers."

Semyon chuckled. "I will try to remember that."

"Do. And keep in mind that we were speaking generally. I

will answer no more questions about Vivienne. She is entitled to her privacy."

"Of course. And so are you, Kyril. I was only curious—you seem changed, somehow."

"Wait until you fall in love."

"Kyril, I fall in love five or six times a day."

"I don't doubt it." Kyril cast his gaze about the room, looking for a distraction. More members of the Pack had entered, taking the vodka the butler served and downing it in gulps. The loud conversation hurt Kyril's ears and he twitched them uncomfortably.

"But I will not allow myself to be led by the nose by some pretty little thing."

Kyril shrugged, irritated by his brother's persistence and his youthful egotism. "Vivienne is not like that."

"Then you are a lucky man."

"Yes, I am. She is a beauty but she also has a fine mind and depth of character."

"Sterling qualities."

"Women possess far more of them than men."

Semyon laughed, missing the point. "Do you really think so?"

Kyril marveled at his youthful egotism. Had he ever been as arrogant? He was only seven years older. But there was a great difference between a man of twenty-five and a man of thirty-two.

Still, Kyril thought, someday a pretty little thing, as Semyon put it, was quite likely to reveal character and spirit that would set his brother back on his heels. It would do him good.

Semyon waved at a friend across the room, losing interest in the subject. "Kyril, you will be clamoring for the rights of women next."

"Mayhap. The world is changing. Have you not heard of *The Rights of Man?*"

"Yes, yes." Semyon said dismissively. "Heard of it. Haven't read it. But I believe it is about men and not women."

"They have only those rights that men are willing to grant them."

"Exactly."

"You are being deliberately disagreeable. I might have to thrash you," Kyril said darkly.

Semyon gave him a cheerful smile. "Like old times, eh?"

"Keep in mind that I always won."

"We are the same size at last," Semyon pointed out. "You might not win now."

Semyon was right about that, but that did not keep Kyril from wanting the last word on the subject under discussion.

"I am quite serious about Vivienne, Semyon."

"Really? That was fast."

"I know my own mind."

"Then I wish you luck, Kyril. And all the happiness in the world."

"Thank you."

"Have you—proposed?"

"No, but she is aware of my feelings for her."

"I see."

"However, she is independent by nature. I understand that the duke valued that quality in her as much as I do. He provided handsomely for her. If she should want me, it will not be for my money."

Semyon snorted. "How admirable. Then what does she want from you?"

"Oh, shut up," Kyril said, exasperated. "You will never understand."

"But I do," Semyon protested. "It is my brotherly duty to give you unsolicited advice. You have given it to me often enough."

Kyril thumped him on the back, hard. Why had he not thought to do that before, when Semyon had thumped him?

It was like thumping an oak tree. His strongly built brother did not even flinch.

"So . . . when do we eat?"

A burning question if ever there was one. Semyon had always been the one to ask it first in days gone by. "Soon."

"Can we stop talking of politics? The subject gives me indigestion."

Kyril laughed. "Yes, my brother. Let us join the others."

"We have not gathered in a while. I am in the mood for a Howl."

"Let us raise our voices together and not quarrel."

"No, we should not." Semyon grew thoughtful for a moment. "I confess that the affairs of ordinary humans are sometimes beyond my understanding. We may look like them in most respects but we are not them."

"No. But we can never go back to what we once were or where we once lived," Kyril said. "Our Pack must live among them and take their women for our wives. When we can find the right one."

Vivienne's beautiful face came to his mind. More than ever, he was convinced that she was likely to be the right one. Her intelligence and her self-possession were qualities he valued most highly. And her gentleness. She had been forgiving about his escapade, as she thought of it, and her healing touch had helped him recover from Volkodav's vicious blow.

She would make a fine mother.

The next generation of his kind would need her. Kyril intended to sire a houseful. Nonetheless, the Pack had welcomed a handful of new members from farther north: Scotland. When first in London, Kyril had noted them upon his visit to the House of Lords. More than one Scots aristocrat had wolfish traits—he was glad to know that a Celtic branch of the ancestral pack still survived, although there were very few of them.

He cared not that Vivienne was purely human. But something about her instincts and her lithe sensuality made him wonder if she had a dash of the Old Blood in her as well. He would have to ask about her family.

His one night with her had surpassed his wildest dreams. Being with her, experiencing to the fullest the sheer animal joy of sex, had obliterated the ugliness of the encounter with Volkodav and the brutish Cossacks in the tavern and given him fresh hope. They would need it. The future could not be predicted.

Semyon snapped his fingers and brought him back to the moment. "Wives, pah. I am happy to keep more than one mistress at the moment. And indulge myself in an occasional *fille de joie*."

"That is as it should be. You are younger than I."

Semyon gave his brother a long look. "I suppose I will find my mate some day as you have. But I really do not understand human females. Perhaps you could recommend a few books on the subject."

Kyril only laughed.

He accepted a glass of vodka from Ivan, who had finally threaded his way through the ever-increasing crowd to them. Ivan picked one up from the tray and handed it to him, then gave one to Semyon. "Your health, brothers."

They clinked glasses, toasted each other, and downed the vodka in one gulp.

"Ahhh. Cold fire. That went down well." Semyon licked his lips appreciatively.

"So it did." Kyril placed his empty glass on Natalya's tray as she went swiftly past, her embroidered skirts brushing against his legs. He resisted the temptation to tug one of the long, gleaming braids that bounced against her back. "Now then. Back to what we were talking about: I will not recommend books, because you will not read them."

"Then how do you, a beast at heart, know so much about men and women?"

Kyril grinned. "I read the newspapers. For only a ha'penny, one can learn much about human nature. I suspect that the sages of ancient Greece and Rome subscribed to many in their day and stole the best bits for their philosophy."

Semyon guffawed. Several more Pack members who had just arrived came over to find out what had made him laugh, and Kyril left his brother with them.

The vodka had gone to his head, and he craved a few moments of quiet before the noisy banquet would begin. There still was no sign of the new member—the chair in reserve for him at the long table was empty and all the men present were familiar to Kyril.

He wandered into the foyer and stopped at a table that held a stack of programmes for the evening. These gave the usual brief history of the clan, outlined the course of the evening, and gave the name of the guest of honor: Alex Stasov. The most important part was, of course, the menu. In true Russian style, there would be far too much to eat.

The programmes would be ceremonially burnt by the end of the night, and the engraved plates from which they had been printed would have all trace of the words upon them seared off in a bath of acid. Kyril picked one up, examining it idly. It had been produced by a member of the Pack who owned a printshop, issuing broadsides, ha'penny newspapers of the sort he had recommended to Semyon, political pamphlets and the like—in short, information.

Which had been the Pack's original business, in a way. Information—secret, crucial information—had been carried by them all over England.

The lean strength of most of the men present tonight had been theirs from birth. Tireless runners who could maintain their swift pace through the thickest forests and most rugged moors, they had been brought from Russia to England more than a century ago to serve as trustworthy couriers for the king and his ministers, swiftly carrying secret messages and military intelligence.

From there, the members of the Pack had moved up into the innermost circles of the court and government, still providing information but in a much less direct way these days. When all was said and done, Kyril reflected, the Taruskins were spies. Highly paid spies.

It could be said that they were on the side of the angels, as God seemed to be on England's side in this new century. At least the Almighty was duly mentioned in all its dealing and adventuring, Kyril thought.

The English won their wars and engaged in lucrative trade with the vanquished, even if the profits were somewhat one-sided and very much in their favor. If not able to trade in peace, they looted and pillaged. The prosperous denizens of the great city of London and its poor scarcely cared. It occurred to Kyril that his newspaper-reading had made him cynical.

He perused the programme to see if anything new had been added. It seemed much the same.

Welcome to the Howl. We join in fellowship upon this night—

He skipped the introduction.

To others we appear entirely human—but the blood of the great wolves of the north runs in our veins. The hidden trait manifests only in males of the clan, and we know each other with one look.

Useful, Kyril thought with a smile, considering how far they had wandered from the land of barren, snow-whipped wastes that had bred them.

Our wolf blood mingled with the blood of the Roemi, mighty warriors from the lands of ice, a vanished race of men. It has proved to be a potent combination. Legend has it that the unholy mixture doubles and redoubles the ferocity and silent cunning of both strains. Yet our loyalty is legendary also, as is our care for their own—brother for brother, cousin for cousin, friend for friend, unto death.

True. His brothers, blood and otherwise, would give their lives for each other, brave to the bone. And here they all were, together in London at last, getting ready for a good old Howl.

"We thank you, o Great One, that we are together on this night . . ." Kyril murmured a ritual prayer to a furred deity that would have been very much a stranger in a Christian church.

But even the supernatural strength of the men of our great clan was no match for the killing storms of two centuries ago. Fierce blizzards lasted for months and swallowed our cubs and our women, the unblooded mothers of each succeeding generation. In time the clan was driven from our homeland.

Not all survived the exodus. Hundreds died upon the road, unseen by human eyes, which wound through the far north of Russia and ended in the port of Archangel. But through the blinding storms, the strongest led the others on along the ragged edge of the known world, the weaker ones following in the way of the wolf, letting their animal senses take over for their useless eyes.

A polite way of saying that they had smelled each other for thousands of miles. The Taruskins still needed to bathe often and Kyril knew he was no exception.

In due time, the survivors found new wives and sired new cubs in their new land, settling upon the shores of the White Sea.

Kyril looked at the programme again. The next part was not as romantic but it was accurate.

In Archangel they were met by stout-hearted men, representatives and factors of the British Society of Merchant-Adventurers, whose interests in Russia began with a lucrative trade in rare minerals and gems, as well as coal and gravel—

He yawned. What schoolbook had this come from?

They also sought tall, straight trees for the Royal Navy's masts—there were few such left in England even then, and Russian forests were vast.

An historical note of interest: The American colonies were another source of such trees but proved uncooperative about sending theirs, duly marked with the King's arrow though they were. A revolution ensued.

Kyril smiled. The Americans had not been as stupid as the English had thought. Nor had they been easy to bully. They had founded a new country of their own. He envied them that.

Ermine and sable and other costly furs were another part of the trade. In return, the Merchant-Adventurers provided the Tsars with silver objects of incomparable elegance to decorate their palaces—urns and ewers and epergnes and bibelots of ingenious design. And guns for the Imperial Guard and the Cossacks . . .

And so forth and so on. But what the devil was an epergne? He stifled a yawn.

The clan's glorious history had dwindled into smug self-congratulation that was far more merchant than adventurer—the Pack in England had been tamed, Kyril thought with a sigh. Many of the men in attendance tonight knew little of the Russian hinterlands. But the vast, lonely steppes that his mother had carried him over and the frost-stricken wastes, beautiful and lethally cold, which she and the clan knew only in legend, were their true homes.

The illustrations in the book of folktales he had given Vivienne had moved him. Cuddled in the afterglow of lovemaking, they had looked at the book together. Her claim that the pictures had actually moved was odd, but understandable. Their vivid colors and beautiful detail, combined with her natural sensitivity, had made her think so. Still, he wished he could see the majestic landscape of white ice and black mountains again.

The cobblestone streets of London were their paths now;

the shrub-dotted squares their forests. Kyril felt a sharp sense of longing for the wilderness and for his own wild self.

Now that they were to be hunted down, under order of extermination for their very success, the Tsar himself turned against them, perhaps the cities of the world were their last refuge on the earth. Ah, there was no use in longing for what he could not have. He put down the programme and went back inside their main hall.

The Pack was in full roar and the noise was deafening. The platters of zakuski—fish in aspic, herring in sour cream, dark bread, pickled beets, cabbage rolls, spiced meat on skewers—looked like, well, like wolves had been at them. There were a few tidbits left, and a scattering of crumbs. Kyril surveyed the assembled company, who had indulged freely in vodka, drinking several glasses to his one. Red-faced, convivial, shouting and joking, they did seem to be having a very good time.

He felt a gust of cooler air when the butler, whose supernatural hearing exceeded that of all the others, opened the front door. Someone Kyril had never seen stood on the doorstep. A man of medium height, with a face that was quite ordinary.

He and Kyril exchanged a glance. Yes. The man was one of them. There was no mistaking that. But something about the new arrival made him uneasy. Kyril gave a slight bow and let the butler lead him in. The ranks of men parted as he was brought into the hall and ushered to his chair.

The members of the Pack consulted their programmes. How damnably dull they seemed. They might as well be Methodists looking through their hymnals on Sunday.

Someone got to the part about the man's name.

"Hail to Alex Stasov!"

The rest joined in. "Hail to Alex Stasov!"

The ritual celebration of welcome proceeded. Kyril commandeered a chair at the corner of the table near the foyer, where he could leave early if he wanted. More bottles of vodka were slammed down in the center of the table and more toasts were drunk. Massive loaves of dark bread were brought out from the kitchen and held high by the serving men and women, then passed around to be split open by eager hands, sprinkled with salt, and devoured in chunks. The main courses came next, served up to raucous applause.

Stasov seemed calm enough. He did not look Kyril's way again. His two brothers, done out of their chairs by latecomers, stopped at his corner of the table and pulled up chairs of their own next to him.

"There you are, Kyril," Marko said. "Pass the damned vodka. The men who stole our seats stole our glasses as well."

"It's all gone."

A servant overheard and promptly came back with glasses and another tall bottle. His brothers poured for themselves and for others, but Kyril refused another drink, concentrating upon the nondescript man at the head of the table.

"Why are you staring at him, Kyril?" Semyon inquired.

Kyril only shrugged. The guest of honor had not looked him directly in the eyes again and, he noticed, had not looked directly at anyone else either. It was odd. But everyone else was far too drunk to notice.

Marko prodded him. "You didn't answer."

Kyril finally spoke. "I have a feeling that Alex Stasov is not who he seems to be. My brothers . . . I smell a rat."

"D'you mean him?" Marko jerked a thumb in the new-comer's direction.

"Yes."

"But he is nobody," Semyon said.

"Brownish. Nondescript," Marko added.

Semyon stared at Stasov. "On the small side too."

"Exactly my point. He even looks like a rat," Kyril said.

Semyon and Marko tried to focus, but the effort made their

eyes cross. They burst out laughing and slapped each other on the back.

Kyril pushed back his chair and got up. His brothers were far gone. He might as well retreat to an upstairs room and write a note to Vivienne. The festivities were far from over and they would continue for days.

He could not invite her to join him, alas.

The room was quiet when he entered and walked to the desk in the corner, where all that one might require for writing was neatly set out.

Pens, ink, blotting sand, blank paper . . . its white, smooth surface was daunting.

Kyril took a chair and tried to think of something witty and romantic to put into the note. He was rather better at both in person. In the end he settled for a few simple lines that made it clear he hoped to see her soon. He was vague about when. He still thought it best to let her take the lead in their affair.

He signed it with a flourish. When the ink had dried, he pressed his lips to the paper and added an invisible kiss.

A while later he came down again and found Alex Stasov by the fireplace in the Pack's library. Natalya, who never, ever seemed tired, was on her knees in front of it, feeding crumpled programmes to the flames.

Kyril nodded to Stasov. It seemed unkind to wonder why he was there.

"Hello," he said. "And how did you like the Howl?"

"It was interesting," said Stasov in a mild voice.

The man still did not quite look at him. It troubled Kyril. He took another chair so he could chat with Natalya for a bit.

"You should go home and go to bed, my dear," he said. "You have been working for hours."

"I will," Natalya answered. "I am waiting for Ivan to walk with me."

"Oh. I understand. But won't your mother worry?"

"No, sir." She held a programme to the fire and threw it in when it caught.

Kyril watched the paper slowly burn, starting with a twisting scarlet flame along its edge to the final, ethereal result. He could still read a few of the printed words on the blackened surface.

... ferocity and silent cunning ... new wives ... blizzards ... the way of the wolf. ... our homeland ...

A final phrase, the most poignant, jumped out at him.

... not all survived ...

The fragment of paper writhed and drifted up the chimney.

He looked again at Stasov, whose head lolled back against his comfortable chair. A faint snore issued from his nose.

"The room is very warm," Natalya said in a low voice. "He is napping."

Kyril could not shake the feeling that Stasov was no more asleep than he was. The man's eyes were closed and Kyril saw no glimmer of white at the edge of his lids. Still, he could be opening them for a fraction of a second now and then to watch him and Natalya with quiet patience. Waiting for his moment to steal some crumb of useful information and take it to—

Kyril quelled his restless thoughts. Alex Stasov's bona fides had been thoroughly checked, he assumed, or he would not have been honored with a Howl. There had never been an infiltrator in their midst, as far as he knew.

"You are right about the room," he said to Natalya. "I think I will go out for a walk."

"Very good, sir."

She did not look up from her task. The fire cast a ruddy light over her exotic features and Kyril smiled. Ivan had chosen well. The girl was lovely.

Her kokoshnik headdress had been set aside and her two braids hung neatly down her back.

On her wedding day her hair would be unbraided and let down to flow freely and dazzle her bridegroom. She would be taken to him by her friends, singing with happiness of the joining of souls.

Kyril was looking forward to that great occasion. For her and Ivan. And for himself and Vivienne.

That lady knew nothing of his plans, of course. It was not the right time to ask her.

6

And a week after that . . .

A pounding sound shattered her dream. Vivienne swore under her breath and raised her head from the pillow. Someone was knocking upon her bedroom door. "Who is there?"

"It is Polly, madam."

The maid. "Not now."

"But I have brought up the bath water that you asked for."

Vivienne could not send her away or be so rude as to complain about the interruption. "Oh—of course. I was still asleep. Give me a moment, Polly."

She got out of bed and swathed herself in a robe, smoothing her hair before she admitted the maid. The aproned girl did not look at her, just picked up the heavy pails of hot water and trudged with them to the bath in the adjoining room.

The refreshing sound of gurgling, falling water followed as she poured both in. The maid left the way she came, her footsteps light, nodding to Vivienne.

She undid the loose knot in the robe's sash and let it slide to the floor. Then she tested the water with her toes, stepping in and sinking down when she found it to her liking. She soaked a big sponge, squeezing the water out of it over her breasts before she pressed it against her cheeks, one by one. Ahh. Lovely.

How nice it would be if Kyril were around to see her bathe. He would dry her off and tumble her upon the bed she had just left, and make sweet, passionate, wild love to her for hours.

She got out. If he was not around, she would have to do the honors herself. Vivienne took her time about drying herself and lay back upon her bed, quite naked, her thighs open as she fluffed the delicate curls between her legs.

As for him . . . she let herself imagine every detail. He would be aroused beyond belief, his huge, thick cock jutting out, holding in tight to control his arousal, making it look even thicker. She wanted very much to watch him roll down the foreskin and reveal the shapely head and the small hole in it.

Yes. She might wet her fingertip and caress only the head at first. Subtle but effective. She looked forward to seeing his groin tighten when she did it. Then, too aroused to wait another minute, he would position his powerful body to thrust into her cunny. Over her body, coming down. His buttocks would clench as she clawed at them to pull him into her, hard and very deep.

Again and again. Until she began to moan uncontrollably, writhing and trembling beneath his big body . . .

Vivienne spread her legs immodestly, as far apart as she could. She knew how tempting and how vulnerable her cunny looked in this position, the open pink slit nestled within a soft fringe of dark curls, a sensual offering of womanly flesh. It amused her now and then to provide her own sexual pleasure while she watched herself do it with a mirror in one hand. Her two slender fingers sliding in and out of her cunny, over her clitoris each time—ahhh. Like an obliging tongue and a ladylike little cock exciting her simultaneously.

There was no mirror at hand, but it was not necessary. Thinking that Kyril would soon see her like this was extremely exciting. Completely relaxed save for the tense, slick flesh between her legs, she moved on the bed so as to enjoy the feel of the velvet comforter, rubbing her bare behind on it and bouncing a little. The velvet felt sensually soft underneath her nakedness, as if she lay upon the fur of some magnificent, imaginary animal. She stroked the silky skin on the inside of one thigh and then the other, feeling like an animal herself.

Had she gone with him in his carriage, she would have talked of this, excited beyond measure by the avid look in his eyes when he would listen, enrapt by her soft voice. He would be instantly aroused to hear her whisper so wantonly, she was sure of that. Her hand moved between her legs, stimulating the tender, voluptuously swollen flesh.

How she wanted him!

Touching herself still more intimately, penetrating her cunny with the full length of her fingers, Vivienne imagined a sexual encounter in every detail—his thrusting tongue, the kisses and nips he bestowed upon her neck and eager mouth, his subtle caressing of her breasts, even the way he'd held her nape and made her submit the first time they had kissed . . . ohhh. She dug her toes into the velvet comforter, lifting up her hips as she rubbed delicately and very quickly. Her bottom trembled as she gave herself what she wanted so much from him: an intense, deep-pulsing orgasm that made her cry out his name in silence.

Kyril . . . Kyril.

She sighed as she came back to where she was. Only he could vanquish the coldness that had ruled her heart and mind for far too long. He had said he loved her . . . she wanted to believe it. She would respond in kind when she was sure that doing so was safe.

A love like his would be powerful enough to blot out her hatred for Donal Sheridan.

The moment she had told her father to go to the devil and left him at Abigail's house, she had felt free. She was no longer frightened by his base accusations, would no longer submit to his appalling blackmail. His eagerness to exploit her could be checked. Not too long ago, Donal had seemed a reputable man, able to keep up appearances and sound authoritative, even concerned for his only daughter. But his taste for liquor had corroded his brain and made him behave strangely. She was sure that Kyril would not believe him if he came around, making insinuations and causing trouble. But she would have to tell him of her youthful mistake and its tragic consequences.

She had not sinned. She had brought an innocent babe into the world, who had soon left it. If Kyril thought the worst of her for that, then she wanted nothing to do with him.

She had looked at the miniature again this morning. Arielle, in some way, would always be with her. Had she lived, she would have been a much loved child. Who would have loved her mother in return and given her courage, as Vivienne had done for her own mother at the very end.

Donal be damned. He could rot in hell. This time Vivienne would not give in.

But he was not around. The family gathering he had mentioned had concluded. She'd had a letter from him, vague but fond, and had gone through a ream of paper to compose a reply that struck the same note. Light. Casual. Affectionate.

She still did not quite believe that he had said he loved her. That sent, she'd waited. And waited some more. No answer.

She had sent her man Henry over with a letter of reply three days ago inquiring politely after his health, and Henry had come back with an answer from someone named Ivan that annoyed her. Kyril had taken to his bed. He was unwell. He remained her obedient servant.

Hah. He had better be alone in that bed.

Could he not write to her himself? She hated the idea that someone else was reading what she sent to him. She'd had Henry deliver another message yesterday inquiring somewhat impersonally as to Kyril's condition and diagnosis, if there was one, and received another answer from the same person. Kyril was better. He would see her soon.

Her sister Pamela, a great gossip, had been unable to find out anything more. Perhaps he was not even in London. That left the rest of the world and not even her sister knew everything about that.

She rang for her maid to help dress her when she was done sloshing about and had dried off. The afternoon stretched ahead, a decorous hell of more letter-writing to friends who had sent her small gifts for her new home. They had been kind. They had to be thanked. And it needed to be done before Pamela's arrival.

Hours later, her sister bustled in without even knocking on her study door.

"Hello!" she called out. "Oh—I see you are working away. Forgive me for interrupting you." She removed her bonnet and stuck it on a marble head of a goddess. "That is new. Wherever did you get it?"

"From a bank masquerading as a Greek temple."

"Do you mean that you stole it?"

"I rescued it. The bank was about to be knocked down and a bigger one built in its place."

"Ah, the march of commerce. London is changing too fast

for me. But a marble head is an excellent place for a bonnet." Her reticule and larger purse she slung over the back of a wooden chair. "So. I consider myself arrived, if not welcomed."

Vivienne put down her pen and smiled. Pamela liked to make a noisy entrance. She was very different from Vivienne in that regard and many other ways, but that was because they were not blood sisters.

Distant relatives, yes. Vivienne's mother had taken in Pamela for a year when she had been orphaned. Donal Sheridan had been away for the same twelvemonth, pursuing a business venture that would, as usual, leave him with nothing but the shirt on his back. He would return in a rage and take it out on his little family whenever he could.

But the two girls were too innocent to anticipate that dreadful day. Nor were they aware of the scrimping and saving that Vivienne's mother did to create a happy home for the three of them. Vivienne and Pamela were nearly the same age and they became fast friends at once. Soon they were like sisters, from their shared joys, such as reading by the fire, to their fierce quarrels over borrowed hairbrushes and the like.

It had been the happiest year of Vivienne's childhood and the only one she wanted to remember. Their bond had endured.

"Don't be so silly," she said, rising and going to Pamela. The two young women embraced lightly and they both laughed. "When have you not been properly welcomed in my house? You didn't give me a chance to speak."

"Let me think." Pamela pretended to do so. "I suppose you are right. You always are."

Vivienne gave her a wry smile. "I am glad you think so."

Pamela nodded briskly and turned her attention to her surroundings. "This room is coming along nicely. There are only fifteen crates left to be unpacked."

"Fourteen."

Pamela waved the lace glove she had pulled off her hand. "It doesn't matter. Turn them over and empty them out in the middle of the floor."

"Why on earth would I want to do that?"

"My dear sister, you will never unpack them otherwise. No one does."

"Whatever do you mean, Pam?"

Her sister cleared her throat and drew herself up to declaim, "To move is human. To unpack, divine."

Vivienne gave a snort of laughter. "I suppose I fall into the first category. As you can see, I have not completed the task."

"Precisely my point, Vivi."

Pamela flung herself into an armchair and rested her feet on a settee. "There, now I am comfortable. Thank you for asking me to sit down."

"As if you needed an invitation to do anything."

"Tra la la. You are right. I never do."

Vivienne took the chair opposite her sister. It was as if she had opened the windows and let a fresh breeze in. Pamela's unconventional manners and warmth truly were always welcome. She was the sunny opposite of Vivienne in every way.

"So how are you, my dear sister?"

"Keeping well," Pamela replied.

"And your husband?"

"The man behind the newspaper?"

Vivienne could not help but giggle. It was an apt description of Richard Bridgefield, her dull brother-in-law. "Yes."

"Richard is always the same."

Vivienne was aware that her sister's marriage was not what Pamela had hoped for. She and her husband dwelled in separate halves of their house in Belgravia, in fact. They had no children and little else in common. But he paid her dressmaker and milliner's bills without complaint and otherwise stayed out of Pamela's way.

"Do you ever . . ." Vivienne started to say and quickly thought better of it. "Never mind."

"Want something more from him? No."

"Why not, Pamela? Surely we are all entitled to be loved."

Her own words surprised her. Never would she have said such a thing until now. Kyril had changed her indeed in a very short time. She thought once more how much his drowsy avowal of love—after the sex and not before—meant to her. And how, with luck, it might change her life.

If only she had been able to see him since. Yes, there had been his letter but it was not enough. If she had read correctly between the few lines that he'd penned, he seemed inclined to leave things up to her.

She had read the damn thing over and over by now. His handwriting was as dashing as he was. She had pressed a kiss to the paper and felt her lips tingle. One more reason to feel foolish about wanting him so much.

Sleepy as he had been after that glorious sex, would he forget that he had said it? He was not the sort of man for light words, although he had—Pamela and others had told her of it—trifled with many women.

Vivienne gave a heartfelt sigh and her sister looked at her curiously.

"And how are you?" Pamela said. "I forgot to ask."

"Much the same."

"Oho. I rather doubt it." Her sister favored her with a close look. "No, I suspect the worst."

"Meaning . . ."

"Your eyes are bright and your thoughts are elsewhere. It's him, isn't it?"

"Him?"

"Do not play the innocent."

Vivienne shrugged and adjusted the folds of her dress. "Well, yes."

Pamela kicked off her shoes and tucked her feet under her thighs. "Tell me everything."

"I do not know much more than you about Kyril Taruskin." Vivienne laughed.

"Hmm. And yet you have—" Pamela looked at her eagerly without finishing the sentence.

"Yes."

"How was it?"

Vivienne had expected that question. "Marvelous."

Pamela sighed with delight. "How wonderful. I envy you."

"I am happy, sister," Vivienne said, adding lightly, "for as long as it lasts." She worried about Pamela sometimes and did not want to seem as if she was gloating.

"Sometimes love does," Pamela assured her. "I myself no longer sleep with my husband, as you know, but that is by mutual agreement. No, I look to romantic novels if I need a gallant hero."

Vivienne laughed. "Do you still read them?"

"By the score!"

"Kyril reminds me of a hero in a book. Of course, I do not know him well."

Pamela got up. She could be more restless than Vivienne. "Speaking of books, what are you reading these days?" She strolled over to the shelves.

Vivienne's gaze moved to where she had placed the book of folktales face out. When she and Kyril had finally looked at it together, the pictures had not moved at all. It seemed safe enough to show it to Pamela.

"That one," she said, pointing to it. "It was a gift from Kyril."

"You are easily pleased," Pamela sniffed. "It looks old and shabby. Should he not be giving you diamonds and pearls?"

Vivienne felt a flash of pique. Her sister had a casket full of such jewels, provided by her dutiful husband. She met Pamela's eyes and glimpsed the loneliness in their depths. The cutting remark meant nothing.

"I have plenty of such trinkets."

"Of course. The dear old duke was very generous to you."

"So he was."

The sisters exchanged a look of mutual understanding that said women, married or not, did what they had to, just to get by, and love very rarely had anything to do with it.

Pamela opened the book of folktales and turned the pages, skipping text in favor of illustrations.

"My word. He is a handsome fellow. Have you seen this one?"

Pamela held the book open, holding the pages at the sides to display the illustration of the Roemi warrior throwing a spear.

Vivienne was relieved to see that it was back in his hand again. "Yes, I have."

Pamela turned the book toward herself again and looked through it. "Are there any more like him?"

"I believe there are."

There was no sound for a few moments but that of turning pages and soft oohs from Pamela over each half-naked warrior.

"I am glad to see that you have not lost your love for literature, Pamela," Vivienne said solemnly.

"Indeed not! Not with men like this to look at!" She walked back to the sofa with her nose in the book, stumbling over a crate. "Blast!"

"Are you hurt?"

Pamela looked down at her stubbed toe. "Will it get me a cup of tea if I say yes?"

"Right away. Forgive me for not having it sent up sooner."

Her sister half-walked, half-hopped to the chaise and reclined upon it, book in hand. "You are forgiven. I believe I will read this, Vivienne. I have never seen such lovely pictures in a book. They seem almost alive."

Vivienne studied her for a long moment as Pamela picked a tale at random and began to read silently.

Almost alive? Were the figures moving?

Unlikely. Pamela would have squealed and made a fuss if they had. No, it was as Kyril had said. She had experienced an illusion, brought on by fatigue.

If only she could make it happen again. Reading the tales of the Roemi warriors with Kyril at her side had been an even more interesting experience. His resemblance to them was so striking, especially when he was gloriously naked and his dark hair was unbound.

Vivienne heard Pamela heave a sentimental sigh. "Oh my. Now this one is the best of all."

She knew which illustration it was before her sister faced the book out to show her.

"Look, he is bringing his bride home on horseback . . . you can tell by her gown and the flowers. How romantic. Isn't it pretty, Vivienne?"

"Yes, it is."

Pamela studied it again. "They seem so happy."

"That is because they are lovers in a fairytale," Vivienne said dryly.

Pamela peered at her over the top of the book. "But they had to climb seven mountains and fight seven trolls and wait seven years together."

"Have you read the story already?"

"No, but that is what they usually have to do, isn't it? Something has to happen in the middle and it is usually bad. Otherwise books would be blank."

"I believe you are right." Vivienne laughed. Seeing Pamela was a tonic for her nerves.

"Lovers must suffer," Pamela said grandly. "And their hearts must break. It is fate."

"Not mine," said Vivienne. "Not anymore."

Pamela gave her a quizzical look. "That is a good thing. But is there something you are not telling me?"

Her sister knew of the lover who had abandoned her, but not of the child or what Donal had done. Nor did she know of Donal Sheridan's disgraceful abuse of his wife and daughter, or of his blackmail. Vivienne had been too consumed by shame to tell her or anyone of it. Still, fiercely loyal and nobody's fool, Pamela loathed Donal and she always had.

"I am no longer speaking to my father," Vivienne began.

"Hurrah!"

Vivienne permitted herself a smile. "That is but the first step in a long journey. I have never told you of what happened when I was nineteen—"

Pamela sat up and looked at her eagerly. "What?"

Vivienne shook her head. "Even between sisters, some things are too—"

"Personal?"

"The word is painful."

"Ah. Please forgive me, Vivienne." Pamela grew quiet and put the book aside. "I will not pry. As we get older—" She hesitated. "Well, we all keep secrets. I have my own."

The next day . . .

Vivienne stood and stretched. She had spent several hours at her desk and finished every little thing that needed finishing. Pamela had ended up staying the night and the sisters had scarcely slept for all the talking they did. In the morning, Pamela had decamped with several romances she had not read, putting the little book of folktales back in its place.

Vivienne glanced at it, wishing that its giver would come to her again. She could not very well march over to his house and demand to see him.

Lost in thought, she barely noticed the commotion in the downstairs hall when it began. Her manservant, Henry Freke, was arguing with someone. A move-along sort of argument that he sometimes had with peddlers. Not worthy of her attention.

Then the housekeeper chimed in. Vivienne heard the whiskery sound of a large broom being pushed over the floor of the hall and then a joint threat from Mrs. Hickham and Henry to push someone down the front stairs and into the gutter with it—

She left the small room that served as her study and library and looked over the banister. Mrs. Hickham was using her broom to force a ragged man with a long beard to pick up his feet. He protested in a piteous voice. Cries, not words.

"Sorry, madam," Henry said. "He has lost his way, I think, or else he is mad. But he will not go!"

Vivienne's brow furrowed as she looked at the man. The beard and that odd hat. The long coat with the enormous sleeves. She had seen him before. But where?

It came back to her. He was the beggar who had stepped out of the shadowy doorway when Kyril had walked past it to his coach and waiting horses, she was sure of it. He had made her uneasy then, but she had thought no more of him when he dodged back into the doorway.

Why had he come back and what did he want with her?

She studied the face that he turned to her. He was careworn and old, but his expression was mild. If he was mad, he was most likely harmless. His eyes were a strange color, almost no color at all, like ice.

The imploring look he gave her said what he could not.

Help me.

She would if she could find out something about him. He might be in need of a meal or . . . there was little else she could give him.

If she could bring him to his countrymen—there were many enclaves of foreigners in London and she was sure he was a foreigner, she had never seen clothes like his—they might assist him. Otherwise he would end up in the workhouse, starved and bullied until he died.

Pamela would scold her for helping him herself and so would Kyril, concerned for her safety. One did not take in a man from the streets. No, she would not. And she would ask Henry to stay at her side while she talked to him. Vivienne thought she recognized a few of the words she had heard him say.

"Stop," she instructed her servants.

"But madam—" they protested in unison.

"Let me talk to him."

"No," Henry said sternly. "Begging your pardon, but he is mad. I am sure of it now. Just listen to him."

She came down the stairs and stood behind both of them. The old man fixed his eyes on hers. He spoke again. In Russian, quickly. Then just a few words in halting, heavily accented English. He was asking for help.

"I think that I understand him," Vivienne said slowly. "Henry, please escort him to my study and remain there with him while we talk. And Mrs. Hickham, you may bring us both tea."

She listened patiently to his garbled talk as they waited for the tea. Henry sat bolt upright in a nearby armchair, his arms folded across his chest, giving Vivienne a frown every time she looked his way.

Mrs. Hickham had made a point of spreading a large rag over the armchair before he sat down, but the old man didn't seem to care.

"What is your name?"

He looked at her hopefully, clutching his strange hat in his hands as if it was a very great treasure. His pate had a few wisps of hair left upon it, nothing that would protect him from the cold.

"Your name?" She gave up and pointed to herself. "My name is Vivienne. And you are—?"

His face creased in a smile. "Ah! Osip."

That was a start.

He nodded. "Osip. I name Osip."

"And why are you here?" Vivienne could see Henry rolling his eyes, as if he at least did not want to know the answer to that question.

Osip shook his head.

"You, Osip, knocked on the door of my house." She explained what she had said with her hands as best she could, pointing to him and then to herself, then raised her palms upward in a questioning gesture. "Why?"

Osip nodded. "Man here. I come."

Did he mean Henry?

"What man?" She pointed to her glowering servant. "Him?"

"Madam!" Henry burst in. "This has gone far enough!"

She raised a hand to shut him up. "I will decide that. What man, Osip?"

The old fellow made a gesture like wheels turning. Big wheels. A wagon? He pantomimed tipping a high hat. No, a coach with a coachman. Then he stretched his hand as high above his head as he could. Someone tall. It came to her then. He was talking about Kyril.

Vivienne sat back in her chair, feeling suddenly tired. They might be at this all night and not very much farther along no matter how hard she tried to understand him.

Mrs. Hickham brought in the tea, glaring at the poor old fellow, who thanked her profusely in Russian over and over. Those were the only words of that language that Vivienne was absolutely sure of. She had picked that much up from Kyril and a few of his friends.

Vivienne poured, ignoring both the housekeeper and her man-servant. He plunked several sugar lumps into his cup. Mrs. Hickham hissed under her breath. The old man's hand, begrimed and wrinkled, shook as he picked up the cup and saucer, making both clatter. The tea spilled into the saucer. He lifted the cup and tipped the saucer into his mouth, sucking the sugary tea in as if he had not had anything to eat or drink in far too long.

"I think he is hungry," Vivienne murmured. "Mrs. Hickham, make sandwiches from the leftover joint and bring them to us."

"Miss Sheridan," the housekeeper said reprovingly. "He will not leave if you feed him."

"Please do as I say."

"You are a great one for taking in strays. Have you forgotten the dog we had to send to your cousin in the country?"

"I still miss that dog."

"And then there was that cat with the kittens."

"We found homes for them all."

The housekeeper turned on her heel and left the room. Henry shook his head in a warning way.

For the next hour, the conversation lurched along, interrupted by Osip's trembling appreciation of the food that Mrs. Hickham reluctantly served up. "I was saving that joint for a cold supper, madam."

Vivienne nodded. The housekeeper had taken the trouble to whisper as if she thought the old man might understand. He didn't seem to, but at least her servants were no longer casting murderous looks his way.

Little by little she extracted some information from him. He was a monk, she believed. On the front of the robe the old man wore under the long coat was an Orthodox cross nearly the length of his body, so faded that she had not seen it at first. And letters she could not make out.

She took the liberty of copying them with a pencil while he talked. Kyril could help her with those.

Osip made wild gestures in the air, moving his hands and arms in broad strokes. A musty smell came from him, embedded in his clothes. What was he trying to say? Wind? Water? It dawned on her suddenly. He had come to England in a ship.

"If only Kyril was here," she sighed.

The old man's eyes grew bright.

"You don't know him," she said. "Or perhaps you do. Kyril Taruskin?"

His eyes positively gleamed. Her mention of Kyril had melted the ice.

"He has brothers," she went on. "Semyon? Marko? No?"

The old man shook his head and his eyes dimmed. How confused he must be.

"I will send a note to Kyril," she said. "You are from his homeland. And you are a man of God." She looked at his uncomprehending face. "You don't understand, do you?"

The monk shook his head again. What to do?

He seemed to brighten up every time she said Kyril's name. Perhaps he did know him, had been looking for him on the night when he'd found shelter in the doorway.

Of course he would have been directed to Kyril's house and not hers, but a well-meaning servant might have sent him to Cheyne Row. Russians were devout people and they would be certain to help a monk or a priest or whatever Osip was.

She did remember that Osip had seemed to be about to speak with Kyril. But he had not. Kyril had been in a hurry to leave that night. To take care of whatever unexplained business he had been about in the East End, rakehell that he was.

She looked at Osip's dirty clothes with dismay and reminded herself that he had taken a vow of poverty.

The old man gave her a tremulous smile and his ice-colored eyes grew watery. He let his chin sink down into his bushy beard, not speaking for the next few minutes.

The next sound was a snore.

Oh dear. He had dozed off. His wrinkled eyelids were shut. But his unexpected nap gave Vivienne a chance to get up. She rose, holding up a hand to forestall Henry's scolding.

The manservant drew in his breath.

"Stay with him, Henry."

"Yes, madam."

Vivienne left the room, racking her brains for a way to get a message to Kyril. She returned to her study, looking for the little book she used when she sent out invitations. She would ask his assistance and explain the unusual circumstances of the monk's arrival. Kyril would understand why she had not turned Osip out to wander the streets once more. He himself had been a stranger in a strange land once.

As Kyril seemed to have withdrawn from society—but surely the family gathering he had mentioned had not lasted this long—and was presently indisposed, writing to him was the only thing she could do. She did not keep a carriage and she would not hire one.

Vivienne Sheridan did not go about knocking on men's doors.

The idea that Kyril might be avoiding her was not something she wanted to think about. She decided to also send a copy of the note to a few of his friends. If Kyril could not come, one of the others might. In any case, his friends would make sure that he knew what was going on and drag him out of bed if necessary.

She had acted on an impulse she was unable to undo. Someone had to help her. She could not put the old man up indefinitely and the servants would not tolerate him in their quarters.

Being an angel of mercy was more difficult than she had thought.

She returned her mind to the task she had set herself: writing more damned notes. To his friends, no less. They were men she knew only slightly, but they had all supped with her and attended her soirées and they owed her this small favor.

Let people think whatever they wanted. There was nothing wrong with trying to help a lost soul. She wrote each note using the same words, adding a quick but careful sketch of the monk's bearded face, and the letters and peculiar cross upon the robe.

Henry groaned when she went downstairs to give them to him. "Five, madam?"

"Yes."

"But I don't want to leave you with that monk. If he is a monk."

"You must. He is asleep. Go."

Two hours later, Kyril had still not come. But Lukian Taruskin had.

His first cousin. Evidently sent by Kyril, because Vivienne had not addressed a note to Lukian. Well, Vivienne thought crossly, Lukian would have to do.

Kyril had once brought him along to one of her Audley Street soirées. The man had been drunk at the time or so she'd thought and she had not liked him then.

She watched from the landing as he entered her front hall, let in by Henry. Lukian ignored the manservant's suspicious look, although perhaps he found it understandable. Henry knew Kyril but did not remember Lukian, who had visited Vivienne only once.

Still, he was handsome, something she had not noticed on their first meeting, perhaps because Kyril outshone him in every way.

Lukian seemed weary somehow, as if of life itself. There

were dark circles under his eyes that betrayed sleepless nights. He lacked his cousin's air of robust health, though he had the same dark, thick hair as Kyril and very much the same features, if more rugged.

She realized how intently she was staring at him and stopped—she sensed that he was about to look her way. Vivienne went down the stairs to him.

"Hello, Lukian. I was not expecting—"

"Kyril could not come," he said flatly. "So he sent me."

"Oh. I am disappointed. I have written to him several times this week and received no reply." She regretted her blunt words when she saw a flash of—was it dislike?—in his eyes. "But that is neither here nor there."

Lukian seemed uncomfortable. It did not surprise her. He was close to Kyril and she could not ask him to account for his cousin's behavior.

"I suppose he received my note at home."

Lukian had seen him. Could she get him to give away Kyril's actual whereabouts? It was underhanded of her, but she had been waiting a very long time to hear.

Osip slept on upstairs, blissfully unaware of the trouble he was causing.

Lukian cleared his throat. He looked nervous. "It took a roundabout path. His page finally delivered it to him at—at the Antwerp Tavern on Threadneedle Street."

"Ah. And you were there with him. That is why you smell of cigars and strong drink." She could not keep the edge out of her voice.

"Forgive me. But it is where we Russians go."

"I suppose I must." She wanted to bite her tongue. Kyril's evasiveness was not Lukian's fault, after all. She had no right to take out her temper on him. She softened her tone. "It seems I have a stray monk in my study. He speaks Russian. I was hop-

ing one of you would be willing to help the poor old fellow."
Vivienne rested a hand on Lukian's arm.

"We shall see," was all he said.

It was his turn to stare at her in a way she found most disconcerting. There was something hungry in his eyes. And something very lonely.

It scared her.

"Please wait here," she said politely. "If you will excuse me, I must talk to Mrs. Hickham for a moment."

"Of course."

He watched her go downstairs to the kitchen and rested his shoulders against a wall . . . then his head. Lukian closed his eyes.

Her note—all of them, actually, at nearly the same time—had reached Kyril at the Pack's lair, of course, and not the Antwerp Tavern, which was all the way over on the other side of London.

His page had brought in the one addressed to Kyril's house. His friends' servants had done the same. Ivan had recognized the handwriting and given Kyril the notes for his friends as well. The butler had a rare understanding of women.

Hell had no fury like a woman waiting too long for a proper answer.

But there was a very simple reason why Kyril had been more or less incommunicado. All hell had broken loose. The Howl had gone on for days. Men who had traveled far, coming to the revels all the way from Scotland, Sweden, and Finland, replaced those who had to be carried to the rooms upstairs to sleep off their liquor.

While the revels continued, the cargo thefts had skyrocketed. There had been arrests and near riots on the docks and

Phineas Briggs was furious. High level contacts within the Admiralty had implored the members of the Pack to return to their spying.

Implored. Not ordered. For the most part, the celebrants were content to keep right on drinking. It had been too long since the last Howl, and it was too bad if mere humans could not understand that.

Kyril and Lukian had assumed responsibility for all of them, taking on the work of twenty men.

They could not be everywhere but they had tried. Lukian was convinced that Volkodav was behind the unrest on the docks. Kyril was not so sure, but he was desperately trying to remedy the situation.

None of which Lukian was allowed to tell Vivienne. Kyril had warned him that she was clever and would figure out everything about them too quickly.

Her cleverness had failed her, however, when it came to the matter of the monk, unless Lukian missed his guess.

He and Kyril had agreed that the fellow was not likely to hurt her. She was too useful as bait. But the men guarding her house in shifts had been told to be even more watchful for Volkodav or the Cossacks or anyone else who seemed suspicious.

Most likely she was being manipulated in a cunning way for one reason: to lure Kyril into a trap. Her note requesting help had been written in all innocence, but the monk—dear Wolf, had she really thought that crafty old Osip was actually sleeping?—undoubtedly knew it was meant for Kyril.

However, Osip had not alerted confederates outside Vivienne's house to follow her servant. Lukian had asked her unseen guards about that before entering. He had taken his time to explore the streets around her house in case they had missed something.

He could have missed something, certainly. He had not slept

for a week. The nights were getting worse and worse. He had to force himself to stay awake during the day.

Lukian thought over what the men had just told him: the monk appeared from nowhere, by himself. Someone was being very careful to make it seem that Osip was acting alone.

Volkodav had to be that someone. The long wait had ended. They were all slated to die and Kyril was being stalked first.

He had come in from night surveillance on the Baltic Dock, looking with disgust at the remnants of the noble Pack, still howling with raucous glee. They were led, to his chagrin, by Semyon and Marko, who had slept for two days, then started all over again.

Vivienne's note concerning Osip had been delivered an hour later. The others had followed soon enough.

Kyril had opened his and read it at once. Covering his alarm, he'd found Lukian and shared the information in it. They had known at once from her sketches and her description of Osip's behavior that the monk was not a monk at all. Lukian was sure the fellow was a criminal, but could not remember where he had seen his face.

He had asked Kyril to read his mind and jog his memory, but Kyril had not been able to do it. Lukian knew then the darkness in his mind had grown stronger. Much stronger.

Lukian had suspected as much. Its shadows protected him and, inadvertently, Osip. But he was too ashamed to tell his cousin why his mind was so clouded. His loyalty to Kyril and to the Pack was still stronger than that which claimed him in secret.

But *that* was devouring his soul.

Kyril had been too preoccupied to ask questions of him. He said only that he could not risk seeing Vivienne, given everything that was going on, and charged Lukian with the task of removing the pretender from her house.

Osip had to be captured at once, by fair means or foul, and

interrogated. If Kyril were to do the deed, he might be captured.

Not that he seemed to care. The most important thing, he vowed, was to continue to protect Vivienne. Eventually she would have to leave the house in Cheyne Row and hide in some safe place, but for the moment, they would remove the monk.

To that end the cousins had left the lair together, Kyril going one way and Lukian the other. He had realized on the way over that all of her earnest, eager notes were in his pocket and not Kyril's, and tucked them well inside so they would not fall out.

He straightened when he heard Vivienne's light footsteps returning.

She interrupted Lukian's thoughts with a light tap on his arm. "I should have offered you a chair. I apologize."

"No need for either."

Brought so quickly out of his reverie, he did not feel entirely well. There was something about her touch . . . it helped . . . *that.* He felt a sexual stirring deep within his body.

No. She belonged to Kyril.

He took a deep breath and forced himself to listen to what she was saying.

". . . I did not mean to be discourteous. You were good enough to come when Kyril could not, and I am very grateful for it."

He inclined his head, feeling awkward for lying, and did not reply. Her pensive face was lovely, far more lovely than Lukian remembered. Of course, he had only seen her once before and not in this house. No, at one of her soirées. Bejeweled and beautifully dressed.

She gave a polite little cough. Once more she had said something that Lukian did not quite hear. The loud howls of the all-male party he had left in such haste still echoed in his ears.

"Threadneedle Street is not a street I have ever walked upon."

"I am sure you have not. It lies to the east, not far from the Thames."

Vivienne nodded. "Is that tavern a favorite haunt of yours and your friends?"

Lukian summoned up an explanation, trying to remember what he had already told her. "The captains from the Baltic seaports gather there. I—we Russians, I mean—have business to conduct with them on occasion."

"Hmm. I have never been to the docks either."

"They are no place for a woman."

"Still, I should like to see them," she mused. Vivienne gave Lukian a look he could not interpret. "I don't suppose you would serve as my guide."

Did she hope to find Kyril on her own? Doing so would be dangerous. She must love his cousin if she would dare it. He felt a stab of jealousy.

The darkness in his mind bloomed briefly in his eyes when he looked down at her, thinking it wrong that Kyril should have such a woman and not he. Lukian had been lonely far longer. He knew the thought was irrational the moment it crossed his mind, but he could not help thinking it all the same.

"No," he said at last.

She frowned at him. A tiny line that he would have liked to kiss away appeared between her brows. He amended his answer.

"Not now, I mean. But perhaps some other time. You must be careful, and dress modestly. There are dark alleys and foul places that—"

"I understand."

Lukian nodded. "Good. Then no more need be said on that subject."

"Will Kyril come to me soon?"

"I cannot say."

Vivienne looked askance at him. "Where has he gone, then, if he was with you? Does no one know?"

"At the moment, no."

She let out a sigh. "Well, he thought to send you. Come with me and I will introduce you to the monk. I hope that you will understand him."

Lukian followed her upstairs and into the study. He looked around, noting the crowded bookshelves and the marble head of a goddess. Her pretty little desk held writing things that showed frequent use. It was very much a woman's room and Vivienne's elegant taste was evident in the décor.

Osip still dozed in his chair. Lukian looked him over, finding something familiar in his appearance that he could not quite put his finger on. The man in the chair seemed frail, his veined, gnarled hands folded on the coarse canvas of his garments.

Lukian glanced over at the windows, thinking of the straight, two-story drop to the pavement below. Even if the man was shamming, he was elderly and would not try to escape that way. He would have to get past Lukian to go out the way he came. Not a chance of that.

"Poor old fellow," she said softly.

Her well-meaning concern for the monk was grating. The damned monk didn't know how lucky he was. Lukian gave a slight cough.

"We must help him, Lukian."

"I promise you that I will find him new lodgings."

"Thank you. It is the least we can do."

"Oh, I can do far more."

"You will not regret it."

"No."

"Where do you suppose he came from?"

Lukian looked at the old man, walking around him. "By his clothes . . . I would say Russia. He must have arrived at the Baltic Dock and made his way into the city on foot."

Mrs. Hickham called to her from the floor below. Vivienne sighed. "Excuse me."

Lukian took the opportunity for a much closer inspection of Osip. The old man was as motionless as a turtle on a rock. Lukian leaned in so close the monk had to be able to feel his hot breath. The tiny veins in his wrinkled eyelids pulsed, but the old man kept his eyes shut.

Lukian was looking for prison tattoos. A trace of blue on his bony wrist, a line ending at his neck, would give away sinister designs hidden under his holy robes. He saw nothing but deep wrinkles and the brown-pink freckles of old age. Lukian straightened and folded his arms across his chest.

Vivienne rushed back up the stairs to be met by Lukian blocking the door. "How is he?"

Lukian walked her outside the room. "Nothing has changed. Keep your voice down."

"I feel that I have brought you here for no reason. But Mrs. Hickham is threatening to quit if he does not leave. To say nothing of Henry."

"Then allow me to take him away."

"No, let him sleep."

Lukian looked at her, his eyes unreadable. "You are kind, Vivienne. To the point of foolishness."

She drew in her breath sharply at his rudeness. "How can you say that? I kept Henry with me the entire time that Osip and I were talking, if you could call it talking."

"You should have sent the man away."

"Well . . . I didn't." In truth, she still did not know quite why she had invited him in. Perhaps something had happened in that instant when she looked into Osip's ice-colored eyes. She had felt no warning prickle of unease, only a sense of purpose, as if something were directing her to help him.

"I will do what I can."

"Thank you for that. As far as Henry, now that you are here and he knows that Kyril sent you, he is willing to relinquish the role of protector and—"

"Henry has your best interests at heart."

They heard the old monk shift position in his chair.

"Is he waking?" she whispered.

They stood together quietly and looked in. A wheezing snore came from Osip and his head tipped to one side.

"No. He seems to find that chair very comfortable."

"Do you know, Lukian—I almost forgot to tell you this—"

"Yes?"

"Osip took shelter from the rain in a doorway on the night when Kyril was here. I did not know his name then, of course."

Lukian thought back. That would have been the night when he and Kyril crossed the river to the docks, just ahead of the *Catherine*. With Volkodav on it. The so-called monk had been put in place well before today. Kyril must have been distracted when he'd left Vivienne, but Lukian could understand that. Beautiful and gentle and bright as a star, she could drive any man to distraction in an instant.

Even him. Toughened as he was.

"What are you thinking?"

"Nothing." Lukian let her talk.

"Kyril had stayed late—he was the last guest to leave. The old monk stepped out of the shadows as if to stop him, but Kyril got in the carriage and went away."

"Did Kyril see him?"

"No. I was watching out the window. I took the old fellow for a beggar or a lunatic. I had no idea that he was a monk."

Lukian only shrugged.

"Can you read the writing upon his robe?"

"Only if I open his coat."

There could be a weapon in it. Lukian intended to find out. But this back-and-forth was taking too much time.

Kyril had told Lukian to bring him to Argunov's house as soon as possible, and Argunov lived in Spitalfields.

Far away from the Pack's lair. Far away from Cheyne Row. It was the sort of neighborhood where people didn't ask too many questions.

Vivienne gave him an earnest look. "I think I know why he came here. He must have been told that Kyril would help him. Perhaps Osip saw him at the dock—it is near the tavern you mentioned, is that right?"

"Yes."

"Then perhaps someone pointed him out to Osip, who then followed him into London."

An excellent guess. Lukian kept a wary eye on the sleeping monk.

"Someone else directed him to my house. A servant, perhaps."

An informer or confederate, no doubt. The Pack planted servants of their own for the same purpose.

Vivienne went on. "And then he waited in this neighborhood after he missed his chance on that night a week ago, hoping Kyril would return."

Another excellent guess. The Pack's guards had not been on the lookout for a frail old man, of course. And Osip would not have gone about dressed like a mad monk in the meantime.

"I think that he summoned up all his courage to knock upon my door and try to talk to me."

"Perhaps."

"He must be very tired. He has not opened his eyes for quite a while, Lukian."

Lukian nodded, thinking that the monk was still waiting patiently for Kyril to arrive. Closed eyes or not, he'd heard

Vivienne say Lukian's name at least twenty times and knew he wasn't Kyril.

"Come, let us go back in."

He obeyed, coughing when the old man shifted his position again. A nose-wrinkling smell of musty canvas filled the room when Osip's long-sleeved coat fell open.

"There," she whispered, looking at Lukian. "Now you can read the letters on his robe. What do they say?"

Lukian bent down and looked closely. "That is an Orthodox cross, as you noted. And the letters refer to a verse from the Bible." He reached out to move aside a fold of cloth. The monk did not stir. "Luke 9:24."

She went over to the bookshelves and pulled out a small, limp volume with gold-edged pages. "Ah, here it is. A traveler's Bible—it will do." She found the Book of Luke and ran her finger down the page. "'For whosoever shall save his life shall lose it: but whosoever shall lose his life for my sake, the same shall save it.'"

Lukian straightened and frowned at her. "The Old Believers of the strictest kind wear that verse upon their garments. He might be one."

If Vivienne wanted to believe that, she could. Lukian was fairly sure that Osip was an old devil trying to shorten his prison sentence by working undercover. No doubt he did not want to die in chains and this assignment had been given him—he certainly played the part well. Ancient-seeming, benevolent, dressed as a penitent in every particular. But there was something about the man that bothered Lukian. The shape of his head—no, that was not it. One balding pate looked much like another.

He put the nagging thoughts aside. The question was how to make him disappear.

Lukian could not manhandle him and risk provoking Vivienne.

Besides, being in her presence, listening to her soft talk, and most of all witnessing her misplaced kindness toward Osip was disturbing him. In fact, he was breaking out in a sweat . . . but not because of her.

His thoughts began to break into fragments and his heart raced. Some part of his mind remained rational—damnation. Not for long.

He knew he might say anything in this disordered state. He would have to be careful. Very careful. It had been too long since he . . . he had not brought *that* with him. He needed it. Now. Craved it—

Vivienne was looking at him solicitously. "Are you feeling well? I am so sorry to have caused so much trouble."

Lukian cast a glance down at the monk. "You are not the cause. Come, let us talk in the hall. The room is stifling."

She followed him out again. "What shall we do?"

Lukian composed himself. "Kyril told me to get him out."

"In just those words? That seems so harsh."

"You trust Kyril, do you not?"

She hesitated for a second. "Y-yes."

"Then do not interfere."

"He will do what is best, I suppose. I really do think the monk knows him," Vivienne said, puzzled. "His eyes are so bright when I say Kyril's name."

"Vivienne . . ."

"Yes?"

"I have to take him away. Now. And—and bring him to some quiet place."

Vivienne peeked through the crack in the door at the slumbering monk. His peaceful breathing ruffled the hair of his beard but his eyes stayed firmly shut.

She turned back to him and searched his face. At last she spoke. "There is something you are not telling me, Lukian. What is it?"

Her green eyes fixed on his and Lukian trembled deep inside. He should not have come here, should have told Kyril to get someone else to do his dirty work.

Lying to her was making his mind split in half. He did not have what he needed to make himself whole again.

The darkness in his mind spread and ached. He fought for self-control.

Lukian reached out for her and then forced his hand to drop to his side. He could not touch her.

"We must wake him up," he said through gritted teeth. "Do not be surprised at anything I do—" Lukian stopped. He had frightened her.

"What is going on?" Vivienne's question was a whisper. "There is no harm in him, Lukian."

He smiled slightly. "He has not harmed you. That is all I will say."

"Why would he—"

Lukian interrupted her. "I must talk to him alone."

"But—"

He rubbed his hand across his burning eyes, then quelled her with a stern look.

"Listen to me. I do know where Kyril is and he has charged me to keep you safe, first of all, and to bring that man to—"

His voice had grown louder. The monk harrumphed and Lukian swore under his breath.

"I think he has overheard," Vivienne said.

"I am beginning not to care!"

"Please tell me what is going on—"

The old monk coughed and sputtered. Lukian grabbed her arm and brought her back in with him. They both watched as Osip woke up with excruciating slowness, peering around the unfamiliar room. His gaze touched Vivienne's face and he smiled almost tenderly.

Then he looked up at Lukian, who seemed thunderstruck, his eyes blazing with fury.

"I think I know who you really are," Lukian snarled in Russian. "But not why you are here. You will tell me, though. Now."

The old man struggled to sit up, coughing even more as he did so. He answered very rapidly, pouring out a story that Vivienne could hardly follow, even with the few words of English he mixed in.

I give you it. Spare my life. Something like that. She could not be sure.

It made no sense to Vivienne. Kyril had sent Lukian to help the old man. It was beginning to dawn on her that he thought Osip was a charlatan, but why Lukian seemed so angry at him she did not know.

The old man rattled on, sweating.

Lukian dragged over a chair and sat down to hear Osip out, interrupting him a few times.

"What does he want?" she whispered anxiously. "What are you saying?"

"I will explain later," he shot back. "Find Henry. He must take a message to a friend of mine. Osip needs a place to stay and he has agreed to go."

"Why has he come here? Will you never explain?"

He made a gesture to ensure her silence as the old monk began to talk again.

Vivienne went downstairs to look for Henry and found him sitting upon the bottom stair, his elbows braced on his knees and his head down in his arms.

He had fallen sound asleep. It was later than she thought.

She touched him gently on the shoulder. "Henry, I am sorry to wake you. But you must do something for Mr. Taruskin."

"Huh? Wha?" He picked up his head and gave her a confused look.

"You are to take a message to someone," she said. "The monk will spend the night at the house of a friend of Mr. Taruskin's."

"I am glad to hear that, madam. Foreigners can't be trusted. That dirty old man is as foreign as they come."

Vivienne glared at him.

"Of course, the Taruskins are a different sort. They are gentlemen." He got up stiffly. Vivienne could hear his joints creak. "Well, where is the note?"

"I will fetch it." She ran lightly back up the stairs and cracked open the door to her study. Lukian slipped a folded envelope with a hastily scribbled address on it through the narrow space.

"Give this to Henry," he said. "Tell him to wait at Argunov's for a reply and come back straightaway."

She heard the urgency in Lukian's tone and did as he asked, running back to Henry and putting the envelope in his hands.

Henry examined the address. "In Spitalfields, is it? I shall bring a stout stick."

"Do that. Off you go." She opened the door for him and looked out into the street. There was no one about.

Putting a foot upon the bottom stair, she heard Lukian's low voice talking in Russian, interspersed with the quavering voice of the monk. Then they were quiet.

Vivienne turned when Mrs. Hickham called to her, waiting for the older woman to lumber slowly up the stairs from the kitchen. She reassured the housekeeper that the monk would not be spending the night, and explained that Henry had gone to arrange lodging for him.

A quarter of an hour went by before she returned upstairs. She ascended quietly, not wanting to startle either of them, and saw Lukian standing at the top, as if he was about to descend.

Then she saw what he had in his hands.

A round thing, green and gold and shining. He turned to examine it in the light from the sconce on the wall. That must have been why he had come out of the study.

"What is that, Lukian?"

"An egg."

She looked at it with wonder. Never in her life had she seen an egg like that.

Rimmed with pure gold, the enameled upper and lower halves were hinged and closed with a diamond clasp. The egg itself was supported upon a stem of gold fashioned to look like a branch with leaves. A snake with enameled scales coiled in a gold channel that served as the base. It was a jeweler's masterpiece.

Lukian touched the top of the snake's head and a tiny, forked tongue of gold flicked out.

Vivienne took a step back. "How did it come here?"

"The monk had it," Lukian said simply.

"That is impossible. He is so poor." She looked through the open door. "Why did he give it to you? But he is sleeping again—"

Lukian made a noncommittal sound. "Have you not noticed how easily he falls asleep?"

"Yes, well, he is old and weary. You ought to be more kind."

Lukian flashed her a scornful look that she chose to ignore.

"Lukian, his hands were empty when he came in and he carried no bag. Where was he keeping that?"

"Under his robe."

"Hm. Well, it is as big as a soldier's tent."

"Yes." It might have been made from one, Lukian thought, along with the coat. He doubted the authenticity of the old man's costume, but he could not blame Vivienne for taking Osip for what he pretended to be: a wandering man of God. "He showed it to me when you left the room."

"It is extraordinary."

"Yes, it is. A mechanical marvel." He touched the snake's tail and the snake began to move around the base.

She heard a very faint whirr. The snake slithered up the branch and around the egg and down the other side.

It coiled around the base again and then repeated the action.

"But why did he show it to you and not me?"

Lukian shrugged. "I happened to notice that he had something under his robe." He shut off the mechanical snake by touching its tail twice. "There. The show is over."

"Who made it?"

"A genius and a madman."

"Two men, do you mean?"

"No. Just one. Jozef Taruskin. A master jeweler and inventor. He was an ancestor of mine and Kyril's."

"Indeed. How interesting. Does this thing belong to your family then?"

"Not anymore. It was made here in London almost a hundred years ago but was taken to St. Petersburg shortly after that."

"As a gift?"

Lukian gave her a mirthless smile. "An appropriation."

She inspected it more closely. "There are Latin words inscribed upon the base." She read aloud. "*Hortus conclusus, fons signatus.* That means . . . a garden enclosed, a fountain sealed."

"Does it?" Lukian seemed indifferent. Almost weary. The shining object he held looked like a toy in his huge hand. An extremely valuable toy.

"It cannot possibly be his."

Scowling, Lukian shook his head. "Of course not. It now belongs to the Tsar. It is the one and only Serpent's Egg."

Was he mocking her? She had heard of such priceless objects created for the Imperial Court, but not this one. But then, if it had been stolen, as Lukian seemed to be saying, perhaps it was kept for private exhibition. She studied the egg from every side, amazed by the ingenuity that had gone into its creation. The eyes of the little snake at its base glittered coldly.

7

She touched the marvelous egg, not of her own volition. Her hand seemed drawn to it. Lukian held it by the base and turned it slowly, allowing her to look her fill in silence. Vivienne let her hand fall to her side. She should not play with it—it had to go back to where it belonged. It occurred to her that she would not want it in her house, should anyone come looking for it.

She could not comprehend how a holy man had come by such a valuable thing. That he might have stolen it seemed incredible. Vivienne glanced into her study at Osip, who had slumped in his chair. His hands were covered by his long sleeves. It would be a shame to wake him once more, she thought absently.

"I expect the Tsar wants it back."

"What do you mean, Lukian?"

He sighed. "As you may have already guessed, Jozef Taruskin was not inclined to give it to Alexander's predecessor upon the throne." Lukian lifted the egg so that she could see the bottom of the base. "That is his mark in our alphabet. J.T."

"And how did it get to Russia?"

Lukian studied her for a long moment. "The Tsar's agents took it by force. They killed a dozen men in the process."

"Was Jozef Taruskin among them?"

"No. His remarkable skills were too valuable, even though he lived in exile. He was persuaded, shall we say, to listen to reason and handed it over. With reluctance. It was his masterpiece. But that was many, many years ago. Alexander I only inherited it."

"I see."

"Nonetheless, although its existence is not widely known, it is worth more than most of the Russian crown jewels."

"Why?"

"The great diamond at its heart is unique in all the world. It could be removed and used to adorn a scepter."

"Ah. As a symbol of wealth and power."

"Exactly. Alexander likes to show off, especially now that he is the most powerful sovereign on earth."

"I am surprised Napoleon did not demand the Serpent's Egg or the diamond for himself."

"It was kept in the Winter Palace in St. Petersburg. Napoleon did not get that far in 1812. The Grande Armée was swallowed by the Russian winter."

"But Lukian . . ."

"Yes?"

"How in God's name did that poor old priest come by it?"

Lukian lowered the egg.

"I have no way of knowing that. I need to examine it thoroughly. It may be only a very good copy, meant to lure—" He stopped himself, not wanting to say *lure Kyril out into the open*.

She did not notice his slip, because at that moment the monk groaned. Vivienne looked through the open door again. "Oh, he is uncomfortable—but why is he lifting his arms like that?" She craned her neck to see. "Good Lord! His wrists are tied!" She looked wildly at Lukian. "Did you do that?"

Lukian glowered at her. "He did not want to stay put." He snarled something at the monk. As it happened, she understood the Russian words.

"Be still? Why should he be still? What on earth is going on?"

"I cannot tell you." He had hoped to get the monk out of the house on some pretext she would accept without her seeing the bonds on the old man's knobby wrists. He had blundered badly, aghast to find out that Osip had the Serpent's Egg in his possession.

"What? Why not? You have hurt him, Lukian!" She rushed into the room and Lukian followed, still holding the treasure.

"H-head," the old man groaned.

"What? Did he hit you?"

The old man nodded feebly. Vivienne looked at his bald pate and saw the lump. Shocked into action, she reached over him and gave Lukian a stinging slap.

There was fire in Lukian's eyes, but his voice was calm. "I suggest that you keep your hands to yourself."

"Do not threaten me! I will tell—"

"Kyril? No. But I will tell him for you."

She gazed at him with astonishment. Lukian must have gone mad. Or she had. Her well-meaning attempt to help the old monk had ended with him being injured. "You will not! I will find Kyril with or without you! Get out of my house!"

Lukian looked down at the glittering egg and tapped the snake's head again. He shook his head. "And leave you with this precious thing and the mad monk? No again."

The snake began its whirring journey around the base and up over the egg. She wanted to smash it to bits.

"The monk is not mad, you are! He is poor—and friend-less—how could you hurt him?"

"It was me or him."

"He is a man of God! I do not believe you!" she raged. She

picked up the old man's hands and scrabbled in the clutter on her desk for scissors—damnation—there they were.

Osip gave her a beseeching look. Lukian just stood there.

She snipped and sawed at the cord around his wrists, and set him free. Osip wept, tears running into his dry wrinkles as he rubbed his wrists with his gnarled hands.

Lukian gave him a contemptuous look and made a disgusted sound. "You may have fooled her, but not me."

"Lukian!"

Her fury was clear on her face. Lukian braced himself for another slap but she controlled her temper. Good. He was barely able to control his. Something in his brain had been jarred loose by the contact of her hand against his face.

"Would you like to see what is inside, Vivienne?" He held up the thing and pressed an unseen button at its base. The hinged egg opened. Inside it was another, smaller egg, just as beautiful, encrusted with emeralds.

Vivienne stared at it, then realized what she was doing. She was angry at him all over again. "Do you hope to distract me with that damned trinket?"

He did not answer, but pressed another button. The emerald egg opened to reveal a third. That one was black onyx. The monk cringed in his chair when Lukian pressed the button to open it.

The black egg was lined with dull metal that looked like lead. Inside it was a small stone. Not enameled. Not gem-encrusted. And far from valuable, at least at first glance.

Not what she had expected. "That is no diamond."

Lukian let out his breath. His eyes were narrow as he looked at it closely. "No," he said, turning the thing this way and that. "It is khodzhite, I think."

She looked at the monk and back to Lukian. They apparently knew what that was.

"And what is that?"

"A very rare mineral. Incorruptible and precious."

"But it is ugly." Her hands were on her hips, and her eyes showed her anger, she knew that. A worthless pebble was no reason to hurt an old man. Or to hurt anyone. She would take the Serpent's Egg from Lukian and return it to—if not its rightful owner, Osip could at least tell her where it had come from. If she could grab it from Lukian and—then what? There was no weapon in the room besides the fireplace poker. Her gaze fell on the scissors and she made a stealthy move to pick them up.

"Khodzhite is strange stuff, Vivienne."

She raised her hand, holding the scissors as if she was going to stab him—she would not but she was infuriated by what he had done. Lukian knocked them out of her hand.

"Oh!" she gasped.

He looked at her impassively. "Do you want to know why?"

"I do not care."

"Khodzhite weakens the one who touches it."

"I do not believe you!"

He only shrugged and held the egg out to her. "I think that is why the monk kept falling asleep. Khodzhite has a strong effect upon the aged."

She scarcely heard what he was saying when she realized she had a chance to take it from him. She reached for it . . . her fingers trembled. Vivienne felt strangely sick. On the verge of vomiting.

She dropped her hand and looked desperately at the monk. He shook his head. He could not help her. Lukian had the strength of ten men combined.

His dark eyes were fixed on her face, as if he were trying to judge her degree of weakness. Her own filled with tears. How dare he.

She could not believe that he had come to help her and then done this. He had changed into a sullen, malevolent stranger who could hurt an old man. And her.

"Should I close the eggs, Vivienne?"

"Yes!" she shrieked.

If only Henry would come back. He would help her . . . she whirled around as if she was about to run to the door.

Lukian seized her wrist. "Henry will be gone for a while. Pay attention before I do as you ask. I want you to understand how dangerous it is."

He held his hand over the small stone.

Her eyes widened. Slowly, his fingers twitched, then contorted into strange shapes, as if the tendons were pulling free from the bones. Lukian clenched his teeth. He endured the pain for a few more seconds, then pulled his writhing hand away.

Vivienne gasped with horror.

Lukian let out his breath as the spasms in his hand began to subside. "Now do you understand?"

"Ah—" She happened at that moment to glance at the monk. He was looking at Lukian's tortured hand. There was an odd expression in his ice-colored eyes. The old man looked . . . pleased.

Osip realized that she was staring at him, and the look in his eyes changed in an instant. Once again his gaze became mild. He ventured a pathetic smile and rubbed his wrists, as if to remind her of his own pain.

She needed no reminding. Lukian had treated him with cruelty.

Lukian tapped and pressed, closing the three hinged eggs one by one. "And now for the finale." He made the little snake circle the egg and flick its tongue.

There was a nasty edge to his voice. At this moment, it was almost impossible for her to believe that he was even remotely related to Kyril. His cousin was warm, kind, sensual—a man who could breathe loving life back into a lonely woman's heart. Lukian was cold and cruel, a man she did not know or trust at all. But Kyril had sent him.

A tiny doubt wormed its way into her mind.

"Why did Kyril not come when he received my letter?"

Lukian reached into his jacket pocket. "Do you want them? I have all five." He threw them at her. They spun in circles in the air, then landed on the floor.

"Why do you have them? Where is he?"

"Someplace safe."

She stood between the monk and Lukian. "I will find him, Lukian. And I will tell him everything."

"Go ahead."

She took a few steps toward Lukian, impelled by a fierceness that thrilled her. It was as if something hidden inspired her to defy him. "Give Osip back the Serpent's Egg!"

"Why should I?"

"It is more his than yours."

"That remains to be seen. I think we can both agree that its sudden appearance is a mystery. But perhaps that is all we will agree on."

"Damn you, Lukian!" She kept walking toward him, taking small steps.

"You are acting as if I brought it to you—as if I caused you this trouble—"

"Give it to me."

Lukian managed to look at her levelly when she finally stopped in front of him. But the dark feeling in his head grew stronger when he gazed into her eyes. He held the thing just out of her reach, silently daring her to grab it.

She sized him up. "You will not hit me, you bastard. I know you won't."

"I want to."

"Oh!" She slapped him for a second time.

He stood his ground. Just like Kyril. The room grew very quiet. The anger in Lukian's eyes was terrifying.

Vivienne edged back. Just a little.

She could scream for Mrs. Hickham.

No. Two women and one old monk against a man his size? They would not win. She tried to stare him down. Useless. His eyes were much darker than Kyril's. Everything about him was darker.

Lukian bore an unmistakable resemblance to a figure of Satan at the moment. His powerful body was tensed, from his spiky hair to his black boots. He widened his stance. His gaze was piercing, flecked with fire, but his face was emotionless.

He surprised her utterly when he handed over the egg.

"Keep it safe. The lead that lines the innermost egg contains the rays of khodzhite. You are young and healthy and it will not harm you if you do not open it. But hide it where he will not know." He threw a look that held the murderous strength of lightning at the old monk, who cowered under it.

Without thinking, Vivienne opened her hands to receive it. The gold base was warm from his. By accident she pressed the button that activated the snake. It began its mechanical journey. Up, around, and down. She gazed at it, appalled, unable to let go.

Vivienne sank into a chair, holding the evil thing as if it weighed far more than it did. The very sight of it was oppressive.

When she looked up again, Lukian had gone. She heard him run down the stairs. Then Vivienne heard Osip cough, as if to remind her that he was still in the room.

Asking him for an explanation would be a wearying struggle. That could come later. Kyril would help.

Her mind raced through a thousand scenarios. How had the old monk come into possession of such an object? Even without the diamond, it must be extremely valuable and certainly it was unique. The most plausible explanation was that he simply wanted to sell it. Or wanted her or Kyril to sell it. So that he could get back to Russia and—what? She told herself to stop her pointless speculation.

She looked at Osip again. He had taken a long, wooden-beaded rosary from some hidden pocket. He touched the beads and muttered prayers that were completely incomprehensible.

The droning chant was unpleasant to listen to, as mechanical in its way as the snake. She glanced at the heavy wooden crucifix suspended from the rosary, noting its plainness. Should it not have a figure of Christ upon it? But then, she thought absently, the rituals and props of his church were unfamiliar to her—perhaps not. Osip gathered up the strand of beads and put them back in the pocket they had come from.

Had she looked a little longer, had the crucifix turned from back to front, she would have understood. It did have a figure on it. Not of Christ, but a mockery of Christ. A small, silver wolf was affixed to it, tiny nails driven through its four paws.

But she did not see it.

Musing, Vivienne was aware that she no longer entirely trusted the monk. There had been that one moment when the old man's expression had changed so—when Lukian's hand twisted in agony. It was as if a mask had dropped away.

No, she told herself. It was Lukian who had dropped his mask. She was troubled, deeply so, by what she had seen in his face and his eyes. She had inadvertently trapped him at the top of the stairs—he must have been hoping to escape with the egg, especially since he'd thought that immense diamond was inside it. He had seemed as surprised as she to find out that it was not.

The monk was a friendless stranger who needed help. Kyril would have to come. If not, she would go to find him. It was not as if she was a prisoner in this house.

"I am going to hide this," she said to the monk. "For your safety and my own."

He gave her another benign smile and raised a hand as if to bless her. She flinched. It might as well have been a blow.

"Hide," he said, nodding as if he understood her.

Good. She would not want him to think that she was stealing it, as Lukian had tried to. Uneasy, Vivienne reminded herself that it had been taken from his ancestor in a way that was tantamount to stealing.

"I wish that Kyril had come—oh, it is no use talking to you," she said, more to herself than to Osip. He brightened at the name.

Very well. She would not put him out upon the street. Her dispirited sigh came from the bottom of her soul. Too many odd and frightening things had happened this day, a day that had started out like any other.

Her sense of what was real and what was not had begun to blur. Starting with the book. No. Starting with Kyril. His eyes had given her a glimpse of a world she did not know. She felt as if its strangest inhabitants had walked into hers.

Lukian left the house in Cheyne Row and strode away. He was headed for Soho and the house of his mistress.

He took his time, walking up Bond Street to Oxford, looking into the windows of the shops. But he scarcely saw the goods on display. The passers-by divided and flowed around him every time he stopped, an immovable island in a river of chattering humanity.

It didn't matter to Lukian. He was in a state of shock. The Serpent's Egg had mysteriously appeared in London, the diamond at its heart gone, replaced by a lump of khodzhite. He was consumed with a nameless horror when he remembered the monk's eyes, when the old man had finally opened them. They were the color of ice. Exactly like Volkodav's. He had been utterly taken aback when he realized that Osip and the Wolf Killer had to be brothers. The irony of that did not escape him.

So. It would be brother against brother, in a fight to the

death when the battle was joined. Each side convinced that they would prevail. Whether the Taruskins would survive was anyone's guess.

Lukian knew he'd handled the encounter with the monk badly. He should report to Kyril but he needed to forget—and he knew how—damnation. His eyes began to water and sting. He rubbed at them viciously.

He walked more quickly and came at last to Soho, turning down Frith Street and going into a mews paved with cobblestones. Pots of scarlet flowers decorated a door in a brick wall. He grasped the doorknocker and rapped three times.

Lily Chiswell soon answered.

"Lukian! I was not expecting you."

He stared at her and she stepped back. "Have you a man inside?"

"No. The last fellow just left."

She waved him in and Lukian brushed by her. He got a whiff of her departed customer. Someone ordinary. Certainly not Russian. The man had belched English ale and the old mutton he'd eaten for lunch. The smell hung in the air.

"Please sit down. Tea?"

"Thank you."

She bustled into the kitchen and he heard cheerful sounds.

Water poured slapdash into a kettle—she had spilled some. Clanking as the kettle was set on the hob. Cups clinked onto a tray. Domestic music.

And back she came.

Lily knew his tastes and she served tea in the Russian style. Very hot and very strong. In a glass set in a holder of pierced silver.

He took a lump of sugar from the bowl on the tray and held it between his teeth, sipping the scalding tea through it.

"It is nice to see you."

Lukian nodded. Just looking at her made him think of what he was going to get. The thought cheered him much more than the tea.

"Have you had a bad day, then?"

"Yes. Hellish."

"I am sorry to hear that." Her voice was sympathetic. He closed his eyes and listened to her soothing prattle, fighting the confusion that assailed his mind. He had very nearly failed in his mission to protect Vivienne, but then he had not expected to see the Serpent's Egg come out from under the monk's robes— he'd thought it was a massive pistol.

Khodzhite had very strange powers. They had all been affected.

The filthy old pretender most of all. Like the stone inside the egg, he radiated evil that Vivienne seemed unable to perceive. Her essential innocence would be her undoing. The only thing Lukian had been able to do was give her the damned thing and tell her not to touch it.

Then leave. He'd had to. She might have come at him in a fury again and he'd become furious in turn, a strong feeling that softened into a strange excitement at the sight of the fire in her eyes.

Lily would do in Vivienne's stead.

"I have what you need, Lukian," she said.

He had almost finished his tea. Swallowing what remained of the lump of sugar, he set the glass aside on the low table that was always there and kept his eyes closed.

Lily kneeled in front of him. She opened his breeches and took his cock out of his small clothes. She pumped and stroked the soft, thick flesh, but nothing much happened.

"Hmm. I will try harder, sir."

Lukian nodded and thought guiltily of Vivienne. His cock responded.

It stiffened to respectable length and Lily seemed satisfied with that.

He opened his eyes when she rose. She turned her back to him and lifted her skirts to her waist, displaying her bare bottom.

Lukian took hold of his cock. "I am ready."

He slumped a little in the chair so she could straddle his long legs, walking backwards over them and positioning herself as was customary. He was grateful that he did not have to look at her face, although it was pretty.

It was Vivienne he wanted. Kyril would tear out his throat if he knew.

"Down you go, Lily."

She bent her knees and did as he asked, squatting slightly and pushing herself back so her cunny was in position over his waiting cock. Free of the foreskin that he had rolled down, the head of it wept for what she had between her legs.

Momentary oblivion. Blessed release.

Her snug, juicy sheath enfolded his cock as she eased carefully down upon him.

Lukian let go of his cock and gripped her hips. She rode him energetically, her arse as round as a pony's.

The sight of his cock going in and out as she rose and lowered herself was erotic. Her plump buttocks were split open like a ripe peach. He liked the way his veined cock disappeared into the juicy flesh, and reappeared wet. He was getting harder. English to the core, Lily nonetheless reminded him very much of a Russian peasant woman he had liked to fuck, a buxom servant at his uncle's dacha. She had been eager to please and happy to accommodate her young master.

He could not imagine a thoroughbred like Vivienne assuming this position. It was ideal for a whore. Lily's strong thighs gave away her frequent practice of it.

She did not have to see her customer's face either. No, all she had to do was go up and down, up and down, as if she were taking exercise. She could daydream if she wished, or think about . . . what did whores think about?

He did not know or care.

Faced with a splendid arse like hers, fondling it freely, most customers shot their wad within seconds.

But Lukian would not.

His mental confusion had cleared, leaving him with an irritable edge.

He needed to fuck.

"How is that, sir?" Lily asked, throwing him an obliging look over her shoulder as she bounced. "Coming along nicely?"

"A few minutes more," he growled. "Then we shall do something else."

She sighed and kept on.

Lukian appreciated her thoughtfulness. He grabbed her buttocks to feel how nicely she flexed them. He used his hands to make her pound down harder.

She braced herself with one hand upon one of his thighs and reached between her legs and his to find his balls.

There was something assessing about her touch when she did. "A heavy load you have today, sir. And they are hot."

Lukian gritted his teeth. "Yes, Lily."

"Do you want me to hold them tight?"

"Y-yes."

He let out a sigh of pleasure, still holding her buttocks and sliding her down on his cock again and again with greater force than before.

He was no longer thinking of Vivienne. Her elegance, her vulnerability . . . these were not qualities that brought out the beast in him.

No, Lily's tough, strong body did that. She had an animal quality of her own.

Down and down. The cheeks of her behind shook as she slammed down on his taut groin.

Unhh. Unhh.

He realized that he was groaning and not her. Too near orgasm, Lukian stopped and lifted her off, holding her in midair.

Lily balanced on her tiptoes, laughing. Her half-boots and striped stockings showed off her sturdy legs.

"Now what?"

"Let me get my breath, my girl."

She looked down between her thighs at the long cock bobbing below.

"Well-slicked, it is. I had a good ride."

"I liked watching." Lukian set her down.

She walked forward, still clutching her skirts around her waist, and then turned around, smiling at him. Her face was flushed pink from her efforts.

Lukian beckoned her to his side. He finished the dregs of his tea as he kept his eyes on her cunny, sliding his fingers in and out of the tight, juicy slit.

She reached down and parted the soft, dripping wet lips to make it easier for him.

Always helpful. "Let's see your tits."

She left off playing with herself and pulled her plump breasts from her bodice, propping them on its stiff edge.

It was a sight Lukian loved. Pushed together and shoved up nearly to her chin, her breasts were irresistible.

The sight made his cock more erect, though it had not flagged since he had pulled her off it.

"Touch them."

"Yes, sir."

She took her long nipples in her fingers and tugged on them hard. Then she rolled them, squeezing until the pink tips turned red.

He watched intently.

"I know you want to suck," she murmured.

"Yes, I do."

"No harm in that. Men love to suck like babies. And get their big cocks jerked off when they do."

"Put your tits in my face." An unnecessary command. She was already leaning over, ready to satisfy his hunger to be close to her, brushing her incredible softness against his cheek.

He wanted to bury his face in her full breasts until he could not breathe, wanted her to stroke his hair like a mother and murmur soft things to him.

Lukian was grateful that she was willing to spend so much time with him. Perhaps it was true that he was her favorite customer.

Lily let him suck to his heart's content, holding onto the back of his chair while he did, humming to herself. She had to let go of her skirts, which drifted down over his lap.

His cock was happy to be enfolded in their warmth and lost none of its stiffness.

Lukian sat up a little to take advantage of her perfect position. He saw nothing but plump breasts and pink nipples and that was all he wanted to see.

Intent upon his pleasure, he sucked one and then the other, stopping only to nuzzle and squeeze, finding earthy comfort in her abundant flesh and stroking her impossibly soft skin.

Lily had no pimp and as a consequence was not ill-used. She maintained a select clientele, which was the reason she had her own house. She was pretty, healthy, and she kept herself very clean. Watching her bathe was a service she offered, in fact, but tonight he would not avail himself of it.

No, he wanted her as she was, without a show of sensuality.

He felt something very like fondness for her at the moment. He planted a kiss exactly in the middle of her breasts, over her heart.

Lily murmured something, a pleased sound.

If it was possible to arouse a whore, he supposed he had done it. She was breathing excitedly.

"You are very nice to my breasts, sir. I do like what you are doing. Sometimes me and another girl will—oh, I should not tell you."

"Minx. Looking for extra shillings?"

"Me?"

"Well, you shall have them. Tell me of your Sapphic play."

She bent to whisper in his ear while he held onto her breasts, still stroking and squeezing. Her wanton words excited him deeply.

"Did you like that story?" she asked, her eyes wide and innocent.

"I did."

She nodded with satisfaction and her breasts bobbed in his hands.

"It is true, sir."

"I should like to watch you two one day."

"A guinea apiece, that is."

Lukian laughed and sat up. "Come. I want you on your back."

"Very well."

She led the way into her small bedchamber, a cluttered room with flowered wallpaper decorated with pictures cut from illustrated newspapers. China shepherdesses and other figurines were everywhere.

Lukian fumbled with her buttons, too hot for his hands to manage such tiny things. He did better with her stays once the dress came off.

He lingered over the laces, pulling them tighter at first. Cinching her waist until she yelped made her behind more round and her breasts overflow.

The soft handfuls were delicious to hold and he took his time with them, eventually deciding that the stays would remain on.

Lukian sat on the bed to remove his own clothes. She helped with his shirt, lifting it over his head and folding it carefully over a chair. She touched the cruel lattice of scar tissue that covered his back.

"Look your fill," he said matter-of-factly.

"Does it hurt you ever?"

"Not anymore. But the skin is tight. Sometimes I cannot move my shoulders very well. But that can't be helped."

"Who did it to you?"

"It doesn't matter. They are dead."

Lily thought that over for a moment. "Did you kill them then?"

"Yes, Lily. I made them eat each other's balls. They choked on them. And their own blood."

"You are scaring me."

"Am I, my girl? You asked a question and I answered it. Come. Lie over my lap."

His breeches had stayed unbuttoned. She obliged him, lying over his thighs and making herself comfortable as he began to fondle her bare behind.

"Do you want to spank me?"

"Not today."

"Well, then. Feel away."

After a short while, she began to squirm with pleasure on his thighs.

"Your customers do not do this so gently, I take it." He cupped her arse cheeks with his big hands, squeezing and fondling.

"No, sir. They only want to hurt me with a whip or a paddle. I don't let them, but you are skillful and considerate." She thrust her buttocks up a little. "I would let you spank me for nothing."

Lukian spread her thighs apart. He moved so he could look at her cunny. "Reach underneath and use your fingers. Touch yourself."

"Yes, sir. I like to do that. Please spank me a little. It goes together nicely with this." He could hear her work her hand into her juicy cunny.

"As you wish." He gave her hearty slaps that turned her white buttocks pink. Lily moaned with pleasure and eagerly thrust her buttocks higher. He gave her more, but finished with caresses over the heated skin of her behind.

"You are a good girl, Lily," he murmured. "And good girls need good fucking."

"You will have to take your breeches and boots off for that." Her face flushed, she rose halfway off his lap and winked at him. "Shall I help?"

"Of course."

Lily got up, turned her back to him and bent over, taking hold of his calf as he stretched out a leg.

The folds of her hiked-up dress had concealed much of her body when he had been in the chair. Now her breasts bounced freely, their hard nipples touching his legs when she bent far enough forward.

He closed his eyes to concentrate on that. Her nipple tips were hot. Not being able to anticipate where or when they touched was a subtle little thrill. She concentrated on his boots.

Her hands smoothed over the fine leather upper and then clasped just tight enough to pull. The snug, smooth feeling was very much like pulling out of her. He was anticipating the popping sound when the boot came off. He opened his eyes. The view of her bare buttocks and the private, puckered hole between them was wonderful.

"And what are you looking at?" she asked. She knew.

"Your arsehole. Do not worry. I want the usual, that is all."

The boot came off and she set it down.

Lukian extended his other leg.

Lily clasped that boot and drew it off. He braced himself this time against her behind, taking advantage of her absorption in the task to spread her and look below.

Tighter than ever, nestled in drenched curls, her extremely swollen cunny tempted him beyond belief. Driving into it would bring the forgetfulness he desperately craved.

She stayed where she was, her hands on her own knees, knowing that he was looking.

Lukian sighed raggedly and pressed his face to her bare bottom, kissing and fondling for all he was worth. She let him, turning around only when his big hands guided her.

He made short work of the stays and tossed them on the floor. He wanted all of her. Soft belly, generous hips, and unconfined breasts. Female through and through.

His for another hour.

"Lie on your back," he said roughly.

She had kept on her striped stockings and half boots, which gave her the look of a performer in a risqué show. But her performance was only for him.

She stretched her legs up to the ceiling, crossing her ankles flirtatiously.

Hardly modest. The sight of her cunny squeezed between the plump tops of her thighs was almost enough to make him spray his come without touching himself, all over the back of her legs.

Then Lily opened herself very wide in a welcoming vee. She patted her cunny. "I am ready."

He peeled off his breeches and small clothes at the same time, and got rid of his own plain stockings. He needed to be naked. And all the way up inside her.

Lukian came down over her and did just that, thrusting again and again as he writhed.

The clouded darkness in his mind was back. And the edge. The frantic pounding did not take away either.

Lily stroked his hair, his back, his clenching buttocks—whatever she could reach. He drove in harder, growling and sobbing against her sweet-smelling neck.

"There, there," she soothed him. "There now. You shall soon have what you need. Come for me. Come."

Lukian clutched the covers above her head, knowing that his grip had grown too strong to risk touching her now. He felt the material tear under his nails.

Lily did not protest. She was aware of what was happening to him, using her body as best she could to lessen his torment. With an agonized scream, he came at last, in a hot sweat that chilled him in the next instant.

Lily held him and rocked him. "Don't move. My turn."

He stayed inside her, still outrageously erect. Gasping for breath, he felt the sweet pulsing begin deep within her cunny. At least he had given her pleasure.

But what he had felt was much more like pain.

When she had cleaned him and herself at the washstand, they dressed without speaking. She was calm, putting on a hat and pelisse against the night air.

"Are you ready?"

He nodded. Lukian did not dare to look at himself in the mirror. The need that had brought him here was so strong now that he knew he would see it in his eyes.

She did not even look up at him.

Just as well.

The fetid air made him wrinkle his nose once they were outside. Was there a street in London that did not smell of death?

Lily patted his arm when she heard his sharp sigh.

"Soon enough, Mr. Taruskin. Ah, I see a light in the window."

The doctor's office was not far ahead. No doubt Lily had arranged for him to be there. Not every doctor saw patients at night.

They entered, let in by an indifferent servant, and went to the room where Dr. Broadstreet sat at an imposing desk.

He looked intently at Lukian.

Lukian barely saw him. He had withdrawn more deeply into himself on the way there. And he had begun to shake.

Lily guided him to a chair.

The doctor sighed and reached for a black case covered in pebbled leather.

"Have you the money?"

Lily helped him find the small bag that held it. She took out several gold coins and arranged them in a neat row on the desk.

"He needs more every week."

The doctor only nodded at first. He looked at Lukian, then at her again. "That is how it happens."

He unlatched the case, which was filled with small glass vials. The doctor picked up one and peered at the liquid in it. "The cork is cracked."

"Come now," Lily said. "It is not the sort of stuff that spoils."

"A chemical solution can change in the presence of oxygen."

"Never mind that. You can see how much he needs it, can't you?"

Lukian's head had lolled back and his mouth was open. He looked at the doctor through slitted eyes.

"Yes." Dr. Broadstreet used a small forceps to extract the split cork. Then he rose and poured the liquid in it between his patient's dry lips. Lukian sighed and licked them.

"After this case is gone, I have no more," he said to Lily. "It is not always easy to obtain morphine of high quality. And I fear this man will never get enough."

"I cannot keep him happy all by myself," she snapped. "Do what you can."

Dr. Broadstreet hesitated. "There is another chemist who sells it. A Russian, like your friend. But his formulation is new. It may be stronger and I am not sure it is safe."

"Do what you can," Lily repeated.

8

That same night . . .

Distraught, Vivienne wandered along the river. It soothed her to walk and walk when she was upset, and she cared not for the lateness of the hour. She had left her house without a word to anyone after hiding the Serpent's Egg under a loose floorboard that was itself hidden by a carpet.

The monk seemed to have lost interest in the thing. He was quite weak, as Lukian had said, and in her opinion, he would get weaker. He seemed to be fading away. Osip had gazed at her mournfully until she could not stand it another second, and bowed his head when she asked him to look elsewhere.

Desperate for a way to distract him, she had gone to the bookshelf and taken down the illustrated Russian folktales. He could look at the pictures even if he could not read it, and tell himself the stories if he liked. Her foolish attempt to do good had done nothing but harm.

And the matter of the egg was very, very curious. Closed up, it was a bauble for display. Open, it exerted a sinister power. She knew of no one she could ask to explain it . . . save Kyril, perhaps.

Wherever he was.

Henry had returned from Spitalfields and the house of Mr. Argunov, surprised to find the monk still there and Lukian gone. Grumbling despite her explanation, he had made sure to bolt all the doors from the inside before he went down to his own room.

Rather than worry Henry if he were to awake and find the doors unbolted, she had scrambled out a window that overlooked the back garden, landing on the soft ground without injury.

She'd been walking slowly for what seemed like miles. The crowded center of London was well behind her, not that she had known it until dawn began to lighten the sky. Vivienne was glad that she'd thought to throw a cloak out the window first. She needed it and she wanted to cover herself.

There were always tramps and rough men by the river, digging in the murk when the tide went out for anything they could sell or use.

Living in Cheyne Row even for the brief time she had, she knew something about their unsavory trade—a morbid friend had told her of it. Sometimes they dragged out the drowned, holding out muddy hands afterward for a few coins from grieving relatives, when any appeared at the dead-house where corpses found in the river were kept for a while.

It happened in the nicest neighborhoods.

The bodies of suicides were not always looked for. Once recovered, they were difficult to bury. No churchyard would take them.

And as for the murdered . . . they were often difficult to recognize, she had heard. The same friend had regaled her with a few more stories that had sickened her, of how they were dragged to the bank as well, stripped of anything that could be sold, from rings to buttons.

The river held unclean secrets. Which did not keep the poorest of the poor from fishing in it.

One such fellow, a crabber by the traps next to him on the bank, glanced at her as she passed, then returned to what he was doing.

Vivienne shuddered. The shy creatures were the first to find what drifted to the bottom of the Thames, she'd heard, delicately picking at clothes that rose and fell in the water, still attached to drowned bodies. Then their claws picked at faces and hands, taking the easy flesh.

She hurried on. The river flowed on indifferently by her, glimmering like dirty silver under the new moon.

By sunrise she was in a part of London she had never seen. In the near distance was a cemetery marked only with a bas-relief embedded in a wall next to the rusted gate. It showed a shrouded woman, weeping stone tears. Vivienne walked in.

She examined the names and dates on the simple tombstones. Most of the cemetery's inhabitants had died young.

An old woman walked between the rows of stones, throwing crumbs for the sparrows. Vivienne nodded to her. The little birds hopped about and pecked at the crumbs. Their liveliness was comforting.

"Good morning," the old woman said.

"Good morning. Do you know—" She hesitated, not wanting to ask where she was.

The woman might take her for a wandering lunatic and with good reason. What if she ended up in Bedlam? She might, if she were not careful. Her hair, tousled first by the hood and then by the wind that blew over the river, was hopelessly tangled. The sadness in her eyes had to show. That at least would not be remarked upon in this place.

Whatever this lonely place was called, wherever she was, her feet were sore. She had walked for hours.

Vivienne summoned up the courage to speak again. "What cemetery is this?"

"It belongs to the Magdalen."

"I beg your pardon?"

"St. Mary Magdalen. Did you not see her in the carving by the gate?"

"I did. But I didn't know who she was." She looked around at the tombstones again. "Who is buried here? They were all so young."

"The sailors' women are in this part."

"Oh. Can you tell me more?"

"There are others." She waved her hand and more sparrows flew down, hoping for crumbs. "All women. Different women, but in one way, the same."

"Why are they all here?"

The old woman looked at her sadly. "Can you not guess?"

"No."

"So many of them were beaten. Some were no more than children. Disease took them soon enough. It was a mercy. Their lives were too hard to bear."

Vivienne understood what the woman was telling her. They had been prostitutes. Beaten wives. Forgotten women. Perhaps the woman's own daughter was buried here.

She would not ask. "Thank you," she whispered.

The old woman nodded and threw another handful of crumbs.

Vivienne walked past her.

"Wait," the old woman said.

She stopped.

"Go farther in. There it is not so grim."

"Where?"

The woman pointed. "Do you see that ruined mansion?"

Absorbed in her reverie, looking down at the tombstones and talking to the old woman, she had not noticed it at all as she walked.

"Yes. Now I do."

The high, crumbling ruins were jagged and black, held up by the thick ivy that crawled halfway up the walls. It would be a magnificent sight in the snow, she thought, when the ivy was covered.

"It was once very grand. But that was a long time ago."

"Who lived there?"

"No one knows. The other part of the cemetery is very near it. It is reserved for those descended from the inhabitants of the mansion, I think. But perhaps that is only a story."

Vivienne was intrigued.

She wondered if it would be dangerous to wander there. She smiled inwardly. She had flirted with danger only hours ago and perhaps it was time to embrace it completely.

"Sometimes people come there. They pluck a few flowers and leave them."

"Is there a garden, then?"

The old woman nodded. "It is hidden. You won't see it right away, but it is there. And there is a way in."

"I would like to see it."

She would leave a few flowers herself. Vivienne felt only sympathy for those who lay here. The quiet graves were truly their last rest, perhaps the only one some of them had ever had.

A few had much smaller tombstones leaning against bigger ones. Children. Babies. She thought of Arielle and said a prayer for her. Her baby was buried in a lovely place, the churchyard of the village where the Sheridans had lived at the time. But her father had refused to pay for the stone. A kind friend had taken care of the matter. Vivienne had visited one last time, planting a little rosebush on the grave before she left Kent forever.

Her mother was buried in London, in a quiet, tree-shaded cemetery. It grieved her still that she would never talk to her mother again, could not give her a pretty room all her own in the Cheyne Row house—or tell her of Kyril.

Nothing could persuade her gentle mama that love was not real—she *was* love, believed in it with all her heart. How was it, Vivienne wondered, that so often the good died and their tormentors went right on living?

She would never mourn Donal Sheridan's passing. Her father had blighted everything he touched. The ugliness in his soul would never be redeemed.

With a start, Vivienne remembered suddenly that she was not alone. The old woman was watching her thoughtfully.

The sparrows' cheerful chirps and hops lightened her mood a little.

"It is good of you to feed them," she said to the old woman.

"It is nothing. Some say that sparrows in a graveyard are really the souls of the dead."

"Oh."

Vivienne looked down at the little birds. There were so many of them. But then, most cemeteries buried coffins upon coffins.

"If you feed the sparrows, then you help the souls fly away and be free."

Struck by the feeling quality in the other woman's voice, Vivienne contemplated the remark for a little while. "I see. Well, it is a pretty thought, and a kind one."

The old woman nodded. "I like to come here. The sparrows remember me."

As she remembered those in the lonely graves. Vivienne was touched.

The old woman looked down at the birds and threw another handful of crumbs, and Vivienne left her to it. She walked on, looking not at the tombstones but at the sky. Clouds covered it, dark, rolling clouds that hid the sun.

She came to the part of the cemetery the old woman had pointed to. If there was a garden here, it was well concealed.

She pushed open another rusty gate and went a little farther. There it was, behind a low, wrought-iron fence that had been recently painted. Someone had been taking care of it.

She came closer and looked around.

The flowers had gone to seed but she saw no weeds among them. The soil was covered with dead leaves that had not fallen there—there were no trees—someone had brought them there to prepare the garden for winter.

In the middle was a small fountain, but there was no water splashing in it. It would have been a fine thing for the birds if there was.

She supposed the fountain had been shut off so it would not crack in a freeze. Winter was not all that far away.

There was nothing special about it. It was a simple column holding up a stone basin from which the water, when there was any, poured into a little pool at the base of the column.

Bone dry.

She left the garden and walked about. The tombstones here were like each other, but not like the first ones she had seen.

More elaborate. More carefully carved. The lettering on them was different. They did not seem to have dates.

Vivienne looked more closely at one. It was very old, but there was something familiar about it.

Of course. The lettering was Russian.

She had learned to understand a little of what she heard but she could not read it at all.

How odd. She had not known there was a Russian cemetery anywhere in London. The Cyrillic lettering was far older in style than what she knew, and her knowledge of that alphabet was limited to begin with.

But she might make out the dates—yes, she could read some.

The stones were different in another way as well. These people—but perhaps they were not all women—had not lived such brief lives as the others in the front of the cemetery.

Curious, she inspected each one and came in time to a part where the stones were somewhat newer. Some of these had English lettering as well as Cyrillic.

These she read carefully.

The names had a familiar ring but that was because of the Russian she had picked up from Kyril and his companions. But she knew nothing about these people.

Goncharova. Leonid. Amvrosy.

Vivienne wished she had brought pencil and paper to write them down, so she could ask Kyril about the names.

He had never mentioned this place, but he might have relatives among them.

Sorsky. Kharuzhina. Dukhobort.

Then she saw it.

Taruskin.

She drew in a shocked breath. How long had his family been in London? She'd understood that Kyril had only been here for two years, if that long. It looked like a family grave. The first names and middle names were listed in Russian on a small tablet carved into the stone, but the eight chiseled letters in English were much larger and very clear.

This grave bore withered flowers. Someone had visited it and placed their modest offering with care, less than a month ago, by the looks of it.

Were they the same as the flowers whose remains she'd seen in the garden, plucked here and left here? She could compare stems and leaves.

Vivienne bent down and reached out a trembling hand.

She stopped herself.

It would be a sin to disturb anything placed on a grave.

What if the visitor came back again and saw that the flowers had been removed?

There was no gravekeeper employed here to keep things tidy for idle strollers. The Magdalen cemetery was not a happy place.

Only the person who had come here would know.

She would rely upon her memory, then. Vivienne went back to the partly hidden garden and walked inside it. The brown stems and desiccated leaves did not seem to resemble the ones she had seen.

She stopped to rest a hand upon the fountain, thinking. Perhaps it had been full when the visitor had come. She noticed an Orthodox cross carved into the column under the basin that she had not seen.

He—or she—might have poured a little water as an offering.

The ghost of a garden and the dry fountain made her melancholy. A little mouse ran out of the withered grass and quickly vanished. She hoped that she would not be laid to rest in such a place.

Another thought beat at her preoccupied mind, as if it had wings. A thought that would not go away.

A hidden garden . . . a sealed fountain.

Vivienne gasped and put a hand over her heart. Those were the Latin words on the Serpent's Egg.

Hortus conclusus . . . fons signatus. There was a link between this place and that—that thing.

Men had killed for that egg, and would kill again. Pretty as it was, it radiated a malevolent power from the small stone at its heart.

She stood for a moment as if struck by lightning, then moved away from the dry fountain.

Agitated, Vivienne plucked a curled leaf from its stem and crushed it in her hand.

A fragrance rose from it that was oddly familiar and she lifted her hand to her nose, studying the crushed leaf in her palm.

She looked at the plant from which it had come. Dry though it was, it was not a plant she knew and she suspected it was not from England.

Vivienne curled her fingers around the fragments of the leaf and then opened them. The warmth of her skin made the smell more potent.

Then she knew.

Kyril's shirt had this fragrance. She had smelled it when she rested her head upon his chest for the first time.

The memory of it was surprisingly strong. He had touched or plucked this flower or herb, whatever it was.

He had been here, probably alone.

The Taruskin grave was the only one with flowers on it. If it was a place of pilgrimage for him, he might come here again.

She reminded herself that Lukian too was a Taruskin. Like Kyril in his outward appearance, inwardly not at all. His violent reaction to the monk and the egg . . . the frightening way he had stared at her and refused to explain . . . no, he was nothing like Kyril. Whatever he might tell his cousin about what had happened, he could not stand between them.

Vivienne walked back to the first gate. The old woman had gone and the sparrows had flown away.

She turned toward home and looked back over her shoulder, glimpsing a forest of leafless trees—no. She turned again and realized that she was looking at ships' masts, clustered together, farther down the river. The docks. Where there had been incidents that Lukian also would not explain. Where he had said the monk had come from.

A fog was creeping upriver, a lighter gray that contrasted with the heavy clouds above it. One way or another she would be drenched by the time she returned home. Vivienne drew her cloak more closely around her face and started back the way she had come.

The wind pushed at her back. A storm was blowing in from the east and it had blown large white seabirds inland with it. Screaming overhead, they flew in circles against the ominous sky.

The next day . . .

"I could not tell her what you and I discussed, Kyril!"

Both he and Vivienne had acted out of fear and anger. Lukian saw no reason to repeat every damned word that had passed between them. The details were hazy. His night with Lily—the extra vials he had obtained and consumed in frantic haste—nothing was very clear.

They were sitting in Kyril's drawing room. It was large and airy but Lukian felt very ill at ease. So did his cousin, by the looks of him.

Kyril raked a hand through his dark hair. "Then what did you tell her?"

Lukian fell silent.

He had explained as best he could to his cousin about the Serpent's Egg—his shock and dismay, her protectiveness of the monk. He thought once again of how badly he handled the whole thing.

"I tried to make it clear that Osip was not who he pretended to be. She did not believe me, because I—I hurt him when I got the egg away from him. I hoped to get him out of there or at least the thing itself, but I missed my chance."

"It is strange that Vivienne allowed him to stay, Lukian."

"She is kindhearted to a fault."

"I suppose you could make a case for that. Anything else?"

"I explained that the Serpent's Egg belonged to the Tsar and that an ancestor of ours had made it. Not much more. The great diamond inside it was gone, Kyril."

"Yes, yes, you mentioned that."

Lukian felt a wave of humiliation pass through him. His best had not been good enough. "Where do you suppose that is?"

Kyril snorted. "Decorating the bosom of the Tsar's mistress, most likely. Alexander is a skirt-chaser first, a sovereign second."

Lukian coughed. "Then he had it removed before he allowed it to be taken to England."

"Of course. It is far more valuable than the egg. I don't think he has the same regard for our ancestor's ingenious craftsmanship that we do."

"No."

"Anyway, you did the right thing. Taking it from Vivienne's house, even by stealth, would have caused a commotion. And it would have raised far too many questions about—"

"About me."

"No, about all of us. And I do not want to reveal more about the Pack than I absolutely have to . . ."

Lukian listened tiredly. He could blame his inattention on the drug that he so craved. But he was just as inclined to blame it on Vivienne. The second he had seen her come down the stairs he had been smitten by an emotion that was perilously close to love. It did not matter that he'd been sent to investigate at his cousin's order or that the entire clan was in jeopardy.

He wanted her. The feeling made him more human than he was. He should have grabbed the damned egg and killed the monk and left her to wonder why.

"And you say she is willing to let the monk stay with her?"

"It seems so."

"And that means she has the egg. The khodzhite stone may

be small but it is still dangerous." Kyril sighed. "The whole thing makes me uneasy. If you think he is Volkodav's brother, then how can she be safe?"

"Osip is very old. And he must have had the egg in his keeping for some time. It has weakened him."

"And will it not weaken Vivienne to a degree, even though she is healthy and young?"

Lukian gave him a confused look. "I told her not to touch it and to hide it away."

"You should have taken it from her, Lukian."

"I tried to. She came at me with scissors."

"And then what? I see no mark upon your face, cousin. Nor your hands."

Lukian almost howled. "I gave it to her and ran away!"

Kyril studied him for a long moment. A very long moment. At last he spoke. "Have you lost your mind?"

Lukian gave him a wild look. "Sometimes I think so."

"We must steal it back immediately. But who—" He snapped his fingers. "Feodor is an experienced second-story man. Vivienne must be got out of the house on some pretext so he can search the place from cellar to attic without her ever knowing it."

"But her manservant—"

"Do not question me, Lukian. You have bungled things." Kyril's tone was suddenly sharp.

"I did what I was told—"

"Badly."

Lukian dropped his head in his hands and looked down at the carpet. Its pattern began to swirl under his gaze. "I am not well."

"You are under a great deal of strain." Kyril's tone was measured, almost polite. Lukian hated the sound of it. "I will ask the housekeeper to bring us food and drink. What would you like?"

"Vodka."

Kyril shot him a narrow look. "That is the last thing you need. I will ask for tea."

Lukian could hear the silent reprimand in his cousin's voice.

So be it. He'd done as he'd been told. Kyril had requested that he try to find out why the monk was there, remove him from Vivienne's house, and report back. He was not supposed to reveal anything about the crisis that the Pack faced or anything about the Pack. Certainly nothing of Volkodav's arrival or what it meant. He had followed those instructions to the letter and now he was being chastised for his faithfulness.

Good dog, he told himself bitterly. You are Kyril's good dog. Resentfully, he recollected the night they had rowed over the Thames, when Kyril told him he was considering Vivienne for a mate.

The same thought had immediately possessed Lukian when he had entered Vivienne's house. Such instincts were difficult to control.

Kyril gave him a cool smile, his thoughts unreadable.

Was his cousin looking into his mind? Lukian hoped not. Kyril was good at it.

Just being in her house, standing so close to her that he could smell her perfume, looking into her beautiful eyes, had awakened the darkness in his mind. No. He told himself to be truthful. The darkness had always been there—morphine made him not care. Sexual desire seemed to stimulate it.

Whores were useful for that. They did their work without emotion, like Lily. And it was that quality in Vivienne that was most dangerous to him. She was deeply emotional, gentle above all, if fiery when provoked. But her compassion, utterly wasted on the pretend monk, had triggered a need so raw in Lukian that it terrified him. A chasm had opened in his mind between his rational self and his wolf self.

His mercurial nature had been the bane of his existence. Of

late it had grown far worse. Lukian suspected that Kyril sensed the chaos in his brain but his cousin had said nothing. Above all Lukian wanted no pity.

He put his head back on the comfortable armchair and closed his eyes. He was weary . . . beyond weary.

Hours later, Kyril came back in with a laden tray.

"I suppose it was for the best that you left Vivienne, Lukian. It was a good thing we stationed two men to watch at Cheyne Row. One to follow her, one to guard her house. The one who followed her just filed his report."

"I did not hear him come in."

"I let you sleep. He told me that she walked along the river for hours last night."

Lukian gave him a grumpy look and ignored the sandwiches and tea that Kyril set down near him. "I had no way of preventing her from going out. You told me to tell her nothing about the situation. I am sorry about leaving the egg with her."

Kyril sighed. "It does not matter now. The men created a disturbance this afternoon and Feodor went in when she and the servants went out."

"A disturbance?"

"They set a fire in an empty house nearby. Everyone in Cheyne wanted to look."

"And?"

"Feodor found the egg under a floorboard. It is at the lair. There are plenty of guards in and about the vicinity of St. James's. Not here, though."

"You will need them soon."

Kyril waved his cousin's worry away. "In time, perhaps. Right now, no. Our resources are not infinite and it is more important to protect the entire Pack than a few individual members. Besides, I am most often at the lair."

"I suppose so." Lukian thought of his own house, a dark place that he hated, on a side street.

"I asked Sergei Abramovitch to look at the Egg. He was once a master goldsmith, as you may know. Not a genius like Jozef Taruskin, of course, but there was only one of him. It is not as if we can take the egg to a Bond Street jeweller's shop and have it appraised."

"No." Lukian fell silent for a moment. "And what of Vivienne?"

"She returned home safely, according to our men."

"Again, I am sorry." Hearing that someone else had rescued her, even if she didn't know it, irked Lukian. "Where did she go last night, by the way?"

"To the Magdalen cemetery."

Lukian raised a dark eyebrow. "Where your mother is buried?"

"Yes. I left flowers there a month ago."

"You are a good son."

"She was a good mother. And a brave one. And I might add, Lukian, that she was also your aunt. I saw no other flowers besides mine."

"I take your meaning," Lukian said quietly. "I will go. In my own time. But why did she go there?"

"Our man said that she seemed to be going where the wind blew her."

Kyril let the matter drop. It was far more important that they predict Vivienne's next move and stay one step ahead of her.

"So. Let us get back to what we were talking about before you fell asleep. You tried to tell her that Osip was no monk."

"Once she saw that I had hurt him, she did not want to listen to anything I said."

"Do you suppose he encouraged her to write those notes?"

188 / Noelle Mack

"I have no way of knowing that," Lukian said slowly. "But I suspect his English is not that good. She did mention that he brightened up at the sound of your name."

Kyril shook his head. "Not good. It is obvious that he had been instructed to use her as bait."

"Oh—she said something else."

"Yes?"

"She'd seen the monk before. On the night when you met me at the river."

"How very curious. She said nothing at all about it to me when—" Kyril remembered that night very well. Their passionate lovemaking had not left time for conversation. Except about the bruise on his face and that book.

"I wanted to know the details but she didn't give me any. And questions asked can reveal more than answers. I kept my mouth shut as much as I could."

"You are good at that, cousin."

The two men sat in silence for a minute more.

"Well then. When we finish this we can head to Great Jermyn Street. The high council is preparing to meet."

"I have had no time to prepare."

"It does not matter. You will not be leading the discussion."

Lukian frowned. "Who is?"

"I am, of course."

"I suppose you have it planned out."

"Not at all. It is far more important that everyone have a chance to speak. We need to rethink our strategy now that we have recovered the Serpent's Egg. That it was brought to London is very strange."

"I don't think so. It is also bait. If one temptation does not work, another one will—someone is thinking along those lines."

Kyril gave him a rueful smile. "I suppose you are right."

"Sometimes I am."

"Well, of course." Kyril took a deep breath. "You may not be leading the meeting, Lukian, but you will present the matter of Volkodav's brother and his odd masquerade. If Osip is in fact his brother."

"I have no doubt of it. Those eyes—"

"It will need to be independently confirmed. Those are the rules."

"Bah. Rules and regulations bore me. I would rather tear out throats."

Kyril leaned back in his chair, a sandwich he was not going to eat in his hand. "And that, my dear cousin, is why you are not a Pack leader. You prefer violence."

"It works."

"It is difficult to undo. And our newer members have turned away from it."

"Speaking of that . . . what of Alex Stasov?" Lukian asked suddenly. "I had meant to ask you about him."

"Why?"

"Because he too has just come to London. His arrival coincided with that of our enemies. More or less."

"A coincidence, I think," Kyril said carefully.

"Will he attend the high council meeting?"

"Yes, probably. All members are welcome. It is one of the founding laws of the Pack."

"But not all members are equal."

Kyril only nodded.

"The newer ones have no vote."

"All the same, he can attend, Lukian. What are you getting at?"

"Nothing, really. How did he like the Howl?"

"Well enough."

"Your brother said you called Stasov a rat."

"I should have kept my mouth shut."

"Why?"

"So as not to offend—" Kyril broke off. "I will admit that I have my suspicions. But he has not done anything that I can put my finger on."

"How does he spend his time?" Lukian was not to be put off.

"Nothing out of the ordinary," Kyril said. "The men say he keeps to his room. They think he is homesick for Russia."

"Then he can go back."

"He seems to want to stay. He is quiet, if that answers your question."

Lukian mulled it over. "Do you know, I can hardly remember his face."

"That is just as well. There is too much excitement around here as it is."

Lukian growled softly. "Not for me."

"Not everybody shares your taste for battle."

"Then let me carry on by myself."

"No," Kyril said firmly. "We are a Pack and we act as a Pack."

"So long as our fearless leader is not questioned." Lukian's voice had a noticeable edge.

"That would be me, I suppose?"

"Yes." Lukian growled.

"No lone wolves in our outfit, cousin. It makes things unstable."

"For you, perhaps."

"I can handle any challenge you throw at me." The same edge sliced through Kyril's tone. "But I think you should settle down."

Lukian growled long and low.

Kyril studied the other man, concern in his eyes. "Let us talk of something else."

"What?"

"Something peaceful. I don't care."

"Vodka. I wish I had some. Then I could be peaceful."

"Do you, Lukian? We are all out. I did ask. Ivan says the potatoes from last month are of a lower quality. It affects the purity of our vodka."

Kyril's bland remark irritated him.

"If his vodka was any more pure, the fumes would blow this house to kingdom come." Lukian wished silently that he could slink off and polish off a bottle right now.

He did not have Kyril's cool head. And he had a feeling that his cousin was lying to him about the vodka.

And as far as his opinions on violence—fie. Lukian had walked into a trap set for Kyril and out again, and missed his chance to kill. The stone at the heart of the egg had weakened him. So had his desire for Vivienne.

He looked up when his cousin spoke again. "I will add a third guard at Cheyne Row."

"She might notice that many."

"I have sent our best men."

Lukian scowled. "But what about inside the house?"

"You said Henry was a good man."

"He is. But . . ." Lukian paused. "I would offer myself but she trusts me even less now. In fact, I think she detests me. Are you sure you don't have any vodka?"

"Maybe there is a little." Kyril set down his sandwich and went to look.

If it was done out of pity, Lukian decided he didn't mind.

Kyril descended the stairs into the kitchen quickly, thinking hard. Perhaps he should not have sent Lukian to Vivienne's house in his stead. A wolf with a past could be dangerously un-predictable. He'd thought often enough in the last year that the physical wounds of Lukian's scourging had healed but his soul had not. Tragedy had stalked his cousin relentlessly. But then he had been born during the white nights of June and July, a time marked by madness.

His near death and the bloody revenge he had taken were not something a man or a wolf could easily shake off.

Lukian was lost in thought when Kyril returned with a glass of vodka.

"Here. Perhaps this will take the edge off," Kyril said, handing it to him.

"What?"

"You know what I mean."

Lukian shrugged and took the vodka, drinking it in one gulp. He smacked his lips. "Ahh. Thank you."

"Come with me to the kennels after the council meets, Lukian. We will pick her out a devoted companion who will watch over her in ways that we cannot."

9

The meeting of the High Council . . .

Whether in the full glory of young manhood or gone gray and grizzled, the members of the Pack still came together in secret when their leader summoned them.

Good. There had been a new development and it did not bode well. Kyril looked down the long table of the council room. The secretary had taken attendance and slid the paper over to him. He glanced at it and cleared his throat.

"Welcome. We are all here and I will waste no time."

There were growls of acknowledgement, but a few men replied in English. "Hear, hear."

"Some of you may not know that the Serpent's Egg has reappeared in London. Sergei, if you would . . ."

He nodded at the master goldsmith, who lifted the lid of a finely made box and lifted the green-and-gold egg from its padded velvet cradle.

Sergei set it on the table.

All eyes were upon it. Kyril let them look their fill.

"It is a remarkable object, made by my ancestor. Jozef Taruskin left no direct descendants, of course, but—"

"He was your great-great-great-great uncle, sir," the secretary whispered.

"Thank you, Antosha. It was taken from him by agents acting on behalf of Russia's ruler at that time. Jozef protested but to no avail. The egg has been kept in the vaults of the Winter Palace ever since."

"Never on public display, eh?" asked a man.

"No."

"Isn't there a diamond in it?" asked another. "A great big one?"

"There was. It is not there now. But it seems that this isn't—"

"Not there now? Where is it?"

"The egg is hinged. Can it be opened?"

"Does that snake strike? I heard its tongue held poison."

The questions came one after another from different people.

Kyril nodded to Sergei. First the goldsmith pressed the button that activated the snake. All were silent as a faint whirr was heard and the coiled snake started up, went around the egg and down to the base.

"Most interesting," an older man murmured. "And did he not also make lifesize automatons of creatures and humans to decorate his house and amuse his guests?"

"Yes, he did," Kyril replied. "But I understand that many were more frightened than amused."

"I see. Well, what were you going to say, Kyril?"

"I will let Sergei say it." He sat down, nodding to the goldsmith again.

"It would seem, gentlemen, that this egg is—not the original."

The questions began again. Some of the members of the Pack even rose to look at it more closely, bracing themselves upon the table with their spread fingers.

"What?"

"Do you mean there are two?"

"More than two?"

The older man raised a hand for silence. "Let him explain."

"I know only of this copy," Sergei said. "There may be more."

Kyril rose again. "It came into our possession through Feodor's efforts. He retrieved it from the house of an—an acquaintance of mine."

He happened to catch Semyon's eye and willed him to say nothing of Vivienne. His brother gave an imperceptible nod.

"It seems that it was given to a man posing as a monk of the Old Believer sect. He went to this woman's house—"

Someone snickered. The older man quelled him with a golden-eyed stare.

"He tried to get her to lure me there. She, in all innocence, fell under his sway. But our Lukian kept me from walking into the trap that was set."

There was scattered applause. Lukian inclined his head with a frown.

"Does that have something to do with Volkodav?" Marko asked.

"Yes, my brother. But I am not sure what, precisely."

"It may be that it is but one part of his nefarious plan. The Wolf Killer will try anything that might work."

A very handsome young man cleared his throat. "I think I was followed from my mistress's house. I sent her to the country to live with her parents for a while. She ought to be safe enough."

Kyril thought again of the guards he had placed in Cheyne Row. With the monk actually in Vivienne's house, was *she* safe enough?

He might have to spirit her away.

Sergei tapped on the table. "Allow me to continue."

"Yes," Kyril said. "Please do."

"The hallmark is the same." Sergei tipped the egg over and pointed to the Russian initials. "But there are slight differences in the way it was made."

"How do you know that?" Semyon asked. His eyes gleamed with avid interest, which Kyril was pleased to see. He did not want to be the Pack's leader forever and one fine day one of his brothers might well step up in his place.

"Antosha found detailed records of its manufacture in our archives."

The secretary looked pleased with himself.

"I will explain the details of that later, but for now . . ." Sergei pressed the button that opened the outermost egg.

The emerald one in the middle appeared to appreciative ahhs.

"And there is one more."

Sergei pressed another button. The black onyx egg appeared. He looked at Kyril. "Should I?"

"Yes. Quickly."

The innermost egg opened and the lump of khodzhite appeared. The assembled men frowned at it. Kyril felt a chill steal over the room. It seemed to emanate from the lump of stone.

Sergei closed it safely away in its lead lining.

"As you may have guessed," he said, "that is khodzhite and not, of course, a diamond."

Excited talk broke out, dispelling the coldness.

"Jozef was clever."

"Clever? He was a master magician. My grandmother told me of his wonderful house. All sorts of strange things happened in it back in the day."

"I think he sent a paste diamond to the Tsar and kept the real one. But where is it?"

"No—he would have been found out and severely punished for such a trick."

"But didn't he die young?"

Kyril held up a hand. "Gentlemen, please."

They settled down and Sergei returned the Serpent's Egg to its velvet-padded box.

"The gold and the gems which went into this are real enough. So perhaps the Tsar was fooled for a time. And the egg was kept in the vaults. It is my belief that it was handed down to the present Tsar as it is."

"I think that the diamond was removed recently, though," said Kyril. "The khodzhite replaced it. So that I would be weakened when—"

"When what?" Semyon asked.

"When I had been captured," Kyril answered calmly.

"I see," said the older man thoughtfully. "It does make sense. You must be careful, Kyril."

Kyril made a gesture of indifference. "I always am, in a reckless sort of way."

His brothers grinned wolfishly.

"But we must move on. Levshin has something very important to tell us."

The Pack's accountant straightened the ledgers piled in front of him until all the corners lined up. Then he unfolded a pair of spectacles and slowly put them on. He took the ledger on top off the pile and opened it in front of him, peering at the numbers neatly written in its columns.

His routine seldom varied. It was difficult to get the members of the Pack to listen to anything boring, and since they never had to worry about money, they seldom listened long to Levshin.

He ahemmed and they looked his way. "Allow me to fill in the blanks for those members who do not read the newspapers."

"A good idea, Mr. Levshin. Carry on."

"As we all know, the Congress of Vienna has met. The fate of nations hung in the balance—"

"Can we leave?" Kyril heard a junior member whisper at the end of the room.

"No," he said severely. "Everybody stay where you are. Just listen."

"As I was about to say, every country of importance was represented. Some of you will recollect the effects of earlier Russian alliances, when British trade was halted . . ."

He droned on. Even Kyril wished Levshin could get to the point.

"It was a time when we, in partnership with the British Society of Merchant-Adventurers, lost millions."

Kyril gave him an encouraging look, hoping he would go faster, even though he knew that the man was about to give devastating news.

"So. Now that the Congress is over, a historic treaty signed, and the great powers have agreed—"

"To carve up Europe like a bloody great cheese," someone said.

Levshin glared at the joker over his spectacles.

The man shut up.

"We find ourselves in the same predicament as we were before the Congress convened," Levshin went on.

"Meaning?" the older man asked quietly.

"On orders of the Tsar, with the cooperation of persons unknown to me in the English government, our assets have been seized or frozen."

A hubbub broke out.

"Silence!" Kyril thundered. "Shall I spell it out for you?"

Some nodded. Others just looked at him, worried.

"Levshin is saying that we have no money to pay our bills. I am sure the greengrocer and the wine-seller will extend credit, but not indefinitely. And those are not our most pressing creditors. The gunsmith is only one of those, but he is the most important one. We have already spent a considerable sum on our counter-investigation of Volkodav and his men, but we have very little to show for it."

For a wonder, they said nothing at all for a while, looking at each other. The members of the Pack were notorious for high living and keeping the women they loved in high style.

Finally the joker spoke. "Pity about the diamond being gone. We could have sold it."

Levshin closed his ledger and folded his hands on its cover.

"I am glad that is over with," Lukian said. "Meetings make me restless."

"But that one was necessary."

"I was glad you were leading it," Lukian replied in a friendly way.

Kyril shook his head. "It was not easy. Some of our brethren have grown too used to a life of luxury."

"Not you, though. And not I."

"No. But then we did not grow up so privileged."

Lukian grinned. "We shall rely on our wits. And our strength."

"Yes. Qualities that enabled us to survive for centuries."

Lukian grinned even more widely. "When some of those handsome young popinjays put aside their fine clothes and gold cufflinks, they will find out how much fun it is to hunt."

"I am looking forward to it."

"And so am I."

His cousin's moodiness had eased, for which Kyril was grateful. They sat on a low bench in the kennels at the back of the St. James's lair, petting the yelping cubs who licked their hands and bit each other's ears.

"Here is a good one." Lukian held a squirming cub in his big hands.

"Yes, he is." Kyril picked up another. "How about this fellow?"

"He is too. It is hard to pick."

"Then close your eyes and point."

"That is as good a way as any."

Kyril squinted his eyes shut and stuck out a finger. A very interested cub promptly sank its teeth into it.

Kyril howled and Lukian laughed. "There, he has chosen you."

He lifted the cub up for a closer look.

"Not a he. I spoke too soon, Kyril. This one is a she. Dear Wolf, she is a big one!"

"She will grow into a long-legged, dominant female. That sort is always—"

"None of your remarks."

The big cub wriggled in Lukian's hands.

"Give her to me." Lukian handed her over. Kyril cupped his hands around the cub's rib cage and looked into her eyes. "Oho. You are beautiful. Your fur is white and silver. Your papa and mama made an excellent combination in you. What pretty black eyes you have. And what fine teeth."

"The better to destroy Vivienne's house with."

"Vivienne likes dogs."

"That is not a dog you are holding, strictly speaking."

"She is not a wolf either."

"No."

The cubs raised by the Pack had wolf and human blood. But the mixture was reversed in several ways. They looked like wolves but they thought much more like humans.

"I wonder what they would say if they had the power of speech."

Lukian shrugged. "Their power of yelping is very well-developed. They are making me deaf." He patted the head of the one whose paws were on his thigh. "Shut up. If you don't mind."

"This one will do nicely for Vivienne."

"She is going to be enormous. Vivienne will have a hard time of it."

"She can be trained."

"Vivienne or the cub?"

Kyril laughed and set the animal down. "The cub will be much easier."

"We agree on that, then. Your lady love is strong-willed."

"I like her that way."

Lukian gave him a sidelong look. "Why?"

"We of the Pack are meant to mate for life, Lukian. I would not want someone weak."

"So I have heard." He rubbed the bristly head of a small cub at his ankles.

"Nor would you. When it comes time for a man to settle down—"

The other man growled deep in his throat. "Not yet. I prefer to keep my relationships brief. The second a pretty miss begins to simper and talk of a thatched cottage and of a little church nestled in the dale under cherry trees, I am gone."

"Do you not want a true mate?"

"I do not want to be domesticated." He was quite content with Lily at the moment. Kyril did not need to know of her.

"Vivienne is not like that. She treasures her independence and will allow me mine. She is ideal."

"But you will control her money if you marry her. She will be under your thumb one way or another."

"Never," Kyril said with some heat.

"You cannot change the laws of England."

"I do not have to marry her under the laws of England. Or in an English church." Kyril patted the head of a cub who was sniffing his boot. "But I will marry her. A mate who is capable and knows her own mind is what men like us need. Hey there! Do not piddle!"

The cub that had lifted a back leg against Kyril's tall boot thought better of it and scampered away.

"How practical you sound."

"One must think these things through, Lukian."

"How often have you slept with her?"

Kyril laughed and cuffed him. "Is that your business, cousin?"

"No."

"I tell no tales. Let me amend that. I will tell no details."

"Ha ha," Lukian said sourly.

"It is no insult to the lady to say that we both enjoyed ourselves very much for one night. Several times. In countless ways."

"One night. Is that all?"

"I know my own mind, Lukian."

"Does she?"

Kyril sobered a little. "That remains to be seen. Of course, I have not yet asked her to marry me. I merely told her I loved her."

"Women do not use the word *merely* in conjunction with *I love you*."

Kyril grinned again. "Good point. But one must not rush these things. She is impetuous, though. I think she likes to be rushed."

"You are a lucky man, Kyril, to have found happiness so easily."

"I am. She is everything I want in a woman—"

Lukian held up a hand. "You have already enumerated her best qualities. But you left two things off the list. Vivienne is extraordinarily beautiful and brilliant, I fear."

"That too." Kyril gave his cousin a curious look. "But I have never heard you describe her that way."

"Does it bother you that I have?"

"Ah—"

"Her charms are not lost on me. I could see why a man would risk his life for her."

"Er—"

Lukian rubbed his chin thoughtfully. "I need a shave."

"Are you—"

"What?"

"Are you in a mating mood yourself, Lukian?"

"Perhaps you have inspired me."

Kyril grew thoughtful. "Hmm. I hope to dance at your wedding someday."

Lukian only growled.

"My own, then."

His cousin thought that over. "Well, of course, I will attend that great occasion. But there are difficult days ahead, Kyril."

"I suppose so. But it is a good feeling to be in love. It will make me fight all the more fiercely and win."

"Hmph." Lukian looked at him narrowly. "There was one other thing I meant to ask you. You told Vivienne you loved her. But did she say she loved you?"

"Hmm. I don't believe she did. But perhaps I did not hear it. I fell asleep."

Lukian growled. "More likely she didn't say it. You are safe, cousin." He slapped him on the back.

Kyril let out a bark of surprise that made all the cubs yelp. "Ow! You do not know your own strength."

"Sorry. Enough of this talk. We must concentrate on finding Volkodav. Nose to the wind."

"Words to live by, as our younger members are about to find out," Kyril said.

Lukian stood up and stretched. The playful cubs had banished his black mood, if not his ever-present suspicions. He might not need so many vials, after all. He would forego tonight's visit to Dr. Broadstreet.

"They seemed impressed by the Serpent's Egg," he said.

"And no wonder. The damn thing does everything but light up and whistle the 'Marseillaise.'" Kyril stood up too. "But the stone at its heart is still dangerous."

"All the more reason to jam it up the Wolf Killer's arse, don't you think?"

"Now that is a plan." Kyril laughed. He knew in his heart that the obscene joke was meant to alleviate fear. He was glad that he and Lukian could be close again and share a little time together, for what it was worth.

They named the cub Tier. Natalya prepared a basket for her—it was a big basket, the one that had held the potatoes. Tier sat at the bottom of it on a folded blanket, looking up at all three of them with eager hope.

"Out? Do you want to go out?" Natalya cooed.

"Dear girl, do not teach her that word," Kyril said.

"But sir—she needs to know it."

"She'll learn it soon enough, along with 'walk.'"

"And will drag Vivienne around all over London," Lukian said.

"Lukian is right. We do not want her to be unhappy with our anonymous gift."

"But she will be if Tier pisses and craps all over her parquet floors," Lukian pointed out. "And if you insist on anonymity, how will she be able to return this little monster?"

"She is not a monster," Natalya said indignantly. "She is a sweet baby—"

"With sharp teeth." Lukian laughed.

"Kyril, Vivienne will know who it is from," Natalya insisted.

"Why do you say that?" Lukian asked. "You have never met Kyril's love. He has not brought her here."

"Are we not both women? Gifts from secret admirers are never a secret."

Lukian laughed and tugged one of her braids. "Ivan is also a lucky man. You are as clever as Vivienne."

"Will I see her today? I will deliver the cub for you," Natalya said eagerly. "Then I will go by the greengrocers and buy vegetables for soup."

Kyril and Lukian exchanged a look.

The members of the Pack had kept the latest news from the servants, discussing strategy in the chamber set aside for that purpose. Not everyone in the household needed to know that they were almost out of money.

And there was another consideration. Natalya, if she chose to wear her peasant finery, would be conspicuous. Of course, the lair's nearness to the Palace of St. James's meant that they were provided with protection afforded to only a few. But that too might change now that their assets had been frozen. There was no telling what was going on where they were concerned in the English court.

Someone at the highest level might be secretly connected to Volkodav and there was no telling what weapon *he* might choose. A hostage was a very effective one.

Blending in was the thing. No matter how many agents were in London, they could not be everywhere and watch everyone. Worst of all, they still did not know precisely who they were up against, besides the tall Cossacks and Volkodav, and there was no more ready money left with which to bribe informers.

Levshin had announced at the conclusion of the meeting that he intended to sleep with the locked cash-box under his head. Only an accountant could be comfortable on such a pillow.

So far they had gathered only sketchy intelligence on Volkodav. He ate, he drank, he visited a whore, he went to the banya—that was all. The man was biding his time, Kyril mused. The strike would be swift when it finally came. And lethal in its force. He was not called the Wolf Killer for nothing.

Kyril had many people to protect—above all, the human woman with whom he had fallen so quickly in love. But he was still not ready to tell her everything. What if she refused him when he explained the delicate matter of his wolf blood? His openness might mean endangering the Pack and all his kin for a love that was not meant to be.

Their relationship had begun with a perfect kiss. It would end with a wedding in the high style of Imperial Wolfdom, if she was willing.

He had hoped to proceed carefully with his explanation of all that, but there was no telling when the right time might be. For all he knew, they were sitting in a trap right now. Making light conversation. Playing with adorable cubs. And not thinking as deeply as they needed to, now that the Serpent's Egg had appeared.

He sighed. He had always relied on Lukian and he always would, but, even with the camaraderie they'd shared this day, Kyril still feared that something was preying on his cousin's mind. His moods altered so rapidly, from aggressive to friendly and back again. It could be his mating instincts, Kyril supposed.

An odd time for those to pop up, so to speak. But danger could do that to men.

"Sir?" Natalya asked. She looked up at him as hopefully as the cub.

"If you dress like an English girl, you may bring Tier," Kyril said. "Thank you, Natalya."

10

In another part of the city...

Volkodav grunted and rolled off the woman beneath him. She did not let go of the sheet she had been holding over his heaving back, using it to wipe herself between her legs.

"Send the next man in?"

She nodded, not caring.

Buttoning his breeches, Volkodav left the room.

He kicked Feodor, who had fallen asleep against the wall with his mouth open. All seven feet of him.

The others were sitting on chairs or on the floor, waiting their turn with the whore Captain Chichirikov had paid for in advance.

Volkodav sniffed his armpits.

Disgusting. His crotch was probably just as rank, but he could not bend far enough to sniff that. Those damned Taruskins and the rest of them would smell him coming.

Chichirikov had given him the address of a banya. He would go there, steam himself clean, get a good birching from a

Ukrainian girl . . . his cock twitched. With any luck, she would be pretty, with large breasts and thick braids.

He saluted his bodyguards and left.

Volkodav found that Chichirikov had beaten him to it.

Flushed red from the steam, the naked captain took up most of one shelf of the banya, reclining on his side. His paunch hung over the edge. Volkodav averted his eyes.

"Hello, my friend!"

"Hello."

He did not want to share the bath attendant with the captain. Polina was pretty. And blonde. He had given her a little bag filled with clinking money and told her to meet him at the inn not far away. She'd winked at him and accepted it.

Volkodav took a shelf of his own.

"All to ourselves, eh? Just you and me," the captain boomed. He slapped his flabby belly. "How do I look?"

"You are repulsive."

The other man laughed heartily.

"Ha ha! Have you been to the whore I bought for you?"

"Yes."

"How was she?"

"Lethargic."

"She is saving her energy. You, plus five Cossacks, makes—"

"Six men."

"So it does. I cannot do sums in a room full of steam."

Volkodav relaxed and said nothing for a while.

"This does feel very good, Chichirikov."

"Doesn't it? I hate the damp cold of London."

Volkodav nodded his head. "It lies in wait for a man."

"I know what you mean. The cold in Russia, now it jumps out and sinks its teeth into you. You know what you are dealing with."

"Speaking of that . . ."

A male bath attendant came in and threw a bucket of water

on the hot rocks. The steam billowed up. The captain's voice came from it.

"Have you found your quarry?"

"They are in a house near the Palace of St. James's. Alex Stasov has successfully infiltrated the place. They have accepted him as one of their own kind."

"Hmm. You will have to be very careful, Volkodav."

Volkodav let his eyes drift shut as he leaned back against the wooden walls of the banya. The planks were saturated with steam and radiated heat. "I have been. But spying is easier here. This is a free country. People come and go as they please and are not always looking over their shoulders."

The captain sat up. He took a towel and scrubbed at his damp skin, then threw it on the floor. "That may be, but don't forget the Taruskins are Russians. I don't care how many generations of them have lived here. They expect the worst and they watch for it."

"Kyril and Lukian and a lot of the others were not born here, though." Volkodav opened his eyes and watched the steam drift up. "I hope to be the worst thing that will ever happen to them. I look forward to torturing the arrogant one."

"Lukian?"

"No. Kyril. He is too handsome. His nose is perfect. That gets sliced off first. And then—the eyelids, I think. He will not be able to close his eyes when he is beaten in front of a mirror. One of the Cossacks can take care of that. Then I will torture the rest of the clan myself."

"Don't work too hard," the captain said mildly. "No point. You could give yourself apoplexy."

"I must earn my fee and it is a fat one, Chichirikov. Like you."

The captain slapped his belly again. "The ladies still love me."

"For a price, you pig."

210 / *Noelle Mack*

"Even so."

"Well, we must not be distracted by quim. The English will fuck anything but I will not. Their women do not bathe enough."

"I had my eye on that Ukrainian girl," the captain said. He belched.

"I am first."

"So be it. How do you plan to catch them all, by the way? The Taruskins, I mean."

Volkodav sat up. "I need only one. The rest will follow."

Volkodav had walked miles to his destination—it helped him clear his mind. He was far from the center of London but he had come to the right place. The stonecutter's yard was decorated with samples of his work. Pedestals. Hideous urns big enough to hide a body in. And tombstones, with standard phrases requested by the bereaved. *Here lies . . . Departed this day . . . With the angels . . .*

He smiled. Angels, eh? Did the devil never get his due? He saw the stonecutter inside the building and went in to talk to him.

Volkodav and the stonecutter made out well enough. The Wolf Killer's English was better than that of Gil Hanratty, the man in the dust-speckled apron. Marble dust had penetrated the skin of his hands and every pore in his face.

Gil looked like a ghost. It seemed appropriate for the man who would make the khodzhite box. He would be dead soon enough.

"I need a sarcophagus made, Mr. Hanratty."

"What is that?" Gil seemed confused.

"Like a coffin. For a new mausoleum. Made all of stone."

"Then it will be a heavy piece, sir. Begging your pardon."

Volkodav only shrugged. "Cut the stone thin."

"How much is there of it?"

"A thousand pounds, I believe."

Hanratty seemed somewhat impressed.

"But it must be cut very thin. Almost as if you were cutting meat for a sandwich."

"Hmm. How brittle is it?"

"Khodzhite? Not at all." Did Gil Hanratty need to know how dangerous it was? Volkodav did not think so. "You could cut the slabs individually, I think. Easier to transport in a waggon."

"Where are they going?"

"To the London docks."

Gil Hanratty gave him a doubtful look. "No one is buried there."

Volkodav shook his head. "You would be surprised. They might not have markers on their graves, but they are there all the same."

"As you say. I will not argue."

They came to an agreement on the price.

"The stone will not take much time to cut, Mr. Hanratty."

"I will be the judge of that."

Volkodav nodded. He pulled a small piece from his pocket. "You may practice on this."

Hanratty picked it up and turned it over in his hand. "Odd stuff. I have never seen the like."

"It is odd. But easy to work."

"Does it last?"

"Forever."

"Then perhaps I will make tombstones if there are any scrap pieces."

"A very good idea," Volkodav said. "I don't want it back."

Hanratty shrugged. "Where is it? There must be a mountain of it."

"Not that much. It is heavy for its size. The sarcophagus will measure five feet by five feet."

212 / Noelle Mack

"Is it for a child then?"

Volkodav thought it over. He had not considered the possibility of imprisoning a Pack child in his deadly chamber. It would be an interesting opening move—but no. He dismissed it. Children screamed too much.

"No. For a grown man."

"He will have to be bent over," Hanratty pointed out.

"That is part of the plan," Volkodav said. His ice-colored eyes bored into Hanratty's until the other man looked away.

"I suppose it doesn't matter if he's dead," Hanratty muttered.

"No. It doesn't. We seem to understand each other."

The waggon brought the load of khodzhite the next day. The carters who lifted it complained of muscle strain.

Unlike Hanratty. His massive arms and hugely expanded chest could pick up the heaviest raw stone. But even he felt weary as he slid it onto his workbench and positioned the saw. The process of cutting was slow, dusty work.

The man named Volkodav had underestimated how long it would take but then people usually did. They wanted their gravestones right away. As if the dead were clamoring to be remembered.

He was surprised by the ease with which the raw rock came apart in thin slabs. Mr. Volkodav would be pleased. There might even be a bonus, although he had paid in advance.

But by the time his strange customer returned, Hanratty was ailing. His wife handled the final details of the job, not noticing that Volkodav had a new team of carters. The first ones had died. In another few days, so would her husband.

Heavy and still, the slabs jounced only once in the waggon going down the narrow road by the Thames. The carter on the box looked back at his load. Volkodav was following in a closed coach. He waved the man on and they went over the bridge to the south side of the river and the Baltic Dock.

Offshore from it was a prison hulk. It loomed over lesser ships. Not meant to be fast. Not meant to go anywhere.

Bledsoe, the ship's master, waved to them from the deck.

He led Volkodav on a tour that ended below. The hulk had once carried coal and every inch of its wood was permeated with black.

It reeked of rot and misery, inside and out.

Bledsoe was proud of his lumbering vessel, though, no matter how much it stank. The broad-beamed hull settled into the mud of the Thames at low tide and floated only when the tide was in, rocking in an ever-spreading slick of its own effluvia.

There were at least two hundred wretched men crowded into its cells. On a fatal voyage to nowhere, they had not the strength to protest their imprisonment on petty charges nor to escape.

The lingering coal dust had embedded itself in every pore of their skin. Still, there were hopeful eyes staring at the visitors from dark faces. Those who had given up all hope stared at the ceiling. Or the floor. Or at nothing.

The silence was profound as they walked down the central area between the rows of cells. Bledsoe stood ready to crack the iron rod he gripped over the hand of anyone who dared to stretch it out or even rest it upon the bars.

The men did not whimper when they were hit, Volkodav suspected. They were undoubtedly used to it.

They walked on, looking straight ahead.

"This part of the ship should do for your purposes."

Volkodav nodded and guessed at its dimensions. "It might."

"It is well forward and far away from the others."

The men in the cells had receded from their view but their oppressive silence was all around them.

"You wish to build an isolation cell, you said."

"Yes."

"Of stone."

"Yes."

"That is unusual, but we are eager for your custom, sir."

Bledsoe fancied himself a man of business, evidently. Not just the master of a hulk packed to the gunnels with ill-treated and dying men.

"And you have the stone—it is in that there cart."

"That is correct."

"Then have your men bring it on board and get to work. Your prisoner will have every comfort."

Which was to say, none. Bledsoe gave Volkodav a brutal grin.

The wood frames that would hold the slabs of thin stone were quickly built. The khodzhite presented the usual problem of killing those who handled it. The second team was soon replaced by a third.

In a week the death cell was ready. It looked like a smooth black box from the outside, not quite large enough to hold a full-grown man.

11

Kyril sat alone in his drawing room, drinking whisky, his feet up on a horses-and-hounds needlework ottoman, looking very much like a proper Englishman. But his wolfish soul wanted to howl at the moon. He could not do without Vivienne indefinitely.

She had written a letter asking for an explanation of Lukian's behavior, if Kyril would be so good as to provide one, and added that she was allowing the monk to stay. She did not mention the Serpent's Egg. Evidently she was not aware that it was gone, but then Feodor had said she'd hidden it under a floorboard and that was under a carpet.

Vivienne was too intelligent not to know that something was going on. But she did not quiz him.

Could it be true that she wanted him so much she was willing to wait weeks to see him? Without an interrogation or fits of the vapors or tears?

He told himself not to be so vain.

He had written back, of course. His letter was a masterpiece of evasion. As hers had been.

216 / Noelle Mack

Sullen and withdrawn again, Lukian was unwilling to analyze the matter. Kyril for one was heartily sick of it, and his cousin's moods. And the juvenile antics of the Pack's younger members, who had taken to swaggering around Pall Mall, trying to pick fights with anyone who looked foreign. They deserved the thrashings they'd provoked. To hell with all of them. He took a big swig of the whisky.

Volkodav and his henchmen were playing a waiting game that Kyril understood very well but he hated inaction. The warrior in him wanted a woman. Her.

He thought it over and convinced himself that his house would be safer than a hotel. Certainly he had no wish to make polite conversation with Mrs. Hickham and Mr. Freke. Her watchful servants might as well have been her mama and papa.

Two people who must be very important to her and about whom he knew nothing. The whisky warmed his veins as he leaned his head back. Judging from the portrait he'd glimpsed on her study wall, her mother had been as beautiful and gentle as Vivienne herself. With tears in her eyes, Vivienne had mentioned only that she was dead and said no more. As for her father . . . he suspected Mr. Sheridan was not his beloved's favorite person on this earth. He had not noticed a portrait that seemed fatherly anywhere in her house and he was an observant man. No explanations from her about him.

But there had to be more.

To be truthful, he did not mind not knowing too much about that part of her life. They had scarcely had a chance to be lovers. Meeting a woman's parents, well—now there was a true test of a man's courage.

A rendezvous was in order. Vivienne could not very well stroll across London all the way from Cheyne Row, and pop in. Especially not with the streets in between swarming with agents and Osip ensconced in her house. The report from the guards said that the old man seemed almost content. Who would not be with Vivienne around?

No, he would have to take the initiative. A responsible voice in his head reminded him of the need for secrecy and security during the interminable wait for Volkodav to make a move. He agreed with the voice. Another mental voice, the one that had told him to pour the whisky and forget about his troubles, told him to do something dashing, such as sweep her off her feet and carry her away in his big, black coach. He agreed with that voice too.

He finished the whisky.

A third voice, that of the butler, was announcing a visitor.

"A Mr. Sheridan to see you, sir."

Kyril sat bolt upright.

"What?"

"He says you will want to know why he is here."

Kyril poured a glass of water and drank it down. It would not do for his breath to smell too much of whisky should this Mr. Sheridan be *the* Mr. Sheridan, the father of his beloved.

He stood up.

The moment the man entered the room, Kyril knew that he should not have bothered. Sheridan reeked of cheap port.

Kyril indicated a chair and sat across from him.

Sheridan settled himself and smiled in an unpleasantly familiar way.

Kyril waited for him to speak. The man had a faint veneer of gentility, but his threadbare clothes and the hole in the shoe he propped upon his knee gave his poverty away.

"I suppose you would like to know why I am here." Sheridan looked longingly at the decanter of whisky.

Kyril didn't offer him any. "You may tell me when you are ready."

Sheridan coughed, a rasping sound from deep in his throat.

Kyril frowned. He could well be suffering from some disease—his skin was discolored and so were his teeth. The few that he had left.

"Very well. I think that you know my daughter, Vivienne?"

Kyril said nothing. He was not persuaded that this ugly little man was her father and Sheridan, if that was his name, had offered no proof.

"I have secrets to share concerning her that you may find interesting." He leaned back in his chair and gripped the armrests. Kyril noticed thin black lines of dirt under his fingernails. "Very interesting indeed."

Something about him—his smell, his manner, perhaps it was everything about him—repelled Kyril.

"Go on," he said at last.

"Vivienne is quite a beauty." He smiled and thrust out the tip of his tongue nervously, licking his bottom lip. "Gets it from me."

I don't think so. But Kyril said nothing. Let the fellow hang himself.

"And she knows how to please a man." Sheridan chewed on his bottom lip, eating the dried skin and scum that clung to it as if it were something delicious.

Kyril was a minute away from throwing him bodily out the front door and down the stairs into the street. But something stopped him.

"I am sure she pleases you, sir."

"Get to the point." He could not possibly be Vivienne's father. No, this hideous person had heard of her, followed her, wanted to invent some association with her in order to—

"But as I say, she has her secrets. Secrets that only a father would know."

Kyril had had enough. "I don't know who you are, but you are not her father."

Sheridan wriggled back in the chair as if he was only just getting comfortable. "Yes, I am. And you will regret it if you don't hear me out."

"I do not think so."

"I can give you a bargain rate."

"For what?"

Sheridan let out the breath he had been holding. "The secrets. Half for telling you everything. And half for not telling anyone else."

"Get out. Now."

Sheridan reached for the decanter and helped himself to a glass of whisky. He gulped it. "All right then. I will go. You will be sorry, though. Here is my card"—he fished out a slip of stiff paper from an inside pocket and put it on the table—"if you happen to change your mind. I can be reached at that address most days. Or you can try the tavern around the corner from it. The Fallen Woman, it is called. If you take my meaning—"

"I said get out!"

Kyril bent over the man and let the full force of his anger shine through his dark eyes.

Sheridan cringed, then got up and bolted.

Kyril heard the front door slam behind him and went to a window to open it and get the man's smell out of the room. He saw him running down the street, his wisps of gray hair flying in the breeze.

No, he could not possibly be Vivienne's father. Another lover of Kyril's had been stalked by just as loathsome a man, someone who hoped to gain her attention by fair means or foul. Kyril and his friends had beat him to within an inch of his life.

This fellow deserved the same. He vowed to send a few men over to the tavern to find out when the fellow came there. He would say nothing of it to Vivienne.

* * *

A few days later, his desire for her had not abated in the least. Sleeping and waking, his mind dwelled on the beauty of her face and her body and her soul—he had to have her. More than before, he needed a reason to go wholeheartedly and bravely toward the ugly conflict that awaited them all.

But do not forget, he reminded himself, *that she has yet to say she loves you. Do not make the ultimate sacrifice and lay down your life without a damned good reason.*

Both thoughts made him smile but not with mirth. Lukian's tough-mindedness must be catching.

For another day, he contrived and schemed to satisfy his concerns for her safety and his own—and when that was accomplished, he surrendered just as wholeheartedly to lust. He was a warrior, after all.

He went to fetch her. It took some persuading and sincere promises of explanations that would come afterward. Two hours later, she was cuddled up against him and whispering in his ear. Vivienne had already confessed to being as frustrated and lonely as he was, in very physical terms. The coach rumbled over the cobblestoned streets, lending its vibration to the sensual atmosphere.

"Go on," he said. "I am enjoying this. I love to hear you talk, softly, Vivienne. I would be happy to listen forever."

She laughed in a low voice and breathed into his ear. "Kyril . . . may I confess?"

"Please do. I already have a raging erection."

She stroked it through his breeches. "Mmm."

He treated her to a long, luscious kiss while she stimulated his hot flesh. The carriage was luxurious but it was still close quarters and the intimacy was greatly heightened by the pulled curtains.

"I am no stranger to sin," she whispered, "nor are you."

"No."

"My thoughts of you have consumed me. Shall I tell you just how I touch my cunny?"

Her fingers squeezed his confined cock.

"Yes," he whispered. "Dear God, yes."

"I lock my door. There you are, already in my room, sitting in an armchair, wearing nothing but breeches and boots, your legs apart, your hand resting on your erection. You are lazy . . . you tell me that you want me to give myself pleasure while you watch. I lift my dress high, holding it around my waist and turn around at your command, half-naked, allowing you to look at me from head to toe."

He began to stroke her thigh through her dress. "Oh, Vivienne . . ."

"For only a moment, I bend over, my back to you, keeping my dress up as I pretend to fix a slipping garter. I hear you sigh with lust as you view my bare bottom. I know my submissive position makes it look rounder and I know that the cheeks are nicely spread."

"You are good at this. Very good."

"The sight excites you. I hear you groan but I say nothing. I tie the garter's ribbon in a pretty bow and straighten up. My face is flushed and my hair is beginning to tumble down."

He ran his hand into her hair and pulled out a few pins. "There."

"When I look at you again, your breeches are still buttoned but you are stroking the stiff rod underneath the leather. Your eyes burn with hot desire . . . but you stay in the chair."

Kyril groaned with lust. She gave his trapped cock an admonishing squeeze.

"Pay attention. It gets better. I keep my dress up with one hand as I go to the mirror and, with the other, remove the pins from my hair as quickly as I can. You tell me to lie down upon my bed and I do. Then you tell me to open my thighs very wide. You can see my tight cunny from where you are—"

"Let go of my cock! I will come in my breeches, Vivienne!"

She did, laughing at his misery.

"But you walk over soon enough. You push down my bodice and bare my breasts. Then you get on the bed so you can really see. You tug at my nipples and roughly caress my breasts . . . what I am doing excites you very much. Then you suck . . . and suck . . . and I begin to moan . . ."

Oh yes, he thought. I want to make you moan. All night long.

"You undo your breeches with one hand and pull out your cock . . ."

He was incredibly aroused to hear her whisper so wantonly, his massive erection tightly restrained by his doeskin breeches. He became more excited with every word and each caress. Considering how closely they sat together it was a wonder he had not pulled out his cock, straddled her over it and given her a ride she would never, ever forget.

That was something he would have to do at his house. In his bedroom. They were almost there.

Kyril went down on his knees in front of the chair he had put Vivienne in. He began to caress her thighs under the dress. The look of crazed desire in his eyes made her feel a little guilty. But she fully intended to satisfy him.

Ten times over.

"Let me undress you, my love."

She was still in a teasing mood and she put her hands on his shoulders to push him away. Then she thought better of it and bent forward to kiss him.

Kneeling before her, he seemed even more proud and masculine.

He returned her kiss ardently. She yielded to the mouth that pressed upon her mouth, and parted her lips when his tongue touched hers. Sensual and wet. His kiss did the trick. She became just as wet between her legs.

Vivienne slipped her hands inside his shirt, reveling in the warmth of his chest, feeling his heart beat faster as the kiss went on.

Kyril broke it off. He rose with a little difficulty, owing to the erection that threatened to burst through his breeches.

He shrugged when he saw her looking at it. How could she not?

His cock was right at the level of her eyes.

He reached down to take her hand and assist her to her feet. She smiled at the gallant gesture, then stood and looked around the room. She had been swept up in his arms and carried in, kissed all the while, and had not seen it. The décor was as masculine as the man who slept here.

The pattern of the wallpaper was interesting. She peered at it curiously.

"Kyril, what is that flower on your wallpaper? A double petal in the center and four small ones above it—I have never seen one like that."

It was, in fact, a stylized pawprint, and the sign of the Pack. He had a few cravats with the same motif.

"Ah—it is a pawpaw flower."

"Really. I have never heard of it."

"I believe it is a tropical plant."

She accepted that explanation. He breathed a sigh of relief.

Vivienne went to the chest of drawers and inspected its top, seeing no sign of another woman.

Not a single hairpin.

Not one snapped corset lace.

No trace of long tresses tangled in the brush upon the dresser. She looked at it and picked at a few short, dark hairs.

"Spying?" he inquired.

"Yes, of course," she said blandly.

"You happen to be the first woman . . ." he began and broke off, obviously not wanting to lie.

He clearly needed help. She would give it.

"To sleep in this room with you," she finished. "I expect you had your wicked way with other women elsewhere."

He crossed his arms over his chest and grinned at her.

"Never mind, Kyril. I do not care."

But she did. She would never admit it to him, but she did.

"Would you mind very much if I brushed your hair?"

She looked at him with surprise. "No."

He took up the brush and ran it lightly over her hair. He did it with skill.

"Were you once a hairdresser?"

"No, indeed not. I think your hair is beautiful, that is all. Now I have an excuse to touch it."

"You need no excuse to do that." She relaxed under the gentle strokes of his brush.

He lifted her hair and kissed her nape.

"Kyril . . ." she said, remembering something else.

He went back to what he was doing. "Mmm?"

"Do you remember how you calmed me with your hand upon my nape?"

"I do."

"I felt that I could not move and I did not mind at all."

"Ah. I will do it again if you like it."

"Do it now," she begged.

He obliged her, cupping her nape in the same way. The warmth of his hand was profoundly soothing.

Kyril knew why. She understood instinctively that he would protect her from every danger. Cubs could be calmed in the same way and it worked remarkably well on females. He still had the touch.

"That is very nice," she whispered.

He went back to her hair, finishing in a few more strokes. It was not as tangled as he had thought.

"Come. Let us get this dress off you."

She raised her arms.

He bent down to pick it up from the hem and lift it and the shift beneath off in one go. The pleasure of revealing her was too good to hurry, though.

Her shapely calves each deserved a kiss. They got one.

The indented bits at the back of her knees were delectable.

And so were the backs of her thighs. He tasted them too.

Her behind . . . poems could be written about that voluptuous double moon. He fondled and pressed a score of kisses upon each side.

Vivienne giggled.

The bunched dress and shift he held moved higher. She had dimples above her buttocks.

His tongue said hello, and hello.

Her small waist received a nip to the left and to the right. Hard nips. The sort that left marks women looked at with pride the next morning.

Still, she yelped.

He sighed and kissed the bumps of her graceful spine. Then he pushed the dress over her shoulders and let it rest upon them, reaching around to cup her breasts. Vivienne sighed too and swayed back against him.

His hot cock moved in his breeches.

It was time to take it all off.

She raised her arms higher to aid him. Kyril slipped the dress up and over her hands.

Vivienne turned around. "And now you."

Her deft hands undid his breeches. He simply tore off his shirt and flung it aside.

"That is a waste of fine linen."

"I do not care."

Her hands caressed his strong, gloriously bare body. He looked down at her with such tenderness that she wanted to melt.

How magical it was to be alone with him, away from the world and safe from all danger.

He swept her up in his arms. Another gallant gesture. The bed was only a few feet away.

Kyril set her down upon it. She rolled a little from side to side, lazy as an animal.

He lay beside her, curving his body around hers. Again she had the feeling of being deliberately protected from harm. As if he would do it forever.

She might not fight him on that much longer.

His wandering hands stroked her belly, appreciating its womanly softness before they moved upwards to her breasts.

There he lingered longer. His cock was in a hurry, bumping her thigh vigorously, but he was not.

The fire cast a soft glow over the room and the white sheets. Vivienne relaxed even more. She opened her legs, silently permitting his exploring fingers to probe her cunny.

Her flesh was slick, yielding to him. He slid in two fingers. The sensation was pleasurable but his cock had felt more like four.

He added another.

Three. In and out. Stretching her for him.

His thumb touched her clitoris and he massaged it expertly.

Being gently fucked by a manly hand felt wonderful.

She clasped her own breasts so he could watch how she excited herself in that way.

Kyril murmured his approval.

"I love to see you touch yourself," he whispered. "The private play of a woman is the most sensual thing I know. Go on. As if I wasn't here at all."

Vivienne had to smile. His three fingers were filling her cunny, which had a very good grip of its own on them. He was most definitely here.

But she would ignore that and please him by pretending he wasn't.

She caressed her bosom in slow, erotic circles, tugging the nipples so high that her breasts formed peaks.

"I like to feel it very intensely," she whispered. "It is not painful. Just strong. A lady's maid showed me how."

"Tell me more." His voice was deep, almost disembodied.

She had never experienced Sapphic love but she was happy to make up an erotic story on the spot to excite him. It was working, judging by the insistent throbbing of his cock.

"She came into the room as I was about to dress. She stared at my bare breasts, then dropped her eyes. But I knew what she wanted."

"Yes."

"I walked over to her and took her hands. Then I placed them upon my breasts. I begged her to caress me. I pushed myself against her. She was fully clothed and modestly dressed. But I was completely naked."

"Mmm."

"She could not disobey. She reached up reluctantly . . . then avidly. Kissing me lasciviously as she fondled my soft flesh. She took each nipple between her forefinger and thumb . . ."

"Do you know what you are doing to me?"

Vivienne cupped her breasts and offered him her nipples.

He sucked eagerly, withdrawing his fingers from her cunny to hold her.

"Then she pulled my nipples into soft points and stepped backwards. I stepped with her. I had to. It hurt a little at first . . .

and then the pleasure started. Her caresses forced my compliance. It was I who had to obey. But I found it a very great pleasure to do so."

Kyril got up on all fours over her, kissing her very roughly indeed. He clasped her chin and forced her to stay still and take the deep, sexually charged thrusts of his tongue.

She whimpered but she enjoyed what he was doing.

He gave over kissing her mouth and moved to her neck, biting expertly in a way that would never leave a mark, but excited her so much her back arched. He slid a hand under the arch and moved her to where he wanted her on the bed.

"Spread for me. Show me everything."

She put a hand on each knee and forced her thighs down before he could do so.

"Open yourself fully for me."

Vivienne's hands moved between her legs. She stretched her labia for him, although they were so swollen with pleasure they did not quite part.

He took hold of her clitoris and rolled it between his finger and thumb. "Your hot little rod is sticking out. You should see it."

His stimulation excited her too much to answer him. Vivienne moaned. He let go of her clit and patted her whole muff.

"Now lift your legs up. Clasp your ankles. I want to see your cunny snugged."

She did as he asked. She would have done anything he asked.

Kyril moved back on the bed but he slid one hand under each of her buttocks and lifted her hips very high.

His tongue thrust deep within her cunny with no preliminaries. In and in and in.

Then he lapped at the outside, still fondling her behind in a passionately sensual way.

He pulled his head up and wiped his wet mouth on the back of her thigh.

"Bounce in my hands," he murmured. "You have a fine big arse but my hands are big enough to hold it. Go on."

She bounced once.

"More. I love a shameless woman."

Vivienne squirmed in his hands. He picked her up by the buttocks and made her bounce.

He was right. It felt very good—and she felt shameless.

She let go of her ankles but he grabbed them and rested her legs on his shoulders.

"Will it be too deep if I penetrate you this way, my love?"

"N-no," she gasped. "I don't think so. Try—then I will know."

He positioned his cock and eased it in, holding himself up with strong arms. The head touched her womb and Vivienne moaned. He was in deep—just deep enough to make her cry out with wild delight.

Kyril began to thrust with delicious slowness. The heavy-laden sac at the base of his cock touched her upraised behind each time he came down into her. Just that touch of skin on skin, balls to bottom, was enough to make her gasp. The pleasure of it was extreme.

And the pressure of his entire body on her clitoris was going to make her climax in just a few seconds. Here it was . . . yes, she was . . . .oh . . . coming . . . coming so hard. For him. Only for him.

He rode her vigorously, sweat beading on his chest and brow as his entire body tightened and he howled her name.

The next few days passed in a sensual haze. She was bundled in his bathrobe into the adjoining room so as to save her the surprise and averted looks of the servants when they showed up with the necessaries of life.

Meals.

Tea.

Hot water for baths.

Champagne. It counted as a necessary thing, when one was in love. And Vivienne was beginning to realize that she was.

He had apparently known from the beginning and not doubted himself. But then he was male.

Their bliss lasted until a newspaper was added to the breakfast tray. On it was a headline that shocked her back to full awareness of what had happened in the mansion before Kyril found her.

Body of Russian Priest Found. Foul Play Suspected.

12

Some time later . . .

The newspaper had not identified the monk in question. It was a very serious newspaper that tended to avoid lurid details, at least until the facts of a case were irrefutable. Especially a murder case.

But that didn't change the fact that Osip had disappeared without a trace from her house. Neither Henry nor Mrs. Hickham had seen him leave and no one had come for the old man.

Kyril's inquiries had turned up nothing. The old monk had vanished into thin air. Vivienne could not stop thinking about him. She had taken him in, weak and sick as he was, hoping that Kyril would assist her with the situation. But he had kept his distance and kept his own counsel for weeks until she was driven to distraction. Unwilling to lose the upper hand with her well-meaning servants, she'd let Osip stay in the spare room and pray upon his rosary.

She had not insisted that Kyril come to her. In truth, it was because she'd been somewhat afraid of Lukian, whose behavior

on that night still puzzled her. What with one thing and another, Osip had retreated from her mind and lived like a ghost
in her house. Her servants' muttered protests she politely ignored, and eventually they gave up. The egg—well, that peculiar
object was also out of sight and out of mind. She had not lifted
the carpet and floorboard to look at it since she'd hidden it.

The time had gone too slowly. And then Kyril had finally
appeared.

Finally.

Lonely, wild with sexual frustration, she'd gone along for a
very interesting ride and stayed with him. She'd had some sort
of plan at first to get him to help her with the matter of the
monk but it had been pushed to the back of her mind, as she
sought physical release with Kyril as her very willing partner.
Again and again.

She was ashamed of her selfishness. Deeply ashamed.

Kyril had brought her home on the very day they had both
read the newspaper with the shocking headline, telling her that
he was paying for guards to secretly watch her. Just in case.

He did not give a reason, but she did not argue. She'd told
him of Osip—but not everything.

Vivienne had walked out today as far as the cemetery, on the
slight hope of seeing Kyril there by chance. The distractions of
London were to no avail. She had not gone out except to be by
the river. From its bank the city seemed oddly distant—even its
outline seemed strange to her now.

The landmarks were the same as ever. Spired churches punc-
tuating the air, ruled over by the noble dome of St. Paul.
Columned buildings of golden stone a stone's throw away from
ramshackle tenements. The streets that tied them all together
seemed to go nowhere.

In the intervening weeks, she had given no thought to society, withdrawing from it and not missing it. Her sister Pamela
had gone to Paris with her husband, so there had been no

cheerful comfort from that quarter. The occasional letters inquiring as to the next date of her soirées or invitations to balls and assemblies she simply ignored.

Lukian visited once, sent by Kyril. He was tight-lipped but he seemed to have gained control of his temper. He had found out nothing more about Osip. Or the Serpent's Egg.

Vivienne resigned herself to inaction. Heroines were not needed to lead the Taruskin Pack, as Lukian referred to his family.

Very well. Life went on. No matter what, she knew she would wait for Kyril. Had he not given her a beautiful dog to keep her company? She still thought it was odd that no note had accompanied the basket on that day. As if she would not have known who would have given her a creature that looked like a plump little wolf. She supposed the girl who'd brought her—Natalya—had stitched her name, Tier, onto the soft ribbon around her thick-furred neck. Tier ate twice as much as one and grew amazingly fast.

Lukian had been happier to see the dog than her on his visit. He said gruffly that Vivienne was guilty of nothing more than impetuousness, but she did wonder if Lukian would give a good report of her to his cousin. She had caught him staring at her in an assessing way, as if he did not quite trust her.

She had asked him flatly if he did. He had given a grave bow and replied that he did not trust himself.

They were mad, the lot of them, she thought crossly. And perhaps she was too. She had been lonely too long.

After Osip's disappearance, she came and went in what seemed like safety. There were advantages to being watched over day and night, but she never saw a soul other than the neighbors she knew well and her own servants. It puzzled her.

Vivienne thought that the dog would sniff someone out, if there were someone. But she patrolled the perimeter on her own, independent from her ears to her paws and never barked.

It was not the only thing she puzzled over. There was the

matter of the inscription she'd seen on the egg. The words stuck in her mind. She had looked more closely at the fountain and the garden and found nothing unusual about either. If they held a clue or a connection to the Tsar's priceless trinket, she could not figure it out.

The basin atop the column that had once held water was now filled with dry leaves. A mouse lived under them—she had touched the twiggy ball it had made for itself and left it where it was. The garden was only a garden, shriveling into itself at the end of autumn. But the cemetery no longer felt lonely to her.

The ruined mansion that loomed over the Russian section was another matter. She'd gone toward it, drawn by its brooding quality, only to be stopped by a wrought-iron fence covered completely with ivy. The mass of dark green was deceptively leafy and light, filled with twittering birds, but she found no gap or gate in the fence beneath it, and gave up.

It was Vivienne's first visit to the cemetery since the arrival of the dog. Sweet as Tier had looked in the bottom of the basket, she had grown so fast she soon did not fit in it at all. The cub was not easy to walk, running off in all directions, barking at other dogs and unwary people.

Tier loved to walk by the river also. The Thames flowed on past them on their way here, past the bas-relief of the weeping Magdalen and the dead she watched over, past the living souls that crowded its banks. Its steady rush was comforting. The cries of the watermen in swift, small craft and the slow progress of the larger ships that sailed past the great docks were too.

She longed passionately for Kyril. There was no replacing him. The sensual explosions he had set off in her body still echoed. She wanted more. She would not satisfy herself by herself. She wanted him.

At least she had the constant companionship of her beautiful dog. The animal went everywhere with her.

Today was no exception. She looked down at the dog at her

feet. There was something almost human about Tier's understanding and nothing doglike about her independence.

Her white-and-silver fur sparkled in the late afternoon sunlight that slanted through the clouds. Tier had grown very rapidly, as her manservant Henry had predicted. He had added that Tier was no dog for a lady. But Tier had turned out well. Her paws no longer seemed too large for her legs, and her big, pricked ears fit the length of her muzzle.

The dog panted, content to sniff this and that. But Vivienne knew it would only be a little while before she felt a tug on the leash and Tier headed pell-mell back to the cemetery gate or somewhere else.

It was less than a minute. The dog stood up and led Vivienne on.

She must look a sight, she thought, what with her gown and coat tangling in her legs. The breeze had freshened and her dark hair whipped across her face. Vivienne looked around for the old woman, whom she had not seen again. She was not there, but the sparrows were.

She reached into her pocket for the dry crust she'd brought and crumbled it, then threw the crumbs into the air. The sparrows descended.

Tier pulled at the leash, though she walked in the center of the path. She did not sniff at the stones—she seemed aware that this was a hallowed place, for all that those who lay here had been outcasts in life.

The dog's head turned from side to side when she yanked Vivienne back once more in the direction of the Russian part of the cemetery. Her big body trembled with eagerness. It was as if she saw ghosts.

Vivienne felt uneasy.

Tier looked at the tombstones intently. She came to the Taruskin one and lay down in front of it, putting her head between her paws and whining.

"There, there. Yes, you do know them. Lukian is their kins-man and so is Kyril."

Tier had gone straight to Lukian when he came to the door of the Cheyne Row house.

But then dogs had simple minds, Vivienne thought. The complexities of human personalities were lost on them. Lukian, who seemed easier with animals than he did with humans, took his time about rubbing Tier's ears and whispering sweet noth-ings into them. That made him godlike in her dog's eyes.

She let Tier pay her respects and let go of the leash, wander-ing again to the ivy-covered fence that separated the graveyard from the ruined mansion. The ivy rustled in the breeze and Vivienne felt the coldness in the air. She was glad Tier was with her.

The dog sprang up and came to stand by her side.

Ever curious, Tier nosed the ivy here and there. Then she stopped and put a paw upon a part of it that Vivienne had not explored. She heard a creak and the dog whined softly.

The ivy had formed a living net over an old gate.

It did not take her long to free it, but Vivienne looked wilder than ever when she was done. Bits of leaves and stems had at-tached themselves to her hair and her hands were scratched. They could walk through. If she dared.

"Come, Tier."

The dog pushed through first. She bounded over the vast ex-panse of ivy on the other side in great leaps. Vivienne went much more slowly, afraid of tripping or turning her ankle.

"Stay with me!"

The dog came back.

The mansion seemed larger on this side of the fence. Every step she took made it seem larger still.

It might have been a trick of the waning light. If Tier had not been with her, she would have gone back.

The dog was nosing under the ivy.

There was something underneath. The ivy had risen in a mound over whatever it was.

Vivienne came closer. "What is it?"

Tier's haunches rose as her head went down. The dog seized something that Vivienne could not see under the ivy and dragged it forth.

In her teeth was a long, tattered piece of cloth with fragments of letters on it that looked somehow familiar. Tier shook it, then dropped it and went back for more.

A shoe made out of rope and leather. And then . . . a human hand. Its wrinkled fingers clutched something. A rosary. The large wooden beads were attached to a cross. And on it was a crucified wolf. Made of silver. Its belly was sliced open—it was hollow. Its paws were pierced with tiny silver nails that held it to the wood.

Vivienne screamed.

Nausea overwhelmed her. There was no saving the person the hand belonged to. She knew who it was. The stench of death was suddenly strong and the dog backed away.

The day's light was beginning to fade. Vivienne looked deep into her dog's eyes and felt a flow of animal courage from Tier to her.

She would look again. Then she would run.

She found a stick and probed the ivy, pulling back the mat of leaves and twining stems.

It was Osip.

His face had frozen into a grimace of fear and surprise.

Had he been killed here? Or brought here and covered up? The mat of leaves seemed otherwise undisturbed.

She let the ivy drop over his body again. It was as good a shroud as any.

"Come," she whispered to the dog.

Tier stayed where she was.

"You must come!" Her voice held a low urgency. If the dog would not, she would leave her here.

Tier bounded away—toward the sinister house.

"No, Tier!"

Vivienne was seized with despair. She could not abandon her dog.

Home seemed very far away.

She followed the dog to the ruined mansion, whacking at the ivy. Finally she caught up with her.

Tier had stopped at the door of the house. Or where the door had once been. The heavy carvings around the door were still there.

Vivienne recognized Russian workmanship and Russian motifs. What the old woman had told her was true. The people in the cemetery had once lived here.

Tier went through the door.

With terror in her heart, Vivienne followed.

She did not do so unobserved.

Kyril was watching her from the shadows. Disheveled, frightened, she was more beautiful than ever. The emotions in her face tore at his heart.

He could not believe Lukian's suspicions concerning her. His cousin had told him she would come here. He had insisted that Kyril wait.

His cousin had fallen into a black variability of mood that was beyond comprehension. The strain of waiting for Volko-dav to make his move was telling on him, on all of them, but Lukian most of all.

Lukian had taken on too much: he had appointed himself protector of Kyril, and watcher-in-chief over Vivienne. And then his obsessions had taken over. He ranted from time to time. He'd tried to convince Kyril that she might have had something to do with old Osip's arrival, even that she had offered herself as bait to lure Kyril from hiding, planning for the bogus monk to bring the egg and thrust it into Kyril's hands—

All of it was absurd. He'd scoffed at Lukian and sent him away angry. But it made Kyril uneasy that Lukian had been right about one thing.

Only two hours before, Lukian demanded to see him. He had specifically said that Vivienne was on her way to the cemetery. And that she would not stop there but continue on to the ruined mansion.

There was something vile hidden in its overgrown garden, something that she had to find, Lukian said. But he would not say what it was and Kyril did not know. He had entered the crumbling pile from the other side. He had not seen her go through the ivy but he had heard her scream.

Why would she scream? According to his cousin, she had been looking for whatever it was and knew that it was vile. Lukian's incoherent stories did not make sense. But Kyril had picked up a strong scent of rot the second he heard her scream pierce the air.

Bah. He dismissed his own suspicions. Most likely there was a dead cat under the ivy. Or two. Strays found homes, sometimes their last, if they were sick, in the mansion. That was rotten itself and on the verge of collapse.

Jozef Taruskin, his ancestor, the eccentric creator of the Serpent's Egg and other marvels, had had it built for himself and lived in it alone. It had been a house of wonders in its day, filled with secret corridors and doors that went nowhere. The automatons he built were just as wonderful: moving, finely articulated representations of real and imaginary beasts, and creatures that were half beast and half human as well.

All had been sold to circuses and freak shows and wealthy collectors of oddities upon his death, many of whom were his friends. He gave famous balls at which half the guests disappeared, only to find themselves in the wrong bedroom with someone naked—or out in the maze in the garden.

But corrosion and decay had attacked the last traces of the mansion's former glory. A greenish slime mottled the old brass fittings and the banisters were cobwebbed and tilting crazily.

Why on earth was Vivienne here? And what had she found outside that made her scream?

Doubts assailed him. He pushed the questions from his mind.

Vivienne had stopped in the middle of the ballroom, reflected in the hundred shattered mirrors on its walls. She did not see him far in the corner where the darkness was deepest. The dog did not seem to perceive his presence—the other smells were too strong. She kept her hand on her dog's collar. Tier's hackles were up and Vivienne's hand stroked them down. She spoke softly to the animal, soothing her. Kyril heard the words and the tenderness in her tone.

"Tier, be good. We must get home. I did not know that—that thing was under the ivy. We should not have come here. There is evil in this house."

Kyril was immediately convinced of her innocence. She had no idea he was there, watching and listening. It had to be Lukian who was lying.

His cousin admired Vivienne . . . a little too much. But why would he try to turn Kyril against her?

At the moment it didn't matter.

She was here and so was he. He loved her. He would protect her. The explanations could come later. He wondered how she had given her bodyguards the slip. No. That didn't fit. He received their reports through Lukian, who had assured him several times that she never noticed the men. Kyril knew well the Packish skill at vanishing in plain sight.

No. Her bodyguards had been told not to follow her.

He took a deep breath at the exact moment she did. He saw her take the dog by the collar and walk away from him, disappearing into shadows of her own.

He had waited a second too long to make a move, not able to see or smell if there was someone else waiting in the darkness. He was sure there was and he dared not call her name. If Vivienne responded, that someone would know where she was. Her survival would come down to which one of them was closer . . . himself or . . . the other man. Kyril was even more sure that the unseen one who watched her was a man.

Still later . . .

The moon had come up. It cast freakishly bright light through the vast holes in the roof and created shadows that were inky black.

Kyril's nerves were on edge and his body was vibrating. The immense mansion seemed to have swallowed Vivienne and the white dog. She never once stepped out where he could see her. He could not smell her. He still did not know if someone else was following him or her or both of them.

His acute hearing did pick up her movements. She started, then stopped. Once he heard her crying very faintly, far away. That stopped too. He had a feeling that she was edging along the walls, looking for a way out.

The endless corridors were a trap. One might enter a room and leave it by a different door and come out upon a balcony too high to jump from.

Kyril had been here before in the night, when he had first joined the Pack. His welcoming Howl had been followed by an unexpected test of his courage and his skill. He had demonstrated both . . . but he had lost his way a hundred times before the sun came up.

The friends who had abandoned him had been waiting for

him outside, rolling around in the ivy, very drunk. Five of them. He had asked them to stand up and then he had thrashed them thoroughly.

Kyril paused in the door of a room that he had been through twice and listened intently.

Nothing.

He had to find her.

He took a chance and called her one last time.

No reply.

If his wolfish skills were not enough, then he would have to use magic. The most powerful magic that he knew.

Vivienne could not find her way no matter how often she re-traced her steps. The corridors seemed to turn themselves inside out as soon as she reached their end. Even Tier, so sure and strong, hesitated.

She went into a small room, certain that there was a door on the other side of it. She saw moonlight. If it led to a balcony, she could climb down the ivy.

But the dog could not. Tier whimpered, as if she understood. Vivienne went with her to the door anyway, her footsteps shh-shhing. She opened it—it was only a closet with a cracked mirror inside.

She covered her mouth, fighting a powerful urge to vomit. In just such a closet had she been locked by her father. Listening to her mother cry for help far away.

Once, only once, her mother had called out to Vivienne. And she had not been able to break down the closet's door or even turn the knob. She had forgotten that moment and her helplessness until this very moment . . . with horror, she heard someone call her name again. Faintly. Despairingly. Was she imagining it?

The body in the ivy . . . no, no, no. Osip had not risen from the dead, there were no ghosts, and even if there were, she had tried to help him.

His corpse would not stalk her.

But she could not shake the feeling that someone was in the house with her.

The darkness breathed.

The old walls echoed sounds as broken as they were. She came into a room that had once held portraits. Most had been ripped from their frames but a few were left.

Dear God, no. All she needed was painted eyes looking at her from painted faces pitted with decay. She would go insane.

But there was no way out save to walk past.

She clutched the dog's collar and went toward them.

The moonlight shone brightly for a moment.

The faces in the portraits were nothing out of the ordinary. Until she saw the last one.

It was the face of an angel. A small face, with closed eyes. Her angel. Her newborn baby. Arielle.

The eyes in the painting opened. Her baby's eyes were filled with luminous tears.

Vivienne began to scream. And scream. And scream.

Crazed with fear and wild grief, she did not see that someone stood in the shadows next to them, shadows that were not so very dark. But when she turned to flee, she glimpsed a tall man with a hard glint in his eyes.

Tier did not growl.

Vivienne felt her heartbeat roar in her ears and she fainted dead away . . .

Moaning, she came back to consciousness. There was no telling how long she had lain there. Tier was licking her face. She urged her mistress up. Vivienne struggled to obey. The animal's wisdom might save her. She could die in this place.

And no one would ever know. She got up and they stumbled on.

244 / Noelle Mack

Corridors. Rooms. Broken mirrors. Empty frames. Doors that went nowhere or opened into utter blackness.

Vivienne heard an unearthly song come through the dark. She sensed rather than saw Tier's ears prick up. The voice was male. Soothing and deep.

But it frightened her.

She pressed herself against the wall, weeping silently. The dog leaned against her leg, offering what comfort it could.

Not enough.

Her sobs grew ragged, no matter how hard she tried to stop them. The song continued. Deep, sustained notes seemed to be coming toward her, growing louder. Vivienne wanted to scream again, scream the sound into nothingness.

She dropped to her knees and buried her face in Tier's thick fur. The dog was still listening, not afraid at all. Vivienne turned and rested her cheek on Tier to listen too.

There were no words to the song. But she understood instinctively that she was being commanded. To stand up. To come forward. Into the moonlight. Where the singer could see her.

Come.

A single, long note hung in the air.

No. She wanted to shriek the single word over and over. Shatter the magic spell of the swelling notes and escape.

Tier turned and licked Vivienne's cheek. Licked away the tears her tongue could reach.

Rise.

The word echoed in her head. She had not said it. Or heard it. Or thought it.

But she answered it. *No.* The song engulfed her. She could no longer think.

Come to me.

As if moved by an unseen hand, she struggled up, supporting herself on the wall. She swallowed the last of her sobs. If she was fated to meet her death, she would do it without cringing. She would go . . . where she would see her child again and her mother. There was life on the other side. There had to be. She took hold of Tier's collar and walked from the darkest part of the shadow into the moonlight.

The shadow on the opposite side of the room broke open, and someone walked out of it.

Kyril.

She looked at him with wonder. His arms were uplifted and his eyes were closed. Tears ran from them. Pure, deep sound came from his open mouth.

He was the singer.

The last and deepest note dissolved every trace of her fear. Then he opened his eyes and saw her. Vivienne let go of Tier and ran into his embrace, screaming for joy now.

"Kyril! Where were you? What has happened?"

"My darling one," he murmured into her hair. "My love. I was afraid—"

"You are never afraid."

"Not for myself."

She pressed her face into his shirt, smelling the faint fragrance of the herb she had crushed in the garden. He was real. He was here. She was safe in his arms.

"I dared not call your name until the very last, Vivienne."

"I heard you. I dared not answer."

He stroked her hair, caressing her over and over without speaking for a little while.

"Why did you sing like that?" she asked. "It sounded so strange . . ."

He kissed the tip of her nose. "Sometimes it is better not to explain. You will have to be satisfied with that."

He held her more tightly. His warmth and closeness made

246 / Noelle Mack

her want to weep again. The song he'd sung still echoed very faintly in the room.

Sobbing with terror and with joy, she told him what she had seen—and what it had made her remember. Her mother, dead too soon. Her father, unworthy of living. And her child, lost but forever loved.

"It was an illusion, Vivienne. A cruel one."

"Who would do such a thing to me?"

"I do not know," he said softly.

"My father, I think," she whispered. "He said that he would . . ." She let the sentence trail off without finishing it.

"What does he look like?"

She described him in a few words. "Have you seen him? He threatened to—"

"Shh. No, I have not seen him." Best to lie for now.

Tears flowed down her cheeks as Kyril began to sing again, rocking her in his arms. It was a lullaby . . . an ancient melody meant to protect the Roemi children, sung by their women and their faithful men.

Tier, faithful Tier, went in a circle around them, wagging her tail. Vivienne felt the brushy thumps against her dress. Even the dog seemed magic, glowing whitely in the moonlight, her black eyes shining when she looked up at her mistress.

"Are you quite sure, Kyril?"

"If I knew your father had done such a thing to you, I would kill him without a second thought."

That much was true. He sighed and rubbed his cheek against her hair. He would think about that later, after he had loved away the last of Vivienne's fear.

Kyril swept her up in his arms. "We must go. I have sung away all the evil, but it may return."

"Oh, Kyril . . ." She twined her arms around his neck. A frightening memory came back to her. "Were you the man who stepped out of the shadows?"

"Not quickly enough. I am sorry for that, more sorry than I can say."

"Tier did not growl at you."

"No, she would not. She does know me."

The hard glint in the eyes of the man she had glimpsed seemed unlike Kyril. But he might have been an apparition, summoned to life by her own fear—she had seen nothing clearly. "Even so—"

"Hush. You were lost in this place. I want you to forget, if you can."

"I am beginning to. I cannot remember anything of how I came here. Something frightened me terribly . . . it was outside this house. Dear God, what was it?"

"Do not try to remember. Let it go. Close your eyes."

He went swiftly through the house, hoping that his echoing song would work as he had said. If she did not look, she would not remember. He wanted another night with her . . . a night with no shadows.

A night of love. Deep and pure.

She was surprised to see his carriage waiting on the other side of the strange house. It was pulled up in front as if he had come there for a ball. The horses stamped and the coachman tipped his hat to her.

"Why is it here? Why are you here?"

"Perhaps you summoned me." Never mind the details. He would have to change the subject if she asked again. She was giddy—it was an aftereffect of the powerful song. Joy chased sorrow, but the sorrow could come back.

He still did not know what she had found in the garden. She might remember. Or not. He could go back and look for himself. Tomorrow. Or the next day.

He put her into the carriage and rapped for the coachman to drive away.

She wound herself around his arm. He could not think about anything except what she was doing right now. Rubbing.

Her body moved sensually against his side as she caressed his chest, tipping her face up to kiss his neck. Her fears had been obliterated in one great burst, replaced by happiness flooding through her. She was experiencing an orgasmic sense of release. A woman of the clan had once sung Kyril to such a climax. It had been unforgettable.

He ran a hand over her thigh, smoothing the silk and catching his finger in a rip. "You need to be looked after. You need food and good red wine to strengthen your blood."

Tier gazed at him soulfully as if she agreed.

"So do you, Tier. But you get scraped beef and water." He scratched the back of her ears. "You can sleep in the kitchen next to the stove."

The dog grinned. She seemed to agree with that too.

Kyril had to hold her for a very long time. Vivienne could not stop crying when at last she did remember more.

"Tier found Osip's body. Under the ivy."

Her dog heard her name and thumped her tail on Kyril's drawing room carpet.

"I was sickened when I saw it."

"Of course," he murmured.

"And terrified."

"Who would not be?"

If there had been a way for him to bear this pain for her, he would have done it in the blink of an eye. And wolves blinked faster than most.

"She ran into the mansion and I went after her."

Kyril nodded and reached down to pat Tier's head. The dog had brought her mistress safely to him in the end.

"And then . . . oh, Kyril. I do not believe in ghosts but that is where they would live."

"You are right about that."

He did not want to explain everything about his ancestor Jozef and his association with the sinister house. He suspected she would be fascinated by it all in due time but not now.

"When I went to look at the paintings, I thought . . ." She hesitated.

"What is it, darling? Please tell me everything. I do not want you haunted by your memories."

"There was a man standing in the shadows of that—that room. I thought it was you."

She had mentioned it. The remark had slipped his mind.

"I was never in a room with paintings."

He regretted the words the instant he said them.

"Oh my God. Then who was he?"

"I do not know."

Her gaze grew distant. "His eyes had a hard gleam. And he was as tall as you."

Kyril could guess. Was it wise to tell her of his suspicions concerning Lukian?

"I went toward him . . . because Tier did not bark."

"You said that she seemed confused in the house, Vivienne. The strange smells and the echoes—"

"She was confused. But she stayed by me."

"She is an excellent dog. The pick of her litter."

Words that Tier agreed with even if she was not, strictly speaking, a dog. She sighed and settled down with her head between her paws.

If only the animal could tell him what she had seen. For the rest of Kyril's life, he would regret leaving Vivienne alone for weeks to wait and wonder.

But there was something else—something that he could not fathom. He felt as if a clue was just out of his reach.

Something Lukian had said . . .

Vivienne heaved a huge sigh and nestled against him.

"Vivienne, may I ask you a question?"

"Of course."

"Why did you first go to the cemetery?"

"I was upset when—when everything began to happen. I walked along the river and chanced upon it."

"It seems like a strange place for you to visit."

"Perhaps I was guided there."

Kyril frowned.

"I saw the Magdalen and the old woman—she talked to me for a little while. I think that perhaps her daughter is buried there."

"Why?"

"I don't know why. She never said and I never asked."

Kyril was silent. Tier had not been with her then. What unseen hand or creature had guided her to that lonely, dismal place?

"The old woman pointed out the Russian part of the cemetery. I was curious—and I was startled when I saw your family name."

"Of course."

"I saw the flowers upon a grave—the dates were right. I thought a woman there might have been your mother."

"An astute guess. She was. And it was I who left the flowers."

"You had visited recently, Kyril."

There was a faraway look in his eyes. "I do not visit enough."

"And then—oh!" She sat up very straight, pressing her fingertips to her tear-swollen eyes.

"There is a clue there. Or what seems to be a clue. It cannot be a coincidence."

"Please explain."

"There is a fountain."

"Yes, I know it. It once held holy water."

"Oh, Kyril. There is also a small garden inside a fence."

He looked at her, baffled. "I do not understand."

"The inscription on the Serpent's Egg. *Hortus conclusus, fons signatus.* A garden enclosed, a fountain sealed."

"Ah," he said. "Of course."

"Do you know of any connection between the inscription and that old cemetery?"

"I do not. But there may be one. Especially since Osip's body was found so near the place."

She got up and began to pace. "Will he be buried among your countrymen?"

"No, of course not. A murdered man who pretended to be a priest? Hell would not have him."

"What do you know of him?"

"Very little."

"Lukian seemed to think that he was an impostor. I did not believe him. I wish I had. But what about the Serpent's Egg? I thought to help him by selling it . . ."

"Vivienne," Kyril said slowly. "The newspaper account of the finding of the body said nothing about the Serpent's Egg. Very few people know that it is in London."

"He might have been killed for it. But I have it—"

Kyril rose as well and went to the window, clasping his hands behind his back. "No. It is gone. I sent a man to steal it from your house so that you would be safe. It is in—my family's house in Great Jermyn Street."

"Not *your* house."

"No."

"Then you are safe."

"No, I am not. No member of the Pack is safe."

"The pack? Why do you and Lukian call your family that?"

"Because that is who we are. And the long and the short of it is that there is a bounty on our hides. Dead or alive."

She gazed at him with wonder. An aura of shimmering black surrounded his body. There were flashes of fire in it. He looked at her steadily, unaware of what she saw.

She fainted again.

Kyril brought her upstairs in his arms. He would come down and instruct the servants to leave them alone until he summoned them the next morning.

Tier waited on the marble tiles where he told her to, thumping her tail.

It was another minute before he came downstairs. Instructions given, dog brought to the kitchen, he was free to return to Vivienne.

He could give her a bath of sorts with the water in the ewer. If he set it by the fire to warm, it would not chill her.

When he came back into his bedroom, he found her curled up in front of it, staring into the flames. He rested his arm on the back of her chair and looked down.

Her hair was matted and wild. He would comb it. Her dress was torn and dirty. He would remove it.

She would sleep in his arms tonight. Safe from all harm.

Vivienne spent a few days within his bedroom, not seeing or speaking to anyone but Kyril. Her dreams were troubled . . . and she was deeply troubled when she awoke to realize that Lukian had appeared in more than one. He too had a black aura.

He'd stood by the edge of the bed, his eyes grim but gleaming with an inner fire. He had to have been the man in the shadows of the ruined mansion, the one she'd thought was Kyril.

His silence frightened her.

Not knowing whether she *was* dreaming, Vivienne had moved into the center of the bed, wrapping herself tightly in the comforter to shield herself from the watching specter.

But Lukian is not dead. Or so said a small voice in her not-quite-conscious mind. He cannot be a specter. He is here.

Drawn out of herself, compelled by a strong force to reach out to him, she extended a hand . . . and it went right through his solid-seeming body. The silent apparition flinched, though.

She heard a sigh in the room. And a vibration of a human voice. The words came from him—they echoed in her soul.

A strange desire consumes me, Vivienne . . . but I cannot have you.

"Go," she whispered. "Just go."

The specter of Lukian loomed over the bed as if he wanted to kiss her. She shrank away and he vanished.

13

A week later . . .

Lukian sat in his parlor. The shades were drawn and an impen-
etrable gloom had settled over the small room. His head was
sunk in his hands.

Why had he followed Vivienne to the old mansion? Tier had
been the easy part. He had convinced her to drag her mistress
there with nothing more than a few soft words. Her bodyguards he had simply dismissed for the day with words that
were not soft at all. If he had been able to growl and seize them
by the scruff of their necks and throw them down, he would
have done that.

The whirling confusion in his mind was getting worse. Only
burying himself in Lily's soft body alleviated the craving for
morphine and then not for long.

She had moved in with him temporarily to look after him.
He was grateful for that. In his dreams she had the face of Vivienne and her own stocky body.

He had wanted to frighten Vivienne. He had succeeded

without knowing how. Something outside the mansion had made her scream. She had been terrified and utterly disoriented by the time she reached the room where he waited for her.

Tier had behaved well.

Lukian had not wanted to frighten Vivienne to the point of injuring her or unhinging her mind. He only wanted her to run to him.

But she had not. She had fainted dead away.

He had gone to her. Made sure she was all right, nothing broken.

Her beautiful face had seemed so serene. The love in his heart for her was overwhelming. And then he realized that Kyril was not far away. Close to finding her.

He should not have persuaded his cousin to go to the mansion. His cousin had listened thoughtfully to Lukian's dark hints about her character. Surely he would cease to love her and set her free.

He beat at his head, which seemed to be splitting in half. He needed another vial. He needed it now.

He screamed for Lily.

She came eventually. In an hour by his reckoning. A minute by hers. They argued about it. She pointed to the clock and Lukian picked it up and threw it all the way across the hall into the kitchen. He heard it shatter and he heard her cry.

He woke up on the kitchen floor. She had dismissed the servants for the rest of the day and seen to him herself. There were two uncorked vials on the table in front of her.

He had asked for only one, he was sure of it.

Perhaps not. He needed more and more. He had never stopped needing it from the day the doctor on the Russian ship had given it to him. The day after he had murdered its captain and the officer who had whipped him to the point of death.

Lukian would not have lived without the morphine. He could not live without it now.

"Feeling better?" Lily asked.

"Yes. A little."

"Then come sit at the table with me." She nodded at a chair, as if she saw nothing remarkable about a man lying unconscious upon the floor.

Lukian struggled to rise and failed.

Lily looked at him and sighed. "You are a big one. I cannot lift you."

"I can get up. Give me a moment."

"Take all the bloody moments you want."

He didn't mind her cheerful rudeness. Lukian scrubbed at his face with one hand and yawned. Then he got on all fours and from there, got up.

The clock lay in pieces on the floor at his feet. "What happened to the clock?" He knew but he wanted her to confirm it.

"You threw it and smashed it to bits."

"Why?"

"You and I did not agree on how long it took me to get to you."

"I am sorry, Lily."

"It is all right," she said evenly.

"What can I do to make it up to you?"

"Stop seeing that Vivienne."

"Who—" He stopped himself.

"You say her name when you sleep. And when you have not had one of them vials."

"I didn't know that."

Lily rattled the newspaper she was reading. She favored the sort with steel-cut engravings of horrible crimes, stories that ran for weeks.

"Who is she, then?"

"She is . . . the mistress of a friend of mine."

"Oh. Well, you think highly of her. Always mumbling Vivienne this, Vivienne that."

Lukian drew in a deep breath and composed himself. He

could not alienate Lily. The sturdy little whore was his lifeline and his salvation.

"But it doesn't matter. You gave me that nice present."

"Oh. I am glad you liked it." Lukian had no memory of giving her anything. Not recently. He had given her a pair of paste earrings but that had been a while ago.

Lily sniffed and studied an illustration. "Now here is an interesting case. A murder. I like them, I do."

He found a piece of stale bread in the bowl and took a bite. The inside of his mouth was too raw to eat it. He choked on the crumbs.

His companion put down her newspaper and patted him on the back. "There, there. We are all going to die soon enough. No sense rushing things by eating a dry crust."

He could not stop coughing.

"Come along with me," she said, pushing herself up from the table. "Hot tea for you. And then bed."

"It is still light out."

"And when did that ever matter to you?"

He stumbled along after her, not able to see the headline in the paper that had caught Lily's eye. The front page was face-down on the table.

Volkodav was still waiting for the moment to strike. But London was a fine city in which to wait.

He had walked its streets and visited its whorehouses. He had bought guns and silver forks and spoons and knives. The guns were for him. The silver was for his wife.

He and his men—not the Cossacks, who had proved worse than useless, for all their vaunted bravery—had made a rough tally of the Pack members who came and went from the house in Great Jermyn Street, evading the constant surveillance around

it with some difficulty. The British were good at it and the men
of the Pack were even better.

Besides the Taruskins, there were nearly a hundred of them,
including some who seemed distinctly un-Russian to him. His
inquiries had borne fruit: they were Scotsmen.

Volkodav had not known there were manwolves outside of
his own land. Well and good. He would enjoy killing them too,
when the time came.

He had commanded his accomplices to gather and all had arrived. Few had known that so many of them were in London,
having been brought from Russia in small groups that answered only to him.

The Cossacks were the most conspicuous, he reflected. And
the least useful. But they would do to break heads.

It was the quiet men, of average appearance, who were truly
the most dangerous. No one saw them coming. No one remembered them leaving. They made the best assassins.

Alex Stasov was an excellent example of the type. He had
been able to infiltrate the lair of the Pack. Of course, his mixed
blood had enabled him to pass as one of them if he did not look
up too often.

Volkodav turned to him. "And what of Kyril Taruskin?"

Alex shook his head slowly. "He has not been near the lair in
many days. He keeps to himself."

"And why is that?"

"He seems to have found a mate."

"Vivienne Sheridan?"

Alex nodded.

"A beautiful woman but an impetuous one. She took Osip
in but did not succeed in getting Kyril to see him."

"She did try," Alex said mildly. "I read and copied their letters to each other."

"She is a fool and she is kind to everyone. Lukian Taruskin
would have killed Osip if not for her."

Alex only blinked.

Volkodav suspected that Stasov was afraid of the tallest Taruskin, who struck him as a renegade.

"We sent Osip, you know." Nel Sarno, an agent of the Tsar, spoke up. "And we gave him the Serpent's Egg. He was supposed to frame Kyril Taruskin."

"He was too smart to walk into your stupid trap."

"Lukian did."

Volkodav steepled his fingers and touched them thoughtfully to his chin. "There is a man who fears nothing. His history is interesting." He glanced down at the papers on the table in front of him. "But I will not share it with you."

"The trap was not stupid," Nel grumbled. "It took us months to put it together."

"It was a foolish move. It called too much attention to us."

"But the egg was only a copy."

Volkodav gave him an icy glare. "And how did you know that?"

Nel blanched. "The master of the Winter Palace vault told me. He said the original was somewhere in London—that its maker had tricked Alexander's grandfather long ago and sent a copy. With a paste diamond. No one ever wanted to admit it."

"Why are you blurting it out in front of so many?"

"Forgive me," Nel said.

The agent would be the first to melt away into the slums of London, Volkodav thought. But he could be found.

Even if he was telling the truth, someone among them had to die first. No, Nel would be second. Volkodav had personally dispatched the captain of the *Catherine* for his talkativeness.

It was easy enough to scald a man to death in a banya. Two buckets of boiling water poured over Chichirikov when he was too drunk to get up and the thing was done.

No more difficult than searing the bristles off a hog's hide.

In this case, the hog had been alive during the process. But not for long.

Nel was expendable too.

"May I ask a question, sir?" the agent said hesitantly.

A small favor for the next man to die was the right thing to do. "Yes."

"What happened to Osip?"

"I murdered him and dumped his body in front of the old Taruskin mansion."

"By yourself?"

"Yes, of course. He was old and weak."

The agent hesitated. No doubt he was imagining his own fate, which would be similar. The man was not completely stupid.

"How did you gain his confidence? Or even recognize him? The man is wary and a master of disguise."

"If you can call a tattered robe a disguise," Volkodav scoffed. "Gaining his confidence was not difficult at all."

"No? You managed to do what the Tsar's best agents could not."

"Are you one of those 'best agents,' Nel?" Volkodav inquired.

"It seems that I am not," Nel said warily. "But I am not wrong about Osip's craftiness."

"Yes, yes. Enough of that." He felt the agent's gaze search his face after his brusque dismissal.

"There is no way that Osip would have—"

Volkodav cut in. "You did not know he was my brother. Much older than I, but my brother. He trusted me in everything. He was very easy to kill."

The agent swallowed hard.

"Anyone else? Speak up."

He had all their reports in front of him.

"Very well. I will continue. Dr. Broadstreet provided us with a means of controlling Lukian by giving him adulterated morphine. He had no choice. We bought up every vial in London and controlled the incoming supply."

One man applauded. The sound quickly died away.

"Of course, such a strong-willed man is not easy to drive insane. But I think we are nearly there. I added a dash of aphrodisiac to the tincture and made him slaver every time he saw Kyril's lady love."

"Vivienne?" a female agent asked.

"Yes."

"How interesting," Nel said.

Sycophant. Volkodav frowned at him before he went on. "The Taruskins and their kind can communicate with animals. Some are better at it than others. Lukian told her dog to bring her to the mansion at my suggestion."

"Ingenious," Nel said.

"Of course, Vivienne has a secret—who does not? We were able to exploit it. Some years ago she bore a premature baby out of wedlock, which died. I arranged for an illusion of it to appear."

"Nicely done," someone said.

"Her father thought first of making money from that sad event—she thinks it is sad, he and I think it was one less brat to burden the world. He was blackmailing her. I encouraged him to continue to do so and engage Kyril in it if possible. Again, he did not take the bait."

He made a bored gesture that indicated that he was done. The others began to take turns talking. The men—and a few women—had fanned out all over London, living in high places and low.

The usual blabbermouths had provided a wealth of information on the movements of all parties concerned. Shopkeepers had been happy to chat if it meant selling a few extra apples. Many servants had been bribed. The disgruntled ones were cheaper. The prettier parlormaids had been thoroughly fucked first before they talked.

Certain ladies of the court, ignored by their husbands, were even more willing. Those who longed in secret for the thrilling embrace of London's legendary manwolves—the ones the handsomer members of the Pack had not got around to—talked the most.

Not all of the information was of equal value. He would have to sift through it well into the night. For now, he would give them their final instructions.

Volkodav unfolded a large map of London. On it was marked the residences of everyone they hunted. Around those dots were red circles that encompassed their territories.

"Most of our prey lives in the west of London. You will each be assigned a Pack member. Follow that one. Kill when commanded. However you can. With the weapon of your choice."

An excited buzz followed.

Volkodav rose. "The battle is joined. Our field is the city. We will win our war in stealth and in silence, a man at a time."

"What about Kyril Taruskin?" Nel Sarno asked hopefully.

Did the agent seek to redeem himself by capturing the leader of the Pack of St. James? He lacked the skill, in Volkodav's opinion. And he did not deserve the honor.

"He is mine," Volkodav said calmly.

A few days later, in the house near Grosvenor Square . . .
"Something is about to happen, Vivienne. I can sense it."
She rolled over and tucked herself under his arm.
"Then we should get out of this damned bed."
He laughed, and hugged her to his side.
"I feel safe enough."
"You are as safe as I can keep you, my darling."
She kissed his ribs. "Thank you."

Kyril flung the arm that was not holding her back over his head. The idle gesture revealed the musculature of his chest.

Vivienne patted him and pinched a nipple.

"Do you want to—"

"No. Five times in one night is quite enough. I am sore."

"Forgive me."

"Never."

She sat upon the opposite edge of the bed, her beautiful arse not quite concealed by the sheets she was draped in.

Kyril moved swiftly, catching her around the waist and nuzzling the twin dimples at the lowest part of her back.

"Let me go."

"Mmm. Kisskisskiss. Why?"

"It is time. We cannot stay shut up in your bedroom for much longer. The servants must be talking about us."

Kyril snorted. "Then I will sack them and get new ones."

"Is that safe?"

"Now?" He swung his legs over the other side and stood up. "I suppose not. But I was only joking."

"I did have your man take a note to Henry and Mrs. Hickham. They would worry if I did not."

"And rightly so."

"Do you trust him?"

"Completely. He has been with me for years."

Vivienne had not quite forgiven that particular servant for aiding his master in laying low after that drinking bout.

"He even interviews new people on my behalf. He knows and anticipates all my needs."

There was a knock on the door.

Vivienne rose and went into the adjoining room, trailing acres of bedsheets.

"Who is it?" Kyril called.

The person on the other side mumbled something that sounded like tea.

"Ooh! I do want some," Vivienne called.

"Whatever the lady wishes." Kyril swathed a towel around his lean hips and went to open the door.

"You may set the tray there," she heard him call. Absent-mindedly, she noted the usual clinking of cups and muffled noises of napkins fluttering open. She stayed where she was, waiting for Kyril to invite her to come forth.

The sounds stopped. Yawning, pushing back her tousled hair, her eyes half-closed, Vivienne came forward, expecting to see Kyril attacking the toast.

He lay on the floor, naked. A strange man in servant's livery was wiping his boot on Kyril's cheek. A fresh bruise bloomed on the site of the old one. A trickle of blood came from the side of his head.

She looked at the stranger. Stared into ice-colored eyes that held no mercy.

Not for Kyril. Not for her. He might be already dead. The intruder would rape her first.

He looked her up and down, and then he slapped her so hard she saw stars. Vivienne gasped and put a hand to her face.

"Do not scream," the man said. "You must learn self-control. Unless you want the dog you let fuck you to die."

She swallowed hard. The man with ice-colored eyes clamped his hand around her throat. She could not breathe. Her tongue thrust out.

Strangling, she pulled frantically at his hand. He only laughed a little. Then his lips parted, coming down over her tongue. He sucked it into his cold mouth and kept it there, grabbing her breast painfully hard with the other hand.

Vivienne saw the room around her fade away. It swam back into focus when he released her, pushing her back. Then his accomplice put a foul-smelling, soaked rag over her mouth and that was the last she knew.

14

Kyril awoke in utter darkness.

He touched his face, felt the crusted blood. He winced. His cheekbone had been broken this time—he felt the bone under the skin move.

Then he reached out cautiously . . . and touched stone.

Buried alive.

The thought floated through his aching head and out again.

He had never been afraid of dying. His warrior blood was too strong for that. But to die like this—like a rat in a trap—would grieve his brothers and his clan.

What graveyard had he been brought to?

The Russian one, perhaps.

No. Volkodav would appreciate the irony but he would not risk it.

Kyril sent up a silent prayer, invoking his mother's blessed soul. He sensed no response. So this was his fate. He would endure as long as he could draw breath.

He touched the stone again.

Its flat feel was strange. He found a rough edge, ran his fingers over it. That part glittered faintly . . . but then he had been hit hard in the head. More than once.

Another injury on the back of his head was throbbing too.

Kyril slid down. He could reach all corners of his cube—it seemed to be a cube—if he stretched out his arms and legs. It was clear that he could not stand up unless he bent over.

All six sides were of stone, joined in wooden frames.

His fingers probed, looking for a crack or weak spot.

There were none.

If he was in a grave, there might be six feet of dirt over his head. He felt weak. He could not shove up the lid and burrow his way out.

He slumped against the wall, breathing quietly. He would soon run out of air.

Kyril shifted his tall body into a corner.

He was quite naked. As he had been when Volkodav had surprised him. There was no bucket for him to sit on or use for bodily functions.

No water. No food.

He wouldn't need either.

If he had to release his bowels or his bladder, he would have to sit in his own filth until he died. Or crouch over it and die standing with a crippled spine.

He hoped his tomb would never be opened.

Then he felt a slight rocking.

There. His mind would go first. He would not even know when he lost consciousness.

But graveyards did not rock.

The wall he pressed against seemed to press back.

Kyril slid a little ways to the other wall.

Understanding dawned.

He was on a ship. But what ship was made of stone?

Permitting himself a slightly deeper breath and directing it to his battered brain, he began to think.

The walls he touched were made of stone. The ship was not.

He had to be in the hold of a cargo ship, bound for Russia. It struck him then that the walls were khodzhite. Its weakening effect would soon kill him, especially if he touched it.

Kyril shrank into a ball in the center of the box. He put his arms around his folded legs and his head down on his knees.

There was nothing for it. He had to touch it. He had to try.

He extended a hand through the blackness, looking for the rough spot he had found by accident. He found it again by its faint glitter. Specks of mica were imbedded in it.

The khodzhite was not so pure as all that. Whoever had cut the raw stone into slabs and helped create his prison must have seen it.

Had the cutting been done here? He forced his mind to recollect the bill of lading for it. The khodzhite had been in raw blocks, not precisely cut slabs.

So a Londoner had done the work. Someone who was now undoubtedly dead. Touching khodzhite was lethal but its effect took time. Inhaling its dust was a faster way to die.

The stonecutter probably had no idea of what he was working with or what it would be used for.

If his brothers or Lukian tracked the shipment to his workplace, the stonecutter might not be able to tell them anything about where the finished slabs had gone.

But the unknown man had given Kyril a chance—a very slight chance—to break free.

His fingers probed the extent of the rough patch. Bracing his back against the opposite wall, he pushed his feet against it.

He invoked his mother's soul again. He felt an infinitesimal crack in the stone. He silently called upon the spirits of wolves and warriors to help him in his hour of need.

No. He did not have an hour. His strength was ebbing away.

Then something flowed through him. A great Being from

the Beforetimes appeared in a vision that floated before his eyes.

Endure. You are stronger than stone.

The vision gave off light. He could see. The crack was wider.

Kyril braced himself again and howled back down the centuries. He sang for the spirits.

We are coming.

Other beings came to his aid. Shamans. Wind riders. Insubstantial but fearfully strong. They howled with him and braced their transparent bodies against the cracked stone.

Suddenly it shattered. The wall fell.

Kyril gasped, dragging in breaths. There was light on the other side, falling on the planks in stripes.

Bars. With shadows behind them.

He blinked and stared at the hopeful eyes that stared back at him half a ship's length away.

He had been imprisoned in a hulk. A floating hell upon the Thames.

Kyril heard the even tread of footsteps and scurried for cover under a staircase. It led to the deck and to freedom, he was sure of it. He could smell it.

The footsteps moved on. Someone dragged an iron rod across the bars.

He heard a murmured entreaty and then a blow. Someone else crumpled to the floor. Shuffling. His fellow prisoners had surrounded the fallen man.

The guard's footsteps moved away.

Naked, weak, and bleeding, he made his escape.

Volkodav and Bledsoe took turns beating the guard. The man swore for the last time that he had seen nothing . . . nothing at all.

Volkodav gouged out his eyes and tossed the pulpy, bleeding orbs to the floor. "There. Now you are telling the truth."

Bledsoe delivered the death blow to the screaming man as he turned in circles, his arms outstretched, looking for mercy. He was granted none.

Lukian took Kyril's place at the head of the table. The members of the Pack looked at him curiously, noting his pallor and the circles under his eyes.

His sleepless agitation was only natural. Vivienne and Kyril had been taken by force. Their whereabouts were unknown.

"Let us pray." A grizzled veteran of the north bowed his head. "First, that our brother Kyril will come safely home and his brothers will meet him, rejoicing with us."

Semyon and Marko were searching every foul cellar and thieves' haunt in London for any trace of their older brother. They had vowed vengeance unto death if either Kyril or Vivienne suffered harm, and the assembled members of the Pack knew that the brothers meant it.

"And that his lady will come safely home," Natalya added softly. She wiped her eyes.

"Hear, hear," the men said. Their voices were raw with suppressed emotion.

"Do you have Tier?" Ivan whispered to her.

"Yes, in the kitchen. I fetched her from Kyril's house."

"Hush!" Someone turned around and glared at them.

Natalya nodded her head and pressed her lips together. A tear trickled into the corner of her mouth and the tip of her tongue darted out to lick it.

Ivan pressed a kiss to her temple, glaring back at the fellow who dared to scold his pretty little mate.

"Second," the grizzled man continued, "that our brother

Lukian will find the strength he needs to guide us in this, our hour of need."

Lukian inclined his head to his fellows of the Pack.

"Hear, hear," said Ivan. He stood by for a little longer as the prayers ended and the meeting continued. Strategies were discussed and most of them were discarded.

Ivan edged out, taking Natalya with him.

"What are you doing? I wanted to listen to the rest."

He put a finger to her lips.

"We have the dog. She knows her mistress well and she knows you."

Natalya's face brightened a little. "We could track her."

"It is worth a shot. I do not think the members of the Pack would handle her as well as you. Tier is very much a woman's dog, for all her size and strength."

"Very well," Natalya said. "I want to do something. I cannot just sit here and wait for news. I will go mad if I do."

Ivan nodded. "We shall take packs upon our backs with everything we need."

"This is not a picnic, you fool—"

He hushed her. "Kyril was naked when he was taken. And so was Vivienne. They will need clothes."

"Of course. Forgive me, Ivan." His hope gave her hope.

"Her clothes have her scent. The dog will need it."

Natalya shrugged. "I think Tier remembers everything."

"That is as it should be."

An hour later, they left by the back door, only to be stopped by Lukian. The ferocious gleam in his eyes frightened Natalya.

"Where are you going?" he thundered.

"To—to look for Kyril and Vivienne," she said.

"With Tier?"

He looked down at the dog, who was pulling on her leash.

"Yes, with Tier. She will help us."

Lukian's anger seemed to soften. "Perhaps."

"We are starting by the river a mile to the east. Unless you think . . ." Ivan left off, waiting for his master's direction.

"The river Thames holds many secrets. I hope that—never mind." Lukian stared over Ivan's head, his eyes moving rapidly as if he saw a crawling insect on the wall.

"Sir?" Natalya asked. "Are you all right?"

"Yes. Why?"

"You seem . . . different somehow."

"The strain—my mind is cracking. Volkodav waited so long. We grew comfortable, perhaps. Not as wary as wolves should be."

"If I find the fellow," Ivan began.

Lukian clapped a hand upon his shoulder. "Allow me the pleasure of tearing out his throat."

Ivan grunted. "If you want it."

"I do. I am going to the Baltic Dock."

"We will be near there—"

Absently Lukian clicked his tongue against the top of his mouth. His fangs and tearing canines descended as Natalya watched, fascinated.

"Can you do that, Ivan?"

"No," he murmured, annoyed that she was impressed.

"Go then." Lukian made a sign of protection over Natalya's head, briefly touching her shining hair.

Ivan nodded at him, mollified. They shouldered their burdens and left with the dog.

Lukian stared out the back door after them. His mind turned over every possibility and came back to where he had started.

The Baltic Dock.

Volkodav had returned there again and again, according to the intelligence he had received. The shipment of khodzhite had turned up in a warehouse there, but had vanished again from it a week ago.

His men had traced it to a stonecutter's yard, but the grieving widow refused to answer any questions about him.

She had known nothing of its eventual destination in any case.

A thousand pounds of valuable stone had more or less vanished in plain sight. It was very odd. The matter undoubtedly held some clue as to where his brother was.

But with nothing to go on, his men could not follow through on it. He thought of asking Phineas Briggs. The man knew everything that went on at the docks on both sides of the Thames.

He sank into a chair and put his head down on his folded arms. The echoing noise in his mind began. If Kyril turned up dead, he would kill himself. But not in this foreign city.

No, he would stow away on a Russian ship returning to his homeland and starve. It would not take long to die. He had not been eating and his ribs already showed. The cold seas would keep his body cold. His carcass would not stink until they were in sight of Russia. When they found him, they would throw him overboard. His corpse would be bloated with the noxious gases of decomposing flesh. It would float. Then the crushing ice of winter would obliterate the last trace of him.

But . . .

Lukian raised his head. Kyril was not dead yet. Faintly, very faintly, he had heard him call.

He himself called to Rudolf Panasenko. No, the word was bellow. The man came quickly.

"Go to Phineas Briggs. And ask him to help us find Kyril. I am going down to the docks."

15

Once over the side and clear of the hulk, Kyril swam weakly. His strength was sapped by the cold water and the current made him go in circles. His hand touched something floating in the river and he stopped to look.

A corpse. Eyeless. Beaten.

He looked up at the prison ship in the near distance and saw men at its side, waving their fists at him.

Kyril swam away, churning through the dirty water.

In another half hour, he was dragging himself ashore, crawling and stumbling over a pebbled stretch of dirty sand. It smelled to high heaven, but it was land and there was no one behind him.

He had escaped. He was alive.

He looked at the thin red clouds in the sky and the bloodshot sun, not sure at first if it was morning or evening. The light grew brighter. It was day. He crawled behind a sheltered rock and hoped the sun would warm him eventually.

But he still shivered, so hard that his jaws banged together. It was too late in the autumn for the sun to do much good, however brightly it shone. There was nothing for it. He would have to wolf up, as the Pack phrase had it. He hunkered down and felt the first pricklings of hair rise on the back of his neck. He concentrated. The pelt came in. Warm fur covered his arms and shoulders and back. His ears rose to proper height and pricked. A thick ruff of fur enfolded the back of his neck.

And last but not least, a massive brush of a tail appeared at the base of his spine. Kyril let the tail curl between his legs and up around his groin. He hated to do it because it was a shameful sign of submission, but he had to keep his balls warm somehow.

"I am here, you dirty Taruskin."

Lukian looked wildly about. The voice seemed to come from everywhere.

He had found Volkodav. Or his disembodied voice.

"Over by the wall." The other man laughed. "No, the window."

"Damn you!" Lukian was sweating profusely. He had not brought the extra vial of morphine that Lily had given him before he left her for the lair. He needed it desperately.

"You are sweating," said the voice. "But it is not hot in here."

True enough. The vast, echoing space of the ropemaking factory was cool. Lukian had come here on a hunch. It was near the docks but isolated, surrounded by the long fields in which ships' cables were stretched before use, hundreds and hundreds of feet of newly twisted rope.

The ropemaking factory smelled pleasantly of hemp, and, less pleasantly, of tar.

Lukian moved about through the complex machinery on which the ropes were made. He rested his hand on a rope that had not been finished. Three smaller ropes leading from three gigantic spools were twisted into this one by powerful machinery.

"Watch your fingers." Volkodav's warning was calm. "I understand these machines can remove them."

Lukian lifted his hand.

He heard a clank. Gears meshed, then stopped.

The equipment was massive, of black cast iron. It would not have looked out of place in a dungeon.

A ponderous hook that must have weighed fifty pounds swung by his head, missing him by a few inches.

"Sorry."

Lukian looked up. The hook swung in a decreasing arc, like a pendulum. It was attached to a chain that slid on a rod high above.

"Sorry you missed me, you mean," Lukian growled.

"That is correct."

He raised his fist in the air. "Come out, you bastard, where I can see you! And fight like a man!"

"No."

"Are you—"

"I am a man. Unlike you and the rest of the Pack."

Lukian heard the contempt in Volkodav's voice.

"But something is missing in me, it is true. Something that makes a man whole."

"What do you mean?"

The voice did not answer right away. And when it did it seemed closer. "Consider yourself warned."

Lukian whirled around. He began to run through the factory, charging like a maddened bull this way and that, bashing his fist into machinery that rattled under his blows.

He almost did not see Volkodav when he stepped out from behind a gigantic spool. He was toying with a piece of rope.

276 / Noelle Mack

"Where is my brother?" Lukian roared. He took the other man by the throat.

Volkodav narrowed his eyes and looked sideways, through the window. His lips formed a single word. *There.*

Lukian tightened his grip and glanced that way.

He saw a hulk anchored in the Thames. An anonymous, battered prison ship. Even from this distance, he could see its ruinous condition. He knew exactly what it held.

Desperate, forgotten men. So crowded together that one might die standing and be held up by the others for hours.

He let go of Volkodav's throat. The Wolf Killer coughed.

"Is he in there?"

Volkodav moved slightly and Lukian grabbed him again, keeping him in place with a bone-breaking grip on his shoulder.

"Answer me!"

"He was."

Lukian brought his sweating face down to Volkodav's, staring into his ice-colored eyes. "Where is he now?"

"I do not know."

Lukian shook him as a wolf shakes its prey.

"Then you will help me find out."

Kyril ran along the waterfront with a wolf's loping gait, tail straight out behind him. Some stared at him curiously, some did not even look. He had to find a tailor—there had to be one here, one who catered to seamen. He turned off from the river bank and made his way into the warren of houses and tenements and shops, although he had no idea of where he was. Somewhere in Stepney, most likely.

He called himself a fool as he ran. He had no money. But he kept on going. There had to be a way.

He stumbled over a drunken old man sleeping in a doorway, who farted and groaned simultaneously, giving off a stench of sour beer. He half-opened one eye and shook his fist at Kyril. "Be damned, you dog!"

"My apologies," Kyril said courteously, getting up again.

The drunk just stared at him. "You are a dog."

"Not really."

He ran on.

And there it was. A tailor's shop. Neat, brass-buttoned uniforms of navy blue wool hung in the window. He stopped running and sidled over to read the sign.

Have A Proper Fit. We Cater To Everyone. Come To Us Before You Drink Away Your Pay.

Everyone, hmm? Kyril took a deep breath and entered. The tailor, a good-looking man with neatly combed hair and a tape measure around his neck looked him up and down. Very carefully. He took the pins out of his mouth before he spoke.

"You are a rum one and no mistake."

"I have—been in a fight."

"Oh really?"

"My clothes were taken. I need a uniform."

The tailor guffawed. "You need a shave. All over."

He looked curiously at the thick fur ruff over Kyril's shoulders and the fur on his arms and head. Kyril flattened his pricked ears in a sign of respect that the man did not deserve. The tailor's eyes widened and he stared at Kyril for a very long time.

"I don't think I've ever seen a man quite like you. But I'm up for some fun." His eyes dropped to Kyril's groin and stayed there. "If you are."

Feeling annoyed by the other man's frank scrutiny of his privates, Kyril whisked his tail between his legs again. The brush tickled his cock and balls but that couldn't be helped.

"Now, now. I was just looking. But I will have to measure." The tailor drew the tape measure off his neck and came closer. Then he kneeled in front of Kyril.

Kyril swore inwardly. He would have to do something he didn't want to do. He grabbed the tape measure and tied the tailor's hands behind his back. The man only laughed.

"All right. But lock the door, would you?"

Kyril nodded and did just that, jingling the small ship's bell that served to announce customers and startling himself. Then he rushed to the rack of ready-made clothes and struggled into pants and a shirt, buttoning up the flap and leaving the shirt open. The fur began to recede as he dressed hastily but it was still there and it itched. Wolves were not meant to wear clothing. He grabbed a heavy wool jacket and a cap with a brim when he was done.

"Now you are a sight for sore eyes," his would-be lover said happily, still on his knees. "You can tie me up and rob me anytime."

"Oh, for God's sake—I can't pay you now—but I will!" He would send someone else.

Kyril rushed out the door.

He was suddenly invisible, dressed like an able-bodied seaman out for a brisk walk—barefoot—along the Thames. He remembered Vivienne and broke into a wild run. He forced himself to slow down and save his strength. He had no idea where she was.

If she had been forced into a khodzhite cell like his—naked and bent over—she would be near death by now. The thought made him frantic. His belly tensed painfully and he leaned over to vomit. There was nothing inside him but bile. It burned his mouth when he spat it out, sobbing wildly. He began to run on.

A dog was running toward him. Damnation! It was a big one, probably looking for a fight—he swerved to the side to avoid it. The animal collided with him and jumped up, knocking him flat, barking with joy.

"Tier?"

She put a paw on his chest and licked his face.

"Tier! But where—"

He struggled to get up when he heard the sound of running feet. Ivan and Natalya were coming toward him, waving wildly.

"She saw you a mile away!" Ivan called. "She led us to you!" They stopped and flung down the packs, gasping for breath.

"Oh, sir!" Natalya said. "We brought you clothes—but you are dressed—and food—"

"Never mind that," Kyril cried. "Dear Wolf, I am happy to see you two!"

They embraced, then split apart.

"Where is Vivienne?"

Ivan and Natalya shook their heads, and she began to cry. "No one knows. All of us are out—Lukian said he would come to the docks—"

"I have not seen him."

A distant howl rumbled through the air.

Kyril listened.

"But I think I hear him."

"Nose to the wind," Ivan said. He turned in all directions, then pointed. "There. The ropemaking factory."

The two men ran on ahead and Natalya followed, carrying the bags and keeping up as best she could.

It was not long before all three were inside.

Vivienne woke up with a blinding headache. Her hands and feet were tied, but not all that tightly. Her mouth was parched. She had been so long without water that her wrists and ankles felt thin. She could move them inside her bonds.

She craned her stiff neck in every possible direction, seeing no one and hearing nothing. Then she used her bare toes to slip out of the strip of rag that encircled one ankle and did the same with the other. Her wrists took longer.

But she was soon free.

She lay on the bed where she'd been dumped, aware that she was naked. The room was nondescript. Through an open door, she could see another room and from it came a single snore, a soft sound that was unmistakably female . . . and somehow familiar.

Vivienne rose and stood, swaying. She moved noiselessly as soon as she was strong enough and looked through the open door so she could not be seen. A stout woman in a house-keeper's dress slept with her head upon a pillow set on a deal table, her lips pursed but her nostrils flaring. Drunk. There was an empty bottle in front of her.

It was Mrs. Hickham.

The woman's limp fingers rested on a note with a list scrib-bled in her handwriting as to the care of her prisoner. Vivienne read it.

Keepe her cold.
Keepe her naket.
Do not fede.
She must use the floore in corner for a necessary. In fronte of you.
Breake her down slowly.

What was the going price for such a hideous betrayal? Vivi-enne felt a surge of fury rise in her chest. Picking up the heavy bottle that was set in front of the woman, she gave her a solid whack on the head. Mrs. Hickham groaned and her mouth hung slack, drooling. Her head rose briefly and then thumped down.

She was breathing.

Vivienne hoped the same was true for Kyril, wherever he was. She looked around the two rooms, then looked out the window, desperate to know more. She was somewhere near the water—farther than she had ever walked. Near the forest of masts that she had seen. Down by the docks.

Where there were women aplenty.

She reached into Mrs. Hickham's pocket and withdrew a handful of coins and a bank note. It was enough. Now to find a whore who had worked all night and was heading off to sleep. She would have to buy some clothes and it was not as if she could walk into a shop.

A bawdy-mouthed redhead decided to believe the wild story Vivienne made up on the spot, on the street, and took her home to get food and drink into her quickly as she dressed. She refused the money.

Vivienne thanked her and ran out, into the bright light of day. She was near the docks, but which one?

She asked a passing man.

"The Baltic Dock, miss. Where them Russians always is."

"Thank you." She breathed the words. She was where Kyril had been, where his friends came—she would find help. And she had enough money to get back to Cheyne Row.

Walking by the canal that led into the vast pool of the dock, she looked ahead and saw a ship being made fast. Like the first threads of a spider's web, long cables reached from her to the dock. The sight was beautiful. But she did not take it in, frantic with worry and fear for Kyril.

A man came up to her, and gave her a calm look. There was nothing remarkable about his appearance—he did not seem menacing. He greeted her in a pleasant way. His voice had a slight accent that she was sure was Russian.

"Can you help me?" she asked eagerly. "I am Vivienne Sheridan and I—"

"Ah," he said, nodding his head. "It is a pleasure to meet you. I am Alex Stasov."

She came to a second time, dimly aware that she was in some kind of factory by the unfinished beams and tall, uncurtained windows. She was someplace high up, close to rafters that arched above her. This time she was very tightly bound with new rope that scratched her bare wrists and ankles painfully. But her assailants had left her clothes on.

Not enough time to remove them, she thought dully. She did not remember what had happened after the nondescript man had introduced himself.

Vivienne heard a voice she recognized and stiffened with fear.

Lukian.

He was talking to another man. He also had a Russian accent but she did not think it was—what had the man on the dock said his name was?

Stasov. Alex Stasov.

The name Lukian was growling sounded something like it—no. She listened harder.

Volkodav. Lukian was cursing at him.

And then she heard Kyril's voice and a thrill of joy went through her.

A warm, strong hand patted her cheek. Vivienne looked up. Alex Stasov was looking down at her. That was when she realized she was gagged.

"How nice of all of you to come," she heard Volkodav say. "You have saved me a lot of trouble by being so stupid."

Vivienne heard a young woman sob, until a hard slap silenced her. Another man comforted the woman. She strained to hear their names. Ivan. Natalya.

For a while there was silence. Stasov said nothing at all.

Then Kyril spoke. "Where is Vivienne?"

"Not far away," Volkodav said evenly.

Stasov called to him. "Up here."

"Ah. There you are."

Stasov went to a railing and leaned over it. "You will never guess who I found walking along the canal. Dressed like a whore."

"Who?"

"Vivienne Sheridan."

She heard the indrawn breaths of the people below.

"Very good, Stasov. A stroke of luck indeed."

Kyril began to bargain with him in Russian. She couldn't make it out, except for Volkodav's one word reply. *Nyet.*

"Hang her over the railing," he called to Stasov. "They will not dare to hurt me. But not by the neck," he added, almost as an afterthought.

Stasov went back to her and looped a piece of rope through her bonds. He lifted her with ease and tied the other end of the rope in a complicated hitch to the railing before he dropped her over it.

Gagged, tied, she swung in the air.

Kyril was the one she saw first. Her eyes met his and fixed on his face briefly. There were two other people with him, a young woman with a bruise on her cheek and a man who was somewhat older. And Lukian. The tallest of the group, looking more like Satan than ever, his face weary with pain and barely checked rage.

She looked at the strange machinery that spun hemp into rope. It seemed to go on for miles. Heavy. Dark. Idle at the moment.

A very tall man, taller than Lukian, stood apart from the four others. A man with eyes the color of ice. Vivienne looked hard at him. That must be Volkodav. But she had seen those eyes before.

The old monk.

Dear God.

She closed her eyes and prayed for deliverance.

284 / Noelle Mack

Then she heard a bark and opened them.

Tier was running around and around the factory. Lukian called her and she came.

"What a good dog," Volkodav said. "And how well she obeys you."

Lukian glowered at him and kept his hand on Tier's collar.

"I want you to do something for me, Lukian Taruskin."

"What?"

"I will trade you Vivienne for that dog."

Lukian was silent.

"Stasov, throw down a rope. You know what I want."

Humming under his breath, Stasov worked on a long piece, tying it securely to the railing before he threw the noose on the other end down to Volkodav.

"Hang the dog high, Lukian. And I will have Stasov cut Vivienne down."

"No."

"Then he will hang Vivienne while you all watch."

She closed her eyes.

"Go ahead, Volkodav," she heard Kyril say. "It no longer matters. We are all going to die."

"One by one. Who goes first? It will be interesting. I vote for Vivienne." He slipped the noose over her head. "Do you like your new necklace?"

Tears slipped from under Vivienne's shut lids. She wanted to scream but the gag prevented her. In the dreadful silence that followed, she heard an infinitesimal click. Then another.

She looked down. Kyril and Lukian seemed to be smiling. But where ordinary teeth had been were fangs—and their faces were drawn tight in menacing growls. In a fraction of a second, they sprang on Volkodav.

He fought them as Stasov watched impassively. He took the rope she hung from and made her twirl. "So that is what you

Taruskins are. Too bad you two are on the floor and I am up here in the catwalk. What are you going to do about it?"

Lukian and Kyril ceased their savaging of Volkodav, who was no longer capable of speaking but still alive, and left him to Ivan and Natalya. They looked up warily, circling under the man who spoke to them.

"All I have to do is lift her up . . . and let her down. In another noose. You saw how fast I made the first one," Stasov taunted.

Vivienne tried to work free. It only made her swing again.

Stasov laughed.

She looked down and witnessed a transformation that she did not believe. Their clothes split asunder, Kyril and Lukian were growing thick ruffs of fur and pricked ears. Their bodies were sleek with lean muscle and at the bottom of their backs were splendid tails.

They were manwolves.

Even Stasov gasped. Kyril leapt up first and his razor-sharp teeth broke the rope she dangled from. Still bound, fearing for her life, she plummeted to the floor far below, with him twisting around her to break her fall.

He grunted, all the breath knocked from his wolfish body. Natalya and Ivan rushed over and worked on the knots that held her. Standing over Vivienne too, Tier chewed at the gag and freed her. Her tongue, agonizingly dry, worked in her mouth. Her lips were cracked open at the corners where the gag had been. Vivienne tried to talk. She couldn't.

Lukian jumped next. The force of his body slamming against the railing shattered it and Stasov backed away as Lukian faced him on the catwalk. Stasov kicked over a can in back of him that he didn't see and a vile-smelling liquid began to spread. He looked down at it, then behind himself, gauging in an instant his path to freedom.

"Catch him!" Natalya screamed. She looked over her shoulder at Volkodav, who had crawled away. He reached up for the rope strung taut between the massive pieces of machinery and hauled himself up with it.

The great spools, taller than a man, began to turn. He hung on. In another moment, he was bound tightly in the other two strands that joined the first.

He groaned. The thick ropes, strong enough to hold a ship, twisted inexorably together. He could not free himself.

His tall body was squeezed and stretched until blood stained the fresh new rope and dripped upon the floor.

In another second he was dead.

Vivienne looked up into Kyril's wild eyes, seeing the man in them. His body was still that of a man. It was the thick ruff and the ears and the pelt on his back that was different.

She looked up at Lukian. In the time that it had taken for Volkodav to die, he had become a full wolf.

Black as death.

On all fours, he advanced toward Stasov, snarling. The man watched him calmly. He took a piece of metal and struck a spark with it, then blew the spark on the spilled, evil-smelling liquid. A ribbon of fire sprang up.

The catwalk bloomed with it. Smoke billowed—and still the great wolf that was Lukian went forward. Stasov turned to jump to another catwalk at the last second.

His jacket caught. Like Vivienne, he hung suspended in the air. If the cloth burned, he would smash into the floor. No one would break his fall.

He decided to take his chances with the wolf. Stasov curled his body and reached up, grabbing what was left of the railing.

In another second the black wolf had him by the throat— and then his fur caught fire. His back ... his ruff ... his ears ...

but he did not scream in agony. He held tight to his prey. The gathering heat of the blaze blew open the tall windows and Lukian leaped, Stasov in his jaws, in a blazing arc that shattered the sky. Far below was the Thames . . . and as the arc of flame descended, the river swallowed them both with a hiss.

16

The memorial service for Lukian Taruskin was held by the Thames. There was nothing to bury. The body of Alex Stasov had washed ashore by the Traitor's Gate upriver, pushed there by the incoming tide—or something else. A swimming wolf, perhaps.

Vivienne did not believe that Lukian had died.

Natalya was crying softly and she put her arm around the young girl's shoulders and held her close.

Kyril nodded to Ivan, who gave him the Book of Wolf, in which the Pack's prayers were written, and went to her.

Vivienne and Ivan traded places. She glanced down at the opened book and saw two illustrations on facing pages. They had an odd symmetry, but were not mirror images. On the left, a Roemi warrior was becoming a wolf. On the right, a wolf was becoming a Roemi warrior.

She rested her head on Kyril's fine linen shirt and cried too, as if her heart would break.

The men comforted them as best they could. Their tears froze on their rugged faces in the cold November wind.

17

In spring, they went back to the Russian cemetery. A stonecutter was waiting for them, his cap in his hand as he inspected the headstone. He said that Lukian's name could be added and arranged to do the work when they were not there.

The place was about to bloom, the sere stems and broken leaves of last year's plants eclipsed by new growth. The fountain was still dry but the enclosed garden was green and full of buds.

She tugged at a leaf of the herb that had scented Kyril's shirts and crushed it in her fingertips, enjoying the fragrance.

"Well, here we are. I thought I would be too upset . . . but I feel I am among friends."

Kyril smiled at her. "You are among your family as well." He touched the plain wedding band upon her finger. "Thank you again for saying yes. I did not think you would when you knew."

She smiled back. "I will always love you."

"And I will always love you. And protect you with my own life if need be." He drew her into his arms and sheltered her there. The day was not all that warm and she was comfortable there. The stone slab underfoot made her feet feel cold.

"May it never come to that again," she whispered. The pressure of his body made the child in her womb kick. She captured his hand and put it over the little foot that was making a nuisance of itself.

Kyril laughed with delight. "Hello, my son. Or daughter? Which will it be, I wonder?"

Vivienne laughed too. "Natalya says it will be a girl. She knows so much."

"Her mother was a midwife."

"I know. Her understanding of herbs helped me conceive."

Kyril kissed her on the nose. "I would prefer to take full credit for that."

"It takes two," Vivienne said pertly.

"Yes, you are right, my dear wife. I only wish I had more to offer you and our babies. The Pack is still scraping by. The Tsar still does not like us."

"I do not care about money."

"Silly. You should." He held her and rocked her, kissing the top of her head. "If the baby is a boy, he will ask for a pony or two. If it is a girl, she will need hair ribbons by the dozen. What's a poor papa to do?"

"Kiss me again."

"Isn't that how all this started, Vivienne?"

"Yes, I believe so."

He kissed her anyway. Vivienne stepped back to get her breath and squeaked when she saw a little snake whiz by, very near her foot. It entered a hole very near the fountain and coiled up in it.

"Look at that, Kyril. Does it not remind you of the Serpent's Egg?"

He sighed. "We had to ship that damned thing back to Russia by royal command. Have to keep the peace in Europe, now that Napoleon is finally done for."

She looked again at the snake. "Is that a ring it is coiled around? I cannot quite see and I don't care to touch it."

Kyril let her go and squatted down. "I think it is a ring. Made of bronze." He gave the snake a light poke and off it went, flicking its tongue. "It is heavy but it lifts up." He slipped a finger under it.

Vivienne heard a sound like the lid of a sugar bowl being moved. A very large sugar bowl. She stepped off the slab of stone underfoot in which the ring had been set and heard the grating noise again.

"Dear Wolf, what is that?" Kyril planted his feet on either side of the slab and pulled lightly on the heavy ring. It made a rusty noise, as if it had not been moved for decades. Then the slab began to rise.

He jumped away, looking at her with surprise.

"Kyril, what—"

"Do not ask me what is happening! I know no more than you do!"

The slab rose halfway and then tilted back, sliding down into the earth.

She saw something white in the grave, but for some reason she was not frightened in the least. The curving lines, the finely worked surface were like a work of art.

Beautifully articulated, a lifesize marble wolf rose up. Next to it was a marble fountain that splashed water so lifelike it was hard to believe it too was made of stone. Underneath its paw was a small box. The marvelous statue lifted its paw and Kyril reached for the box. Then he hesitated.

"What if—no. It cannot be harmful. This must be Jozef Taruskin's last and greatest work."

He took out the box and rose as he did so. Vivienne stepped back. She was not so confident.

Kyril lifted the lid. She saw a flash of green and gold, and gave a cry.

"The real one. It has been here all along." He lifted the Serpent's Egg from the box. It had been nestled in dry hay—a final jest of its maker. He brushed away a fragment of it. "Shall I open it?"

"Yes. But look—the serpent at its base does not move."

"No, that little creature crept away into the grass."

She pressed the first button as he watched, holding the precious thing carefully. The outermost egg opened to reveal the second. The emerald egg appeared. Then the one of black onyx.

Vivienne hesitated before pressing the last button. Kyril put his hand over hers. Then her fingertip connected with it and the innermost egg opened.

The massive diamond inside it caught the sun and refracted it a thousand times over, dazzling them both.

"Oh my," she said with wonder.

He held her hand up to it.

"It would make a beautiful ring for you."

"No, no," she said, laughing breathlessly. "It belongs to the Pack."

"We are no longer poor. Imagine that." He closed up the eggs one by one and put the Serpent's Egg back into the hay, bending down to set the closed box aside.

"My dearest Kyril, I have the ring I want."

"Do you, Vivienne?"

"Yes," she answered simply. He kissed her again and she felt the baby move.

"Then we will always be happy," he whispered.

Enjoy more supernaturally sexy romance
from Noelle Mack!
The story of London's immortal Pack continues in
WANTON: THE PACK OF ST. JAMES,
available August 2008 from Brava.
Here's a sensual sneak peak . . .

London, 1816. The Pack of St. James meets in secret in their elegant lair. An unknown assailant has begun to prey upon the women they love—and a poisoned communication threatens worse things to come. Marko Taruskin begins to investigate and finds the trail leads to a scandalous beauty known as Severin. Well aware of how a clever woman can hide more than she reveals, Marko must employ all of his powers of sensual persuasion . . .

The last chord died away and Marko heard the almost noiseless click of a piano lid closing. The woman who had been playing so beautifully sighed as she put the sheets of music in order before she rose, pushing back the padded bench with a faint scrape. He heard the faint miaou of Severin's cat, following her mistress about the adjoining chamber. Silk skirts rustled over polished floors. Then Severin swept through the double doors that led to her bedroom and stopped, her lips parting with surprise.

296 / Noelle Mack

"What are you doing here?"

"Waiting for you."

Severin glided past the bed upon which he lay to her mirror-topped dresser. "I do not remember inviting you." She began to take down her hair, looking at his reflection in the silvery glass, her back to him.

"No, you didn't."

"Then how did you get in?"

Marko shrugged. He was quite at his ease stretched out upon her featherbed, luxuriously so, in fact. He rolled to his side, bracing himself with one arm and letting the other rest upon his hip. "Through the front door."

"Hmm. Unusual for you."

"What do you mean?"

Severin gave an unladylike snort. "You're a great one for trellises and balconies. Ever the romantic hero."

Her gleaming hair ripped over her bare shoulders. He longed to bury his face in its fragrant softness, lift it away from her neck, kiss her madly—but he stayed where he was.

"It is raining."

"Oh? I did not notice," Severin said, turning to face him. She put her hands on her hips and looked him over.

Marko could almost feel her gaze. He was nearly as aroused as if she had actually touched him. Since he was fully dressed, from his fitted half-coat to the breeches tucked into his high black boots, the sensation was not entirely comfortable. He drew up one leg and bent his knee to conceal his reaction to her cool study of his body.

"Boots in the bed?" she murmured. "How uncivilized of you."

"I could not very well strip, Severin. You might have screamed."

She permitted herself a small smile. "I don't think so. I've seen you naked before."

He remembered that night with chagrin. "Yes, but—nothing happened."

Her amber eyes glowed with amusement. "You wanted something to happen. But I was not ready."

"Are you ready now?"

The question was bold, but she was bolder.

"Yes," she said. And she came to him . . .